STUD MUFFIN

DONNER BAKERY BOOK #2

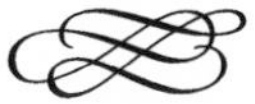

JIFFY KATE

Made in the United States of America

Print Edition

ISBN: 978-1-949202-16-8

PROLOGUE

TEMPEST

I'm getting really good at peeing on sticks.

Setting the small white tester on the counter, I stand, flush, zip up my jeans and thoroughly wash my hands. After drying them and applying enough hand sanitizer to kill a small infestation of small pox, I begin to pace the bathroom. Counting off my steps as I go, I try to keep from watching the stick.

It's kind of like a pot of water. If you watch it, it'll never boil, or turn blue… or say YES. Whatever.

One, two, three, four … pivot … one, two, three, four … pivot … one, two, three—

"Em?"

"Two more minutes," I call back through the closed door, biting at the cuticle on my thumbnail.

"I'm sending all the good juju your way," Jenn replies and I can hear the smile in her voice.

It's no secret I'm trying to get pregnant.

My husband, Asher, and I have been trying for quite a while, but I had a miscarriage six months ago, so this is the first cycle we'll be actively trying to conceive again. My hands are starting to sweat a little as I continue to pace.

I want a baby so badly—more than I've ever wanted anything in my life.

I've done all the tricks. Pomegranate juice is my new drink du jour. It's supposed to increase blood flow to the uterus. Prenatal vitamins are my new best friend. I kicked my coffee habit, which was no small feat, and I'm completely avoiding alcohol. Of course, I exercise and eat healthy. Not to mention, there aren't a pair of tighty whities to be seen in my house.

Asher is freeballing twenty-four-seven.

"Any results yet?" Jenn's voice startles me this time. I assumed she'd be back to baking. There are over a dozen custom cake orders and she is the queen… the Banana Cake Queen and absolute ruler of Donner Bakery. She and I are often the only workers this early in the morning at the newer location, downtown Green Valley. It's a satellite location, but fully equipped with the best kitchen equipment available. I love it here. I love the original location too, but this place is a bit less hectic and allows me time to feel inspired and create.

Glancing over at the stick, I notice the screen is still flashing, which means it's still thinking… or testing… or whatever the little contraption does. It's kind of inconvenient taking this at work, but when you have to report to your place of employment before the butt-crack of dawn, you make it work.

"Not yet," I call back, opening the door to see Jenn standing there with a bright smile and violet-blue eyes staring back at me, hopeful.

She peeks around my shoulder and then steps back, a sly smile creeping up on her beautiful face. "Looks like someone's gonna need an early lunch."

"What?" I ask, whipping my head around. My heart chooses that time to kick into an even higher gear, skipping a beat on its way to overdrive—blood pumping so fast, I feel a little woozy. The smiley face blinking back at me brings immediate tears to my eyes.

"I'm ovulating," I whisper, to myself… to Jenn… to the universe as a silent prayer of thanks.

"Yep," Jenn says with an even wider smile and a quirk of an eyebrow.

"Asher works from home today," I add absentmindedly as I think out loud and try to get my head on straight. My ovulation is a bit unpredictable, so I have to act fast. "I've already prepped the batter for the Muffin of the Day—Back in Baby's Arms. The Sweet Dreams and Tennessee Waltzes are already in the oven. South of the Borders are on deck," I gush out, grabbing the test and tossing the test strip. It's been a Patsy Cline kind of week, what can I say? Waving the still-blinking smiley face at Jenn, I finally take a breath. "I'll be back in thirty minutes."

I'm already halfway out the back door when Jenn calls out, "Take your time! Oh, and make sure you have an orgasm! I heard that helps!"

Laughing to myself, I jump in my car and start it up as another rush of excitement floods my body.

We're gonna make a baby.

Driving as fast as I can without drawing the attention of local law enforcement, I make my way across town. Even though I'm in a hurry, I still abide by the laws. I'm looking to get knocked-up not booked-up in the county jail. Although my daddy *is* the local bail bondsman and he's in pretty tight with Sheriff James, I've never been one to make a scene or abuse my privileges.

When I approach my house, I note that Asher's truck is still in the driveway, right where it was when I left a couple hours ago. If I'm lucky, he's still in bed and I can wake him up with a nice surprise to get things cooking. His morning wood will be working in my favor this morning. He's always been frisky when he first wakes up and finds it annoying that my first thought has always been coffee instead of sex.

Well, Asher Williams, today is your lucky day.

As I'm unlocking the front door, a wicked thought comes to mind and I start shedding my clothes before I've even approached the landing of the stairs that lead to our bedroom. Sex and orgasms and sperm making their way to an egg are my only thoughts as I balance against the doorway of our room, just long enough to kick off my shoes.

And I freeze.

Curled up in my bed—in my fluffy white comforter I picked out at

Dillard's on my last shopping trip with my mama in Nashville and my most-favorite one thousand thread count sheets—is my husband of eight years, sleeping soundly… and right beside him is another head of brown hair that looks suspiciously like Mindy Mitchell.

Been around the block more times than the ice cream truck on a hot July day… Mindy Mitchell.

Screwed the entire football team back in 2009… Mindy Mitchell.

Naked as the day she was born and curled up next to my husband… Mindy Mitchell.

Standing in the middle of my bedroom in my bra and unzipped jeans with one shoe on and the other in my hand, I feel something snap on a cellular level.

I've always been a relatively calm person.

But in this moment, as red clouds my vision, consuming my mind, I lose control over everything.

I feel as if I'm hovering above my body, watching it all play out like a scene from a movie.

The shoe in my hand flies across the room, making direct contact with Asher's head, waking him abruptly. When his eyes meet mine, he looks sleepy and confused. Then he turns to look at the sleeping body beside him. I watch as everything registers, just how bad this is. His eyes grow wide and his mouth gapes like a fish as he scrambles for words—an excuse, a plea, an apology? I don't know, but I don't allow him the luxury of figuring it out.

Blindly, I begin to grasp for something… anything. Whatever my hands find becomes my next weapon as I begin launching objects across the room. Anything I can lift becomes airborne.

Glass breaks, things shatter into a million pieces—picture frames, the vase my mama bought us for our wedding flowers, the lamp on the dresser… my heart, my past, my present, my future.

Everything splinters into a before and after.

My throat burns and it's then I realize I've been screaming. Coughing, I brace my hands on my knees and try to take a breath, but it gets lodged in my throat on a sob.

"Tempest!" Asher yells, taking advantage of the pause in action to get off the bed. Hands raised, he looks at me like I'm a stranger, not his wife of eight *fucking* years. "Get a damn grip on yourself. What are you doing? Have you lost your mind?"

A harsh bark comes out—deep from the pit of my stomach. "Me?" I yell back. "I think the better question, Asher Williams, is have you lost your goddamn mind? What is she doing here? What have you done?" I scream. My voice sounding foreign, like it's sourced from the pits of hell—torn and feral. "How could you do this?"

"I can explain—"

I don't let him finish that sentence, instead, I pull a dresser drawer open and start throwing clothes at him. "Get dressed and get the hell out of my house!"

"Em," he says, pleading as he eases toward me like I'm a caged animal. Maybe I am, because right now I feel like I could chew off his right arm and shove it up his ass… and then… I finally allow myself to look over at Mindy who's standing on the other side of the bed with the sheet covering her naked body.

My fucking sheets.

My fucking husband.

"You," I say, voice trembling as I redirect my ire. I begin to take a step toward her, but Asher tries to intercept, so I turn back to him. "Get. Out." It's half cry, half plea, all demand. I need them both out of my house right this second. I need space. I need air. I need … I don't even know.

I came home to make a baby … to make love to my husband.

And this ...

"Maybe you should …" He starts to suggest something, bringing my gaze back up to him, and his expression changes—self-preservation, regret, resignation… I don't know. But he thinks better of whatever he was going to say. "Okay. We'll go," he says, climbing onto the bed to make his way over to her … to Mindy. The way he slips an arm around her waist, protectively, like he's done to me so many times, it makes me lose what tiny grip on sanity I have left.

When the dresser hits the ground, my eyes go wide.

I didn't even know I could do that.

As I'm inspecting my work, the door to the bathroom that's attached to our bedroom shuts behind me and I hear the lock slide into place.

My head whips around as I glare at the closed door.

Oh, that's rich.

"Are you seriously locking yourself in the bathroom?" I scoff. "Are you scared, Asher? Not man enough to face me?" A humorless laugh escapes and I begin to pace around the room and that action brings me back to the reason I'm here in the first place. Pacing … Ovulating … Happy …

When the lump in my throat becomes too much to bear, I finally let the tears fall.

My insides begin to rip in two, part of me wanting to stay angry—fired up, and downright pissed the hell off—while the other part wants to crumble into the used sheets and fall apart.

When I open my mouth to speak this time, it's broken and small. "How could you…" About the time I let the tears break free and collapse to the floor in front of the bathroom door, I hear sirens from a distance.

They get closer and closer until they're right outside the window.

The next thing I hear is the front door open and my daddy's voice coming from downstairs. "Em," he calls out. "Em, it's Dad. I'm gonna need you to come down here, honey."

I shake my head as the lump is back and it begins to squeeze, making me unable to speak.

"Emmie," he says a second time, firmer, but I can't talk. I don't budge. I can't. I won't.

This is *my* house.

Asher is *my* husband.

I came home to make a baby.

How did this happen?

"Tempest?"

This time it's Sheriff James's voice that's carrying up the stairs. "Honey, can you please come down here so we can talk this out like adults? I don't want to have to take you in."

"Did you seriously call the cops on me?" I ask quietly, banging my head against the bathroom door.

Asher's sigh is muffled, yet audible, and I can only assume he's mimicking my position on the other side of the door. "You were acting crazy," he says. "Mindy was scared."

Bolting up at the mention of her name, my anger fueled anew, I bang my fist against the door.

"Are you fucking kidding me, Asher?" Next it's my foot that kicks the door and then I'm using the piece of wood like a punching bag. "How long, Asher? How many times?" I scream, letting out all the hurt I'm feeling on the sad excuse for a door. When I kick it again, my foot makes contact with the knob and I hear Mindy scream when it breaks off and falls to the floor.

"EM!"

A second later, my dad and Sheriff James are standing in my bedroom, surveying the damage. "What in the—" My daddy's words break off and he looks over at me with wide, shocked eyes. "Are you okay?"

I finally step away from the door and let my back thud against the bedroom wall, shaking my head, I begin to sob.

Sheriff James walks to the bathroom door and gives it a quick knock. "Asher."

"Uh, yes, sir."

"Gonna need you to step out, son."

"Uh," Asher opens the door, but only exposes his head. "Do, uh… do you think you could hand us some clothes?"

At least he has the decency to sound embarrassed.

Good, I hope he's ashamed of himself.

I hope he's fucking humiliated.

Most of all, I hope he's fucking happy.

"Could you—" Sheriff James looks to me for some assistance, but quickly changes his mind, obviously deciding that's a bad idea and goes about collecting articles of clothing from around the room. "Make it quick," he says, handing them to Asher through the partially open, mostly broken door.

"You know I'm gonna need to take her in," Sheriff James says to my dad in a hushed whisper. I see my dad give a resigned nod. Closing his eyes, he breathes deeply and then walks toward me. I pretend I didn't overhear their conversation and cross my arms as I stare out the window. It's now light outside and I realize I have no idea what time it is or how long I've been gone from work.

"I need to call Jenn," I say biting on my bottom lip to keep myself from crying. The pain is a good deterrent.

My dad sighs and walks to stand in front of me. "Sheriff James—"

"Needs to take me in," I finish for him, kicking off the wall just as the bathroom door creaks open and a clothed Asher and Mindy walk out, still looking at me like I'm their mortal enemy. I glare at Asher and turn the rage up a notch as I let my eyes slide to Mindy.

This bitch is in my house.

In my bed.

With my husband.

My stare intensifies and she flinches.

Good.

I hope she's scared.

I also have no clue what's gotten into me, but there's no turning it off now.

"I'm gonna need all three of you to come down to the station," Sheriff James begins, addressing the room. "Since this has been logged as a domestic disturbance call, we'll need to take statements from the three of you.

He gives me a tight-lipped, apologetic smile. Then he lets out a huff and steps back so Asher and Mindy can walk out ahead of him, obviously putting a barrier between them and me. The absurdity of this entire situation settles in my chest and I can't help the incredulous laugh that erupts.

"Em?" my dad asks from somewhere behind me. "You okay?"

"Fine, Daddy."

Except for the fact I still want to rip Asher limb from limb.

And Mindy too.

And maybe break some more shit.

And burn some shit.

My mama and daddy named me Tempest not because of my red hair, but because I was born on a stormy night. According to my mother, I was howling like the wind. The nurses and doctor even joked about my lungs being overly developed and that maybe I'd be an opera singer when I grew up … an auctioneer … pig caller.

However, for the majority of my life, I've been quite the opposite —calm, cool, collected. I was born in October and am a true Libra, quite often the peacemaker, never making waves. Sure, I've been known as a bit of a spitfire, my red hair mirroring my tenacity and determination, but that's where it stopped. The cliché of a redhead having a fiery temperament has always been lost on me.

But something snapped today.

Something has changed and it's a little frightening to acknowledge the emotions boiling beneath my skin. I want to hit something *or someone*. I want to break things. I need some kind of outlet to release this pent-up anger and resentment roiling through my body.

My eyes bore into the back of Asher's head as we make our way out to the driveway, my daddy ushering me to the back of Sheriff James's police cruiser. After securing me in the back, he slides into the front, while Sheriff James orders Asher and Mindy into the backup squad car that's parked behind my truck.

As we drive off, I turn back to look at the perfect yellow house with white shutters. All of my dreams were wrapped up in that picturesque setting. We were going to have babies and raise a family. And now, the only thing I know for sure is that somewhere—deep inside me—a dormant beast has been awakened.

CHAPTER 1

TEMPEST

Three Months Later

"Mama," I grumble into the receiver of the phone, "Please talk Daddy into getting me out of here."

"Baby, I know this is hard. Believe me when I say that this is harder on him than it is on you, and don't even get me started on what *I'm* going through," she replies with a deep sigh into her end of the phone.

I can picture her sitting in Daddy's chair, since he's here at the police station with me. I'm sure she has her housecoat on and she's probably watching her stories, which she taped earlier today because it's Tuesday and she volunteers at the Community Center on Tuesdays. And when I say "taped", I literally mean "taped". She and Daddy probably own the only working VHS machine in Green Valley, Tennessee. They've yet to catch up with the times and invest in a damned DVD player and don't even get me started on the DVR Debacle of 2015. I've tried and tried to talk them into it, but I always get the same response—the response they give to any modern technology—they're not letting the FBI into their home.

Yeah, that's what I'm working with.

According to them, anything made in the last twenty years is bugged, wired, or tracked.

I still suffer from second-hand embarrassment that they believe in all that Area 51 bullshit. Big Brother. Shark Spies. Fake Moon Landing. You name it, they subscribe. My mama keeps tin foil wrapped around the end of their television antenna for better reception and to block satellite spies from coming into their living room.

"Mama," I plead once more, trying my damndest to work up some legitimate tears, but I'm sad to say, I'm all cried out.

"You've made your bed, Sweetie. Now you're just gonna have to lie in it." Mama's voice takes on the no-nonsense tone she uses when dealing with me or my daddy, especially when we're not living up to Shauna Cassidy's standards. My mama is an ideal southern women—prim, proper, big hair, close to God.

"Mama?" I ask, hoping she's still there, but then there's an audible click as the line goes dead and I feel defeated. She was my one phone call. I can't believe they really only give you one phone call.

"Did she hang up on you?" My daddy's expression is serious, but I also see a small twitch under his thick mustache as I hand the phone back to him through the bars. I feel like he's getting a kick out of seeing me in this situation, knowing I've already used my get-out-of-jail-free card one too many times. As he sighs and stuffs his hands into the front pockets of his jeans, the term *tough love* swirls through the air. It's unspoken, but it's there. My chest feels tight as my dad's head bows and he tucks his chin to his chest, scratching the back of his head with a deep sigh.

Disappointment.

My father, who's always been proud of me, is disappointed.

Until a few months ago, I was an upstanding member of society. I recycled, voted, and braked for dogs, cats, and squirrels. I went to church on Sundays. My husband was my high school sweetheart. We had a life cut from the pages of *Southern Style* magazine—a yellow house with white shutters and a fence to match.

Now, here I am, sitting in jail. *Again*. The only thing keeping me company on this side is a flimsy mattress and an even flimsier blanket folded neatly at the end.

"Can I get you something to eat? Maybe a glass of water?" Sheriff James asks, walking over from a desk in the corner of the room. I know he's only being nice to me because I'm Butch Cassidy's daughter.

And before you get to thinking I'm famous, let me stop right there. We're not *the* Cassidy's—Hollywood actors or legendary outlaws. And no, I am not the Sundance Kid.

The next person who calls me that might get shanked, especially with my recent track record.

But my daddy is the bail bondsman, so he and the sheriff are buddies. Sheriff James books 'em. My daddy bonds 'em. They play for the same team.

"No, thank you," I huff, with as much menace as I can muster.

"Tempest, now you know that this is—" my daddy starts.

"Hurting you more than it's hurting me?" I interrupt. "Yeah, I already know."

And I call bullshit.

Funny thing is that most of my anger is not directed at the man walking out of the jail at this moment, leaving me behind, it's directed at Asher.

He brought all of this on himself.

I was a perfectly calm individual until I walked into *my* bedroom and found him and Mindy snuggled up in *my* thousand count sheets. *My* bed. *My* sheets. *My* husband.

Not that I even want him now. I don't.

At least, that's what I keep telling myself.

But I also didn't want him to have that damn truck.

"I don't really see what the big deal is, anyway," I mutter to myself and the three concrete walls. "I mean, who says it's a sin to drive a truck into a pond?" I pause for my own contemplation as I begin to pace the short length of the bars. "The last I heard, this was still a free country. Seems to me that I should be able to park a vehicle wherever I see fit."

One, two, three, four.

Pivot.

One, two, three—

"You know, I've always thought Mr. Miller's pond was a nice place for a swim," a familiar voice says from behind me, halting my pacing and self-reflection. Glancing up, I see my cousin Cole standing a few feet away, hand on his holster as he gives me his signature smile, dimples on full display. How any criminals ever take him serious is beyond me.

Fighting back a smile, I turn to face him. I should've known he'd be on duty tonight, or if he wasn't, once he heard my name on the police scanner he'd be here. "I don't need your smart mouth tonight, Cole Cassidy. I've gotten enough of a lecture from my daddy, who, by the way, left me to rot in this damned jail cell."

"Aww, now. It's not that bad. Sheriff James just had the beds upgraded last month and I can have Anna bring an extra piece of meatloaf when she drops by later to bring me supper."

Spinning on my heel, I grip the bars and stare him down. "Oh, no. Don't you dare tell her I'm in here," I warn. That would be even worse than my daddy leaving me here or my mama calling her prayer chain.

Cole shows a sign of zipping his lips and tossing an imaginary key over his shoulder. "Your secret's safe with me." Walking over to the desk, he perches on the edge, crossing his big arms across his chest.

"How long are you holding me here for, anyway?"

Giving me a small smile, he shakes his head and glances over his shoulder before turning back to answer. "As long as no charges are pressed, you should be free to go in the morning."

Letting out a deep, resigned sigh, I walk over to the cot and plop down.

"So, you really drove that truck right off into Mr. Miller's pond?"

I take a second to make myself as comfortable as possible, seeing as though I'm going to be here for the night. Kicking my shoes off, I place them neatly on the floor and then lay back, staring up at the ceiling. "Yeah, drove it right past the dock and straight into the pond."

"Holy shit," Cole replies with a chuckle. "I always knew you were a little crazy. It was just hidden down under all your cardigans and china patterns."

"Shut up," I tell him with a laugh. "I'm not crazy. Just pissed the hell off."

"So, what made you want to do that?" Cole asks and I sit up to look at him.

"Is this Cole the deputy asking or Cole my cousin?"

"Always Cole, your cousin."

"Asher called me today and said since the truck was in his name, he was gonna sell it. At first, I told him fine and that he could come and get it, because I don't want anything of his anyway. The divorce will be final in another few weeks and I'm ready to be done with it, you know? But then, after I hung up the phone, I really started thinking about, thinking back on when we bought the truck and how happy I was… how happy he was. He wanted me to have something nice to drive. We were happy…" I drift off, unable to finish for a second as my memories bring up fresh emotions. It's not Asher I'm sad about; it's the possibilities… my future. "I just couldn't let him take one more thing from me."

We both sit in silence for a few minutes until Cole's walkie talkie starts rattling off some mumbo jumbo I don't understand. I hear him shift and then clear his throat. "I've always got your back. You know that, right?"

I offer a small, sad smile to the ceiling. "Thanks, Cole."

"But no more truck swimming," he says, tapping the wall on his way out.

It's strange to think that I, Tempest Cassidy, am in jail.

I'm not your typical criminal. I didn't drop out of school. Actually, not only am I a high school graduate, I also graduated from college… with a degree in culinary arts… that I use.

Which brings me to my other contradictory quality: I'm a hard-working, contributing citizen of society. I take my job very seriously. I'm passionate about muffins, well, baking in general, but since I got hired on at the Donner Bakery and put in charge of the muffin making,

I've owned it … taken it to a new level … revolutionized muffin making and given them flair.

If Jenn is the Banana Cake Queen, I am the Duchess of Muffins.

Which, by the way, I'm glad it's Saturday night and I don't have to work tomorrow. I'd hate to have to call into work ... from jail.

However, this isn't my first *episode*, as my mama likes to call them. I wish they really were episodes, because then, maybe I could figure out a way to stop them … cancel their subscription.

I don't want to be a person with a rap sheet. Orange is not a good color on me. Driving that truck into Mr. Miller's pond was definitely not my finest moment. Believe me, I know the law, but when my soon-to-be ex-husband is in the picture, all my rationality flies out the window.

It usually goes something like this:

I'm minding my own business, trying to live my life.

He shows up out of nowhere, his presence alone reminding me of everything I had and have lost. I get pissed off… sometimes just because he's doing something as simple as breathing.

My vision gets hazy.

My body tingles with untapped aggression.

Then, the crazy sets in and there isn't a lick of reason to be found.

From that point on, I have somewhat of an out-of-body experience and I just do whatever feels right in the moment—whatever will ease the pain or let me vent my anger—and hope to hell I don't get caught.

CHAPTER 2

CAGE

As the car I'm riding in passes a sign that reads "Green Valley—population 12,539", I sit up in my seat a little straighter, focusing on the scenery. But there's not really much to look at besides trees and hills and the occasional car, until we come across an old farmhouse and a wrecker's flashing lights gets my attention.

Craning my neck as we drive past, I notice it's pulling a truck from a pond.

Smirking to myself, I shake my head. There's bound to be a story there. But what do I know about small towns? Nothing. Absolutely nothing. I've lived in Dallas my whole life, so this, along with everything else that's transpired in the last couple months, is a serious change of pace.

"Hey, thanks man," I tell the guy I paid to give me a ride from the bus station, tapping the side of his car once I have my two duffle bags unloaded from the backseat. I could've flown into Nashville and rented a car, but the less-traveled path seemed to suit me better right now. Besides, I don't know how long I'm going to be here and I didn't want the hassle of returning a rental car.

A few months ago, I felt like I was in the prime of my life—finally fighting on the professional circuit. Everyone always tells you it won't last forever. My mom has always been on my case about the future and making plans for the next phase of my life, but I've always felt like I'll either die young or fight until I'm ninety. I've never seen an in between for me. There's never been a second love or a Plan B. It's always been fighting or nothing.

A career-ending injury was definitely not on my radar.

I eat well, train well, take every precaution to keep myself in top shape. Physically, I'm in the best shape of my life, but my right shoulder no longer allows me to have full-range of motion. I can't complete an uppercut without excruciating pain radiating through my arm and up my neck, which leaves me vulnerable in the ring.

Cage Erickson is synonymous with champion.

I've only lost a handful of fights in my life and most of those came during my amateur years. And no, I don't normally refer to myself in the third person, but I've made my name my brand and I refuse to let that be tarnished. With forty-nine wins under my belt, seven draws, and five losses, I was on my way to a title and a lucrative career as a UFC fighter.

I can still remember feeling the tear, something foreign, a pain I wasn't used to, but I kept fighting. I won the round and eventually the bout. Initially, I thought the injury wasn't so bad. Maybe a few weeks in PT and I'd be good as new, until the doc sent me for an MRI and showed me the extent of the damage.

Less than a day later, I was in surgery, having my shoulder cut open.

Ruptured right subscapularis and bicep tendon tear.

I spent six weeks in a sling and another six weeks doing physical therapy. And another six weeks going fucking stir crazy. Without an outlet for all my pent-up energy, I feel like breaking walls and smashing windows. The slightest thing sets me off these days.

Which is what brings me to the quaint town of Green Valley, Tennessee.

As the dust from the gravel parking lot whips up with a gust of wind, I feel like I'm in one of those apocalyptic movies. Except for the blinking sign on the building in front of me and the few cars parked in the lot, this place feels like a ghost town compared to the big city life I'm used to.

"Cage Erickson." A familiar voice brings my attention to a side door and Hank is standing there with a smirk on his face. "I wasn't sure if you were gonna take me up on the offer."

"Well, I wasn't sure myself …" I tell him, walking toward where he's standing, kicking up a little more dust as I go. A few hours back up the road, I was still deciding on whether or not I'd get here just to turn right back around and head back home, or if I'd actually stay. But something about the green trees and mountains and fresh air makes my mind up for me. "But a few miles back up the road, I decided it sounded like a good idea."

His smile widens as he lets out a laugh. "Well then. Welcome to Green Valley."

"Thanks," I tell him, giving the building another once over. "So, this is your club?"

Hank sighs, stepping out of the doorway to peer up at the building. "Yeah, she's a beaut, huh?"

Chuckling, I nod my head and toss one of my duffles over my good shoulder. "Not too shabby," I agree, walking toward him. "How about a tour? And where can I find some food in this town? I'm starving."

When Hank slaps my shoulder, I wince.

"Sorry, man." He grimaces, giving me a hard look. "About everything, really."

"Yeah, me too."

"You're a hell of a fighter, best I've seen."

"*Was*," I correct.

"*Are*," he insists. "Which is why I hired you to be my bouncer. I need someone around here to keep everyone in line. My girls are too pretty to be harassed."

As we walk into the building, he escorts me down a dimly-lit hallway and into the open expanse of the club. Surprisingly, it's well-lit and well-furnished. I'm assuming it's dark in here during the evening hours, but with the house lights up, everything is exposed, including a scantily dressed waitress walking our way.

"Hi, Hank," she drawls in a sweet southern accent. "Who's your friend?"

The blonde winks in my direction as she pushes her boobs together to bring them to my attention, which isn't really necessary. They're big. And her top is tiny. Along with the equally tiny shorts, she's giving Hooters' girls a run for their money.

"Cage Erickson," I tell her, dropping my bags and offering her a handshake. If we're going to be co-workers, we might as well get off on the right foot.

"Cage is our new bouncer," Hank informs her. "He's gonna help me get this place in order."

She raises her eyebrows and places her dainty hand in mine. "Sarah," she says with a seductive smile. "Nice muscles."

"Thanks," I deadpan.

She's pretty enough, but I'm not interested. I'm here to do a job and I'm not looking to get involved. One-night stands have been my style the last few years, but that never goes over well in a place of employment. It's been a while since I've worked a day job, but the rules never change.

"Well, let's get you fed and then I'll show you around," Hank instructs, guiding me over to a table as he calls out to someone that he needs two burgers and fries.

"Thanks for this, man."

"Don't thank me," Hank replies. "You're doing me a favor. I really need some muscle around here. So, don't act like I'm giving you a free ride." He laughs and glances over his shoulder before turning back to face me. "Where are you planning on staying?"

I sigh, leaning back in my chair. "I don't know. Haven't really thought about it. Just packed up my shit and headed for Tennessee. All I knew was I had to get out of Dallas before I lost my damn mind."

"Well, you came to the right place."

Glancing around, I smirk, shaking my head. Never in a million years did I think the road would lead to a strip club in the middle of nowhere Tennessee. "It's a change of pace, that's for sure."

"Yeah, and it'll keep you out of that damn head of yours while you continue to heal up." Hank nods, thinking to himself for a second. "How is the shoulder?"

I give it a test spin, wincing when I get halfway around. "Still not back to fighting shape, but it's better."

Won't ever be, I think to myself.

Hank huffs his response, his eyes boring into mine. "You'll do just fine. Pretty sure you could take most people if you were blindfolded and hogtied."

We both laugh, and I know he's probably not too far from the truth. Fighting is in my blood. It's what I've always known, what I've always been passionate about. Somehow, I've got to find a way to channel all of that into something productive.

Over the past couple months, I've felt the adrenaline building. There's always this underlying current, something I've never been able to put a finger on, but it's there. Fighting has always been my outlet, keeping it to an electrifying buzz instead of an overwhelming gong.

Anger?

Anxiety?

Excess energy?

I don't know, but my father, being a boxer, recognized that when I was in the ring with him, I was a calmer, more collected version of myself. It gave me discipline, taught me respect for myself and others, and even helped me focus on tasks outside of the sport.

I've always been determined, motivated, and one of the best fighters in Texas, and most recently, the country. That is until my injury. Now, everything feels like it's in slow-motion. A few months ago, I was cruising down a highway with no speed limit, and now, I'm on a back country road, trudging through the mud.

Without the rigorous schedule of training for fights and the reward of putting all of my hard work to use, I'm feeling pretty fucking lost these days.

Who knows? Maybe somewhere in this roadside strip club and quaint town, I'll find myself again.

CHAPTER 3

TEMPEST

The way people look at me nowadays makes me feel like a stranger. It's the same way they look at out-of-towners, or people they don't trust—guarded and suspicious. My mama has given me one too many talks about putting on a good appearance, and Lord knows, I've been trying.

Fake it until you make it.

Put on a good face.

But I've never been good at lying and that's what it feels like.

My bullshitter has been broken since the day I was born. I couldn't lie my way out of a brown paper sack. For the life of me, I can't understand what's happening... why I'm acting the way I've been acting. My only explanation is that Asher brought out something in me, a level of anger and vindictiveness I've never known until now.

"I've raised you better than this," my mama leans up and whispers as we sit in the courtroom and wait for the judge. "Tempest June, are you listening to me? You do whatever this judge tells you to and get a grip on yourself."

"Not now, Mama," I hiss back. I love her. God knows I do, but I'm so tired of everyone telling me how I should feel and how I should act and how I should turn the other cheek. Normally, she'd full name me—

first, middle, and last—but since she knows the mention of Williams causes my blood to boil, she did me a favor and stopped at my first and middle.

Small mercies.

"Tempest Williams," Judge Carson says, as if on cue, and I grit my teeth.

Apparently, he didn't get the memo.

"Here, Judge Carson," I say, standing from my spot in the second row and making my way to the podium where I try not to fidget. Forcing a smile, I smooth out the pale-yellow skirt I picked out for today. Not sure why, but it makes me feel pretty and I need any little help I can get these days.

The last time I saw Judge Carson, we were arguing over the last slice of Mississippi mud pie at the church Pie Supper. When he gives me a stern, serious stare, I wince and give an awkward wave. "Seems to me you've been in a little trouble, Mrs—"

"Miss," I correct, cutting him off and clearing my throat, because if I have to hear *Mrs. Williams* one more time I'm liable to do something that'd earn me a permanent spot in Sheriff James's jail and as nice as those upgraded cots are, I'm not looking to change my address. "*Miss* Cassidy. I'd prefer Miss Cassidy."

"Is your divorce final?" he asks, looking down through the reading glasses at the tip of his nose as he flips through the stack of papers in front of him.

"Uh, no sir, but it will be next week."

Sighing, in either frustration or reluctance, he cuts his eyes back up at me and repeats, "Seems to me you've been in a little trouble, *Miss* Cassidy."

"Yes, sir."

Honesty is still the best policy, right?

"Also seems to me that the trouble stems from your… well, temper, Tempest."

Temper. Tempest. I see what he did there and the pun isn't lost on me, but I decide to plead the fifth on this one, keeping my lips in a straight line … and shut.

"In the last three months, you've been brought in on a domestic dispute, disturbing the peace, vandalism … and the most recent count, destruction of personal property. How do you plead?"

I swallow, wanting to turn around and see if my mama is still sitting behind me, but if I saw her, then I'd see my dad, and the look of disappointment I'm sure I'd see on his face would be a little too much for me to bear. "Guilty, your Honor."

Judge Carson nods, pursing his lips, as he flips back through the pages, obviously thinking … thinking of what my fine will be … or sentence, perhaps. Cole told me that my worst-case scenario is a few days in jail and a thousand dollar fine, neither of which I want.

The fact of the matter is, this divorce has cost me in more ways than one. Not only did I lose my husband, but I lost my vehicle and soon I'll have to give up my house, along with half my savings to cover attorney fees.

Can you believe that shit? He cheats and I still have to pay. But it's fine because I don't want anything from him and I'm ready to be done with everything involving him, so the faster this is over the better.

At least, that's what I keep telling myself.

There are a few people in the courtroom murmuring, probably talking about me, but I tune them out. I don't really care what people are saying or what they think of me. I can't explain the reasoning behind the crazy things I've been doing. They don't really make sense at all.

However, I know that with each incident—a pile of burnt clothes, a vehicle dumped into Mr. Miller's pond—I feel a little better inside, like a small piece of myself is coming back.

The truth is, I want Asher to feel what I feel—to hurt like I hurt—but that's impossible. What I've come to realize lately is that he's not the person I thought he was. He doesn't care about me. He doesn't love me. If he did, he never would've broken our vows. I thought they were sacred. I thought we had something special. But I was wrong.

There's no way I can hurt him like he hurt me, because I loved him.

I was ready to go to the ends of the earth for him.

But he threw all that away.

Metaphorically, he burned everything we'd spent years building to the ground in one afternoon.

The damage was already done.

It kills me every time I see him and Mindy around town. I wonder what he'd think if the tables were turned, but again, I'd never do that. I'm Tempest Cassidy and I'm loyal to a fault.

I also realize that even if I went out and fucked the whole town, I'd just be the new town whore with a broken heart… and maybe a few STDs. I wouldn't be doing myself any favors.

So, I've settled for a different kind of revenge.

The first time I was arrested was the night I was standing outside of Asher's new house. I'd been sleeping and had one of my nightmares—this vivid dream where I'm walking into the house all over again. He's moaning. She's moaning. Practically the whole house is shaking. And then I'm standing in the doorway of our bedroom and I see them.

One time, I was pregnant—round belly, my hands protectively placed.

When I woke up, I had tears streaming down my cheeks and my heart literally ached.

That particular night, I decided if I couldn't sleep, then neither should he. So, I went over there—to his new house. In my fluffy pink house slippers and my red plaid pajama bottoms from Christmas, I stood in Asher's front yard and yelled out every feeling I'd pent up inside me—the hate, the betrayal, the disgust. I just let it all out, yelling so loud I probably woke the dead, but then the neighbors had called the cops. Before the sirens and flashing lights, I remember feeling completely exhausted and laying down in the cool grass because it felt good on my hot, tear-stained cheeks.

The liquid courage I drank prior to going over there probably hadn't helped the situation.

And even though I landed myself in jail, I felt better. That time, my daddy bailed me out pretty quick. I was barely there long enough for the whiskey to wear off. He just drove me home and told me to go back to bed.

A week later, after I ran into Asher and Mindy at the bank, I went straight home and ran around the house like a crazy person, gathering everything that belonged to him. Clothes left in the closet, shoes left in the garage, his stupid baseball magazines—I piled them all up in the driveway and lit the sons of bitches on fire.

Apparently, the Homeowner's Association frowns on fires in the driveway.

"*All fires must be contained in a fire pit, fireplace, or grill,*" Mr. Ramirez, the HEA president, had said.

Is this still the fucking south?

Can't people burn shit if they want to, damn it?

That time, I only received a citation and a hefty fine of two hundred and fifty dollars, which initiated my next run-in with the law.

I figured that since all of this was Asher's fault in the first place, he should have to pay my fine. So, while he and the missus were at work one day, after I finished up my Duchess of Muffin duties at the bakery, I drove over and broke in the back door of his new house and stole his pride and joy—an autographed football from the University of Alabama National Championship team.

Rammer jammer, my ass!

I'd like to have rammed that football up Asher's ass, but instead, I hocked it.

I know all of these *incidents—episodes ... whatever you want to call them*—make me sound exactly how everyone labels me these days —*crazy, unstable, scorned*—but at the time, my actions seemed completely logical. I'm not even mad anymore, really, just hurt. I'm also sorry I wasted all those years putting him on a pedestal, because he never deserved it.

"Tell you what I'm going to do," Judge Carson finally says, bringing my attention back to him. "I'm going to fine you the minimum five hundred dollar fine, plus ..." he says, pausing. His bushy, gray eyebrows furrowing as he looks at me. "Twenty-four hours of anger management. You can either find a class or I'll appoint one for you."

I swallow, partially grateful and partially pissed off. I don't have an anger problem. I have an Asher Williams problem, and as soon as he's out of my life, everything will go back to normal.

"Is that understood, Miss Cassidy?" he asks, waiting for me to acknowledge his decree.

I nod, swallowing again. "Yes, sir."

"And if I see you back in my courtroom again, I won't be as lenient next time."

As we're walking out, my mama on one side and my daddy on the other, she lets out a huge sigh of relief. "Praise the Lord. See, I told you, prayer works. That could've gone so much worse, Tempest. God was looking out for you today," she says, squeezing my hand and adding under her breath, "and every other day for the past three months."

"Yes, Mama," I say, placating her until I can get to the solace of my house. Even though it feels tainted with memories of Asher and Mindy, it's still mine, for now, and the only place I feel like I can go these days without people staring at me. Although, I have moved into the spare bedroom downstairs, hardly going upstairs in the past three months.

"We should celebrate," she says as we approach the parking lot. "Butch, take us for steaks. It's been a while since we've been to the Front Porch. I think today calls for a nice supper. And Lord knows I'm too exhausted to even think about cooking."

I bite my cheek and let out a deep exhale through my nose, willing my patience to hold out a little while longer.

My daddy walks to the car and opens the passenger door for her. Before he opens the rear door for me, he pauses, leaning on the hood. "You wanna grab a bite to eat?"

"As lovely as a nice steak dinner sounds," I manage. "I really just want to go home." I try to put on a convincing smile but he doesn't buy it.

"Don't let him win," he says quietly, just for the two of us, looking me square in the eye. "Take your punishment, get this mess over with, and move on with your life."

Swallowing the lump in my throat that comes out of nowhere, I nod. "Yeah, I'm planning on it."

He sighs again before giving me a quick hug, kissing the top of my head. "You're gonna be alright."

"Okay." I needed that. I needed someone to tell me that so hopefully I'll start believing it myself, because right now, things seem dismal, and that's putting it lightly.

My mama doesn't say much when my daddy turns the car in the direction of my house instead of the restaurant. When he pulls up into my drive, I get out and shut the door, without preamble.

"Call us tomorrow," my mama says, rolling her window down. "And I expect you to be at church on Sunday."

"Yes, ma'am," I call out over my shoulder, offering her a consolatory wave as I'm halfway to the door.

I know she means well, but she has been downright stifling lately. She's constantly checking up on me, coming by the house unannounced, and unloading all of her wisdom whenever she sees fit. I know I need some of it. We all need our mama's words of wisdom from time to time, but I also need a freaking break.

I need to breathe.

I need to forget.

I need some time for my heart to heal.

I need to figure out how to fall out of love with Asher Williams.

Because as hurt and mad as I am, there's still a part of me that loves the man I married. The one I was planning on starting a family with. The guy I planned to spend the rest of my life with. He was in all my plans … five-year, ten-year … retirement. And now, I'm left figuring out who I am without him.

Today's soundtrack would include *Choices* by the late, great George Jones. Maybe I'll pour a glass of wine and listen to him on repeat. Sometimes, the only thing that can soothe my soul is the steel guitar.

It's been two weeks since my last run-in with the law, which is something to celebrate in itself, but I've got something even better than that: my divorce is final.

I met with my lawyer yesterday after work and it's a done deal. After a short trip to the DMV and the Social Security Office, I'm officially back to being Tempest Cassidy. I'd like to say it feels good, and in a way it does, but I'm also fighting off the impending doom of being alone.

How did I get here?

The thing I try to keep reminding myself is that, for the rest of my life, I won't ever have to look at Asher's face again, if I choose not to. After months of living under the weight of his betrayal, I feel the first ease of tension, like I can breathe again.

And tonight, I feel like letting my hair down.

Earlier, I contemplated calling someone to go out with me, but most of the people I know have either joined Team Asher or refuse to take sides, which in my book, means they're Team Asher. The few people who actually *are* on my team would never be caught dead in a bar. They're either knocked-up or are your typical wholesome southern woman, which I am neither—with child or a stereotype.

I'm more than certain my mama and daddy would frown on my choice of location for my celebration, but one thing I've learned since my life got turned upside down is that from here on out, I'm doing things *my* way.

Operation: Make Tempest Happy.

Because if *I* don't, who will?

For years, I let my happiness reside in Asher Williams. Twelve years, to be exact, since I was sixteen years old, and look where that got me—cheated on and divorced, with a rap sheet.

Not anymore. From now on, I answer to no one but myself.

So tonight, I'm going to the Pink Pony.

Sure, it's not my usual scene. Let's face it, my usual scene for the last eight years has been my house, the bakery, or an occasional night out to dinner. But it's precisely what I need—half-priced ladies' night, music to drown out my thoughts, low lighting to keep me as inconspicuous as possible, and half-naked girls to keep the men folk distracted.

I know, I know. You're probably thinking, what the heck, Tempest? Can't you at least go where there are naked men? But the truth is, I don't want to see any naked men. I just want to feel the numbness that comes from drinking one too many margaritas.

After I get ready, I pull up my Uber app and pray that someone is available tonight. Being in a small town has its perks, but public transportation is not one of them. And I know good and well that I won't be in any shape to drive home, so I take my chances.

Worst-case scenario: I call Cole, but seeing as though he's a deputy and is married to a nun, he probably wouldn't want to be an accessory to my night of debauchery.

When my app shows no availability, I sigh, feeling a bit dejected and kind of like crying.

"Are you kidding me?" I shout to the ceiling. *Looking at you, Big Guy.*

Letting out a frustrated huff, I lean against the wall and for a split-second, I consider changing out of these clothes and letting ice cream and baked goods lull me into a false sense of serenity. But that's a weak substitution for what I want: a night of no thoughts, no feelings … just the warmth of tequila running through my veins.

Nothing is ever freaking easy for me these days.

One night. That's all I want and I can't even make that happen on my own.

Taking a look in the mirror in the foyer, I give myself the once-over —favorite sweater, skinny jeans that make my ass look great, and a new pair of shoes I've never had the chance to wear. I'm not wasting this.

So, I dial Cole's number and pray.

"Is this Tempest the Burner, or is this Tempest the Ball Buster, *or* . . ." he asks, pausing for dramatic effect, "is it possible that I'm talking to the one and only Tempest the Beautiful?"

"Always the charmer, Cole," I deadpan, rolling my eyes. "It's

Tempest ... *Cassidy*." I put heavy emphasis on my last name and smile, trying to convince myself it's a good thing.

I'm divorced.

I'm moving on.

"Well, well, well. Sounds like congratulations are in order," he says, his voice depicting his pleasure in my current marital status. "Proud of you, Tempest. Really."

"Thanks. I'm not sure everyone feels the same, but—"

He huffs his displeasure at that statement. "You did the right thing. Regardless of what anyone thinks, none of this is your fault. He's the asshole. Don't doubt that. And you've been nice for far too long, so no matter what anyone else says or thinks, I'm proud of you." He pauses and I wish I could reach through the phone and hug him. "So, to what do I owe this pleasure? Please tell me you're not calling from jail, because I don't really think—"

"I'm not calling from jail," I interrupt, rolling my eyes again as I lean back against the wall, chewing on my thumb nail. "I need a favor."

"Okay, shoot," he says, then adds, "Not literally, that's a felony."

I huff a laugh, knowing I'll never live down the past three months of my life. "Haha, very funny," I say, fighting back a smile and working up the courage to ask him what I called to ask. "I was, uh, wondering if I could get a ride ... somewhere?"

"You could call Anna, she'll probably be heading out to the Piggly Wiggly later for her Saturday night grocery run … don't know how that woman can find entertainment in that, but whatever."

"Well," I drawl, breathing out deeply. "I was actually thinking more like the Pink Pony." The last few words are expelled in a rush and I squeeze my eyes shut in hopes he won't instantly shut me down.

"Ah, man. Tempest, I don't feel good about this," he whines. "Anna will kick my ass when she finds out, and don't say she won't find out because we both know that's a lie. Nobody gossips like the barflies and the Baptists."

"Cole," I say, opting for a different angle. "I'd do it for you."

"You're gonna wind your ass up in jail. Again." I can almost hear him pacing the floor, and I feel bad for putting him in this situation—really, I do. If I had another friend to call, I would, but I don't. "Why you wanna go there anyway?"

Guilt trip in three, two, one ...

"Listen," I say, mustering what little self-assurance I have left and try to put it all in a nutshell, needing him to understand where I'm coming from. "I spent the last eight years answering to Asher Williams's every whim. I worked while he went to college. I bent over backwards for everything that man ever wanted. And he repaid me for all of it by fucking Mindy... Mindy Mitchell, Cole! Do you remember how mean she was to me in middle school? And now, she's living with my ex-husband. I don't know how to feel these days. I have all these misplaced feelings and tonight, if I don't let off some steam, I'm gonna blow and I really might end up back in jail. Do you want that?" I pause to take a breath and then go in for one last blow. "Besides, I haven't had any *real* fun in a *long* time. After all the shit I've been through, I deserve this. Don't ruin it for me. It's not like I'm going to apply for a job or dance on the stage."

After a few seconds, he finally acquiesces. "I'll be there in five."

Ten minutes later, Cole is dropping me off at the front door of the bar. The gravel parking lot is full and dark and Cole is scoping out the perimeter, making sure it's safe before I get out.

Also, he's probably trying to see who's witnessing the drop-off. And who's going to be on the phone to Anna before he can even get back home.

"Cole," I say, stepping out of the cruiser. "Do yourself a favor and just tell her when you get home. You'll worry yourself sick over her finding out if you don't." Leaning back into the car and reaching across the seat, I give his big, burly arm a squeeze. For such a large guy, he sure is a pussy sometimes. "Tell her it's my fault and she can come over tomorrow and pray over me or whatever, okay?"

His eyes grow wide as he gives me a look of pure shock, unbelieving I'd give Anna Cassidy permission to unleash her wrath on me. It's almost worse than God's.

Finally, he nods. “I’m on patrol all night. Promise me you’ll call when you’re ready to leave. I’ll come pick you up.”

“I will. Thanks, again,” I tell him, leaning over further to kiss his cheek. “And, I’m sorry if I get you in trouble.”

“Wouldn’t be the first time,” he says with a chuckle.

Nope, it wouldn't be the first time and I’m pretty sure it won’t be the last. Cole and I are known for getting in and out of trouble together. When he became a cop, things changed a little, but he’s still the same Cole I grew up with. Except, now he’s an adult who works for the law and is married to the most pious person in the Appalachians.

“Maybe I should go in with you, just to make sure it’s …” His words trail off as he makes hand gestures toward the bar.

“It’s fine. I’m a big girl,” I tell him, smiling as I shut the door and wave over my shoulder.

CHAPTER 4

CAGE

The past couple of weeks have been good, slow but good.

My shoulder is feeling moderately better, my mind is clearer than it's been in months, and I haven't had much time to dwell on the demise of my career. All good things.

Hank is letting me live in an apartment he owns above a vacant storefront downtown. It's quiet and spacious. When he mentioned it to me the day I arrived, I assumed it'd be some rundown space that I'd make do with until I decide what I'm doing with my life, but it's nothing like that. It's oddly something I would've designed for myself —high ceilings, exposed brick, and old wooden floors. It's old, but new and it has character in spades.

I found a cool old bedframe at an antique store just a few doors down and bought a new mattress for it at the furniture store. Hank had already furnished the kitchen with stainless steel counters and open shelving. There's not much in the space right now, except for the few things I brought with me—clothes and few books—along with an old radio I also bought at the antique store.

Every day has been spent at the Pink Pony, learning the business and getting to know everyone. For the most part, it's an easy job. Hank runs a tight ship—no touching, no drugs, no drama.

There's been a few guys who've gotten a little rowdy, but other than that, I've been just standing around keeping an eye on the place, helping bus a few tables from time to time, and filling in where I'm needed. Hank had mentioned needing some muscle around, but now that I'm here, I'm pretty sure he created a job for me.

Tonight's crowd seems pretty average.

A girl named Fuchsia, apparently her God-given name, is on stage and the customers seem to be eating it up. With her bright pink tail feathers, she looks like a cross between a flamingo and a peacock. I've seen her routine a few times and am prepared for when the feathers come off, exposing her ass cheeks.

I guess for some guys, working in a strip club might be a problem, but not me. Sure, I know an attractive woman when I see one, but I'm not interested in anything these women have to offer.

"Hey, baby," one of the waitresses croons as she walks by and grips my bicep.

I smile and give her a wink, but she's harmless.

"Do me a favor and clear table eleven?" she asks, setting her tray on the bar top beside me and calling out some orders to the bartender.

"Sure," I tell her, pushing off the bar and walking over to the table. There're just a few glasses and used napkins that I quickly gather up. When I turn around and head to the back, I see that in my absence, someone has slipped into the barstool where I usually stand.

After I set the dirty dishes in the bin behind the bar, I catch my first real glimpse of her.

Shoulder-length, fiery red hair and a petite frame. She's not exactly what I've come to expect from the patrons of the Pink Pony. Her low-cut sweater and skin-tight jeans draw a little attention from men around her, but most of them get one look and turn their eyes back to the entertainment on stage.

"Can I get you something?" I overhear the bartender, Floyd, ask.

"Tequila," the woman says, sliding her credit card across the bar. "Start me a tab."

Checking around for a date or a friend who might be with her, I come up empty-handed and my curiosity is peaked. What is a girl like her doing in a place like this … alone?

"How's it going, Tempest?" a man to her right asks as he takes his beer and puts down some cash.

Tempest.

Curiouser and curiouser.

"Good, Joe. How are you?" she asks and her voice is husky for such a small person and my dick takes notice.

What the fuck?

"Not too shabby. Heard about you puttin' that truck in Miller's pond," he adds with a chuckle before taking a drink of his beer.

"Yeah," she says with a sigh and a grateful smile as the bartender places the requested tequila down in front of her. "Good times." There's a heavy dose of sarcasm coating her words and I notice the way her shoulders tense a little.

Without a lick of salt or a second thought, she picks up the shot glass and throws it back.

No lime.

No chaser.

"I'll have another," she tells Floyd, who quickly obliges.

That's when I realize this could get ugly.

So, I decide to stick close, just in case my services are needed, but far enough away that I'm not tempted, because for some unknown reason, I'm definitely fucking tempted.

Maybe it's the red hair.

Maybe it's the raspy voice.

Maybe it's the way she's throwing back the tequila like a fucking badass.

Maybe it's her name … *Tempest.* It's different. She seems different and I haven't even officially met her.

I decide, standing there at the end of the bar, watching her from afar while I keep my eyes focused on the rest of the club, I'm not sure if I want to. The last time I was this instantly attracted to a woman, I fell hard, and she broke my heart.

The big, bad cage fighter, crushed by a blonde heartbreaker.

I wasn't driven, according to her.

She needed to marry someone like a lawyer or a doctor. I'd confided in her about my real dreams—dreams beyond getting a degree from a prestigious university like Harvard—winning belts, being on the UFC circuit.

She couldn't be with someone like me, someone who *beat the shit out of people for living*. Her words, not mine. Her parents' perception and opinions meant more to her than my love. I should've known better. I should've seen it coming.

But I was in college, with my entire life ahead of me, and I felt like I had the world at my fingertips.

When she broke up with me, she broke me. It came out of the blue, on a night I was planning on giving her a promise ring. I knew we were too young to get married, but it didn't mean I didn't want to. I did, but I knew she wouldn't. I knew she'd freak. But instead of slipping that small gold band with an eternity symbol on her finger, I got slapped in the face. Not literally. Although, I wish I had. That would've been easier to take.

Shaking my head to clear the memories, I turn my gaze to the red head down the bar and notice there are now three empty shot glasses sitting in front of her and what looks like a margarita on the rocks in her hand. At least she's smart enough to stick to one liquor.

Maybe she won't be a problem.

Maybe she can handle more than one would expect.

More than her petite frame might insinuate.

Forcing myself to face forward, I watch a few more numbers. The crowd grows a little, a few people I've seen before and have started to notice as regulars. I've never thought much about strip clubs and the people who frequent them, but it's interesting, that's for sure.

Old men.

Young men.

Wealthy men.

Blue collar.

White collar.

And women.

All kinds.

There seems to be a little something for everyone.

Especially Candy, the girl who is currently on stage, dancing to *Pour Some Sugar on Me*, because … *Candy*. She really draws the crowd and the whistles. Noticing a few guys getting a little close to the stage, I push off the bar and take a few steps toward them, just in case.

"Yeah, baby," one of them yells, counting out dollar bills as he holds his beer in the crook of his elbow. "Pour it on me!" When he gets a little off-balance trying to place the bills on the stage, his beer pours over the side of the glass and onto the guy who's sitting at the table beside him.

When he stands up and puffs out his chest, I walk forward, placing myself between the two men.

"Hey," I call out, getting his attention quick. "It was an accident." I cock an eyebrow and motion for Sarah to bring the guy a towel. "How about a beer on the house?"

His nostrils flare and he glares at the other guy who's still luring Candy with his sweaty bills. Finally, the song changes and she blows a kiss, waving over her shoulder about the time Sarah walks up with the towel. Dabbing at the man's shoulder with a sweet smile, I finally see his anger start to ebb.

"How about her?" he asks with a wink to Sarah.

"She's off the menu," I inform, giving Sarah a roll of my eyes.

"I'll take the beer then," he says, settling back in his chair.

Sarah smiles and walks off to the bar, while I take the mostly empty beer glass from the guy by the stage. "How about you have a seat, buddy?"

"How about you don't tell me what to do," he says, before turning around and getting a glimpse of who he's talking to.

Yeah, that's what I thought.

"Have a seat," I reiterate and he obliges.

Catastrophe averted, I turn to walk back over to my post at the bar when I see her. Tempest.

With a break in on-stage action, the house music is turned up and

Crazy by Aerosmith is blaring over the speakers. And Tempest is now climbing onto the bar.

Onto the mother fucking bar.

For a second, I'm frozen in my spot … in place … in time … as she sways her body to the music, arms above her head. The blissful look on her face makes me not want to disturb her. She looks … happy. But I can't let her dance on the bar.

That's another one of Hank's rules.

If you're not a dancer, you don't get a stage.

Walking over to her, I tap her leg, but she continues swaying and now she's belting out the lyrics, her expression making me believe she's feeling every word down to her toes.

"Hey," I call up, loud enough to cut through the music.

Her eyes pop open and she frowns down at me and I see the glassiness, the tequila shining through. When she goes back to dancing, closing her eyes and blocking me out, I huff, bracing my hands on my hips.

The guys two seats down are now fully invested in the show she's giving and I growl in their direction. I want to ask them what they're looking at, but I know.

I see it.

I see her.

She might not be a Candy or a Fuchsia. There aren't any double Ds. But she's got something they don't have. I can't even put my finger on it, but it's there.

Red hair flying around her peaches-and-cream skin.

Nice, tight little ass, poured into the jeans she's wearing.

Plump lips wrapping around the lyrics of the song.

And moves like a porn star.

"Off the bar," I bark out, gripping her calf to get her attention. I don't know if I'm more pissed off at myself for being affected by her or her for putting me in this position. Or the mother fuckers down the bar for looking at her like she's their next meal.

"No," she says, yanking her leg out of my grip and I swear, I just saw her teeth.

This one might bite.

When she squats down on a low note, I take advantage of her proximity and grab her under the arms, scooping up under her legs, as I whisk her off the bar top.

"Put me down!" she cries, her fist banging on my chest.

I get a glimpse of sexy kitten heels coming way too close to my face and back away. "Whoa," I whisper, not trying to gain an audience, and I'd rather not have to restrain her, but I need her to listen to me and promise she won't get back on the bar.

"I said," she starts, her voice getting louder, fists stronger. With my good arm, I hold hers down to the side of her body as I reposition her back on the barstool, my hand going over her mouth.

When her gorgeous green eyes, full of fire, hit mine, I feel it as if it were an actual punch.

With her chest heaving and my dick springing to life, I swallow. Hard.

"I'm going to need you to calm down, alright?" I ask, hoping for a nod or something to let me know she's feeling me right now, but all I get is a sassy glare. When I finally take my hand off her mouth and release some of the hold on her shoulders, she sags a little in what feels like defeat. "No more dancing on the bar."

"Floyd," she calls out over her shoulder. "I'm gonna need another shot of José."

Floyd's eyebrows shoot up in question and I just shrug. Someone should probably cut her off, but I don't really want to be that guy. She's obviously got something going on … pretty girl in a strip club, drinking alone. That doesn't exactly scream typical Saturday night. I want to press, ask her what her story is, but seeing that we haven't even officially been introduced, I decide to leave it alone.

I should leave *her* alone, but instead, after I'm convinced she's back to occupying the barstool instead of the bar top, I walk back to my spot … well, my new spot … and watch.

She throws a couple more back and I start cringing every time she holds her hand up for another drink. I want to tell her that this is probably going to hurt more than whatever she's nursing … break-up, job, shitty friends … She'll probably regret her choices tomorrow.

But sometimes, we've just gotta live and learn.

And sometimes it's worth it, anything to drown out the pain.

I've definitely been there before.

"A round for all my friends," she calls out a while later, motioning to the few men sitting down the bar from her. They smile, shaking their heads in her direction, and I wonder if they know her. The way they're eyeballing her, I'd have to guess they do.

What's her reputation?

What's her story?

Curiosity killed the cat, Cage.

Leave it alone.

"Crazy bitch," I hear one of them mutter and my head cocks to the side. Clearing my throat, I cross my arms over my chest and glare at him until he feels my stare and looks up to meet my eyes.

Nervously, he looks down at the bar and then offers a small, apologetic smile.

That's what I thought.

Again, I don't know her, but I'm not going to let anyone get away with calling her names.

When she motions to Floyd for another, I catch his attention and shake my head. He walks back toward the back of the bar, grabbing a clean glass, and I'm about to say something when I watch him pour straight mix over the ice, trim it with a lime, and set it down in front of her.

"You're so good to me, Floyd," she says, her words thick and slow. "You don't think I'm crazy, do you?"

Floyd smiles softly, holding a hint of something I can't quite put my finger on, and shakes his head. "Nah, I think you're quite all right, Miss Cassidy."

Cassidy.

Tempest Cassidy.

I roll her name around in my mind while continuing to eavesdrop on their conversation.

"It's official, you know?" she asks, like he should. "I'm officially a Cassidy again… no more Williams bullshit for me." When she laughs, it comes out as a snort and it's fucking cute. "D-I-V-O-R-C-E."

"Heard that," Floyd says, pulling a beer for another customer as he continues to engage her in conversation.

Divorced?

That just doesn't seem right.

What kind of guy would have a girl like her and mess that up?

"He's with Mindy," she drawls. "Mindy… Miiiiindy… Minnnnndy." Repeating the name over and over, she licks salt off her glass. Her pink tongue darting out to the rim and sending chills up my spine. "She used to work here, remember?"

Oh, fuck.

"Mindy," she muses again. "She was so mean to me in high school … and I was *always* nice to her." There's nothing but pure disgust and injustice in her tone. "Can you believe that, Floyd?"

He's basically just listening to her talk now, arms braced on the bar, lending her an ear.

"What happened to the nice guys finishing first … or girls …" She mumbles something I can't hear. "I'm a girl… well, a woman." She laughs, tossing her head back. Good ol' José. He makes everything funny. "Wouldn't you say, Floyd? I'm a woman, right? I mean, I've got boobs … they're not big ones, but they're a handful." She's now cupping her tits, over her shirt, thankfully, and I have to force my eyes in the other direction. "I always thought they were enough … I thought I was enough … but I guess …" When I hear her tone shift from appalled to so fucking sad, I turn back to see her laying her head on the bar. "I guess I was wrong. I'm not …"

"Hey," Floyd says, squatting down to get eye level with her. "You're great. And you're going to be fine …" He hesitates and I can tell this is a little out of his comfort zone, but I'm already putting Floyd up there with some of the better people I know, because she needs someone to tell her that. I would, but again, we haven't even officially met. "And you know what," he asks, forcing her to turn her head to look at him. "What goes around … comes around."

I can't help but keep my eyes on her, waiting for her response.

"Thanks, Floyd."

"You're welcome, Em."

Em?

Nickname?

I find myself filing away each little tidbit of information about her.

"Want me to call your dad?" he asks and this brings her straight up in her seat.

"No!" she says, practically crawling over the bar. "No, Floyd. Not my dad. And not Sheriff James," she pleads. "I'm not going back to jail … not tonight."

He chuckles, hands up in a placating gesture. "Okay, alright … no Butch and no Sheriff James. Who else can I call?"

"Cole…" she says, sleepily putting her head back on the bar. "Call Cole."

The next thing we know, the fiery redhead, who was dancing on the bar thirty minutes ago is now snoozing on it. Like, full on snores. They're cute snores, don't get me wrong, but they're snores nonetheless.

He looks up at me, as if to ask what to do, and I just shrug.

Turning, he picks up the phone behind the bar and dials a number. I go back to watching the rest of the club, Fuchsia is back for her second routine and the crowd is behaving nicely, as they usually do.

Before I came, Hank hadn't had a bouncer in a while. He stuck around to keep the peace when needed, but me being here frees him up some, or at least that's what he claims. Part of me wonders if he really needed someone or if he's just being … well, Hank. He's always been good people … giving more to others than they'll ever be able to give him in return.

"No answer for Cole down at the police station," Floyd says with a sigh.

"Maybe she has a phone?" I ask, glancing over at her small purse on the counter beside her.

Floyd's hands go back up. "I ain't touching it." Shaking his head.

"My mama about beat me one time when I went digging in hers for a stick of gum."

Sighing, I glance around before walking over and slipping her purse from under her arm. It's small, so the only thing in it is her phone and a house key. Pulling the phone out, I swipe my thumb across the screen and see that it needs a passcode. When I show it to Floyd, his head drops in defeat.

"Man," he says on an exhale. "She really didn't want me to call her dad, but I don't know what else to do if we can't get ahold of Cole."

"Who's Cole?" I ask, feeling nosy, but I can't help it. "Is he the ex?"

Floyd huffs a laugh. "No … no way, man. Cole Cassidy is her cousin, deputy … good guy."

I nod, running a hand over my short hair. "So, what do we do?"

"I guess we can keep trying Cole," he says, looking down at his watch. "Bar's still open for another three hours."

"She didn't even make it to midnight." I smirk, looking down at her sleeping form. My fingers itch to brush the hair off of her face, but I can't do that. That's too intimate … too familiar. I didn't even get to introduce myself. Who am I to brush hair out of her face?

What the fuck is wrong with you, Cage?

"Pretty girl, huh?" Floyd asks, his eyes on her too. "Sweet girl, too … definitely doesn't deserve what she's been through lately."

And what's that? The question is on the tip of my tongue, but I bite it back.

"Walked in on her ex screwing someone else," Floyd adds under his breath, eyes cutting down the bar to see who might be eavesdropping.

"Are you fucking kidding me?"

Floyd shakes his head. "Nope." Looking around again, he asks, "wanna know the worst part?"

Did I? Did I want to know the worst part? I know it's common in small towns for people to gossip, but I don't feel right gaining information about Tempest, even though I want it, without her knowing. But Floyd takes my silence as a yes.

"She was going home to…" He cocks his head and eyebrows suggestively. "You know."

My eyebrows shoot up. "What?"

"Yeah, apparently, they were trying to get pregnant and she was going home early for some … you know."

"Damn."

"Yeah."

We both look down at Tempest, who is still snoozing on the bar.

"She kinda lost it," he whispers, but it's not in disapproval, more in sympathy … understanding. "But can you blame her?"

No, I can't. I remember what it was like when I thought my life was going one way and then suddenly, it wasn't. I've had that happen to me on more than one occasion. It's jolting, disarming. Can't say I've always handled it in the best way myself.

"What are we going to do?" I ask, my eyes still glued on the softness of her cheek and the way her lashes rest on the pale skin.

"I'm stuck here until close, but you could drive her home."

My eyes snap up. "Me?"

"Yeah, she just lives a few miles away. I can give you her address." He motions to her purse. "You've got a key. She'll probably wake up by the time you get there … just make sure she gets into the house okay."

I guess I could do that. Looking around the bar, everyone seems to be doing fine.

"I'll keep an eye on the place," Floyd continues. "You won't be gone long."

Right. Sure, I can just take her home. I mean, she can't sleep on the bar all night. I wouldn't want her to. And she obviously doesn't have a husband or boyfriend to call. Her cousin isn't answering. She was adamant that she didn't want to call her father, so that leaves … me.

"Okay," I say, taking a step toward her and pausing to think it through. "Should I just?" I ask, hands in limbo.

"Carry her?" Floyd offers, looking at me like maybe I'm not as smart as he thought I was.

"Right."

When I slip my arm around her back and cradle her to my chest, scooping up her legs, she stirs and so does my dick. Earlier, when I dismounted her from the bar, I hadn't really been thinking about how she felt against my chest, but now, it's all I can think about—her small, soft body against my hard torso. Her warmth. Her scent—vanilla and something else—lavender, maybe? It's soft and subtle and sweet.

Grabbing her purse, I wave to Floyd. "I'll be back."

He smirks and nods his head. "Address is on the slip of paper in her purse."

I hadn't even noticed him writing it down, too preoccupied with the half-asleep, completely drunk girl in my arms. Walking toward the door, we garner some looks, but I just stare them down and dare them to say a word. No one does. I tip my head to Sarah when she grabs the door for me.

"I'll be back in a few," I tell her.

She offers a small, gentle smile, and I wonder if it's for me or Tempest.

What has she been up to?

What makes everyone think she's crazy?

I almost want to pry, but I know I won't.

That's an invasion of privacy and I know what that feels like. It's one of the reasons I'm here in Green Valley. Back in Dallas, everywhere I went—the gym, the dojo, the bar—the only thing people wanted to know was how I was holding up and what I planned on doing with my life.

Will you fight again?

If you do, will you fight to get your title back?

This isn't how we saw your career ending.

No shit, Sherlock. Never in a million years did I think I, Cage Erickson, would be taken out by a shoulder injury. Maybe too many concussions, which I was approaching the danger zone, but hadn't been forced to address that … yet. Maybe winning so many belts and keeping my title for so many years that I got bored. Maybe meeting a girl I could see myself settling down with and leaving the fight behind for a family … yeah, that's one I'd never told anyone about, but it's been there for the last couple years in the back of my mind. Regardless, when I left the sport, it would be under my own terms.

But being forced out, that shit made me angry … displaced … bitter.

"Put me down," Tempest mumbles, trying to put some force behind the words, but failing. "I can walk. Put me down."

"I'm taking you home," I tell her.

She shakes her head, her eyes still closed. "No, no home … home is lonely … and sad."

My heart, the one that usually didn't care too much for sentimental bullshit due to the nice sturdy wall I'd built up over the years, crumbled a little at her confession. When my steps falter, I think about taking her back into the bar. Something inside me sparked to life and I knew in that moment I didn't ever want to do anything to make her sad. But I couldn't leave her at the bar. She needed a bed and some water and ibuprofen.

"It's going to be okay," I mutter, my lips a fraction away from touching her hair before I stop myself.

What the fuck, Cage?

She still doesn't even know your damn name. You can't go kissing her hair, you creep.

And maybe that was a lie. Maybe it wasn't going to be okay, but I had to believe it was for her sake.

Walking around the side of the building, I approach the truck Hank has been letting me borrow, another benefit of working for him. Those just seem to keep coming lately. I'm starting to feel like he just makes shit up to get me to agree to accepting his help.

Sitting her gently in the passenger seat of the truck, I pull the seat-belt across her chest and buckle her in.

"Don't want to," she says, her eyes cracking open and blinking furiously, as she tries to get her bearings. "What are you doing?" Her words are slurred and I know what she's feeling. Sometimes, when you drink, you don't even realize how drunk you are until you stop, and then it hits you like a ton of bricks. When she swipes the back of her hand across her face, I realize she may not be feeling so well.

"Hey," I say, ducking back into the cab of the truck and trying to force her to look at me. "You okay?" I ask. "Are you feeling sick?"

She shakes her head, groaning slightly. "No, just don't want to go home …"

"Well, I think it's the best place for you."

"What do you know?" she asks, a hint of spitfire presenting itself and I smirk.

Laughing lightly, I make sure her seatbelt is secure before leaning back. "Not much," I tell her, shutting the door and walking around to the driver's side.

"What's your name?" she asks, as I start the truck up and put it in reverse, her head lolling to the side to look at me. "I don't even know you. I don't go home with strangers… strange," she repeats, drawing the word out a little like she did when she was stuck on Mindy. I don't even know her, but I already hate her. "Strange… men." She laughs and rolls her head back the other way, leaning over until her cheek is pressed against the window. "This feels good."

Slipping the paper out of her purse, I check the address and pause before pulling out of the parking lot to put it into the GPS on my phone. Just like Floyd said, it's less than a few miles away, so I turn out and head back toward town.

"Cage," I tell her, answering her original question, but I'm not even sure if she's still awake. Her breathing is quiet and I can't see her face. "I'm Cage Erickson."

"Like an animal … cage?" she asks, laughing once.

I shake my head. "Yeah, kinda like that."

"Or a bird cage. Are you a bird?"

She's making no sense, but I love the lilt of her voice, so I don't stop her.

"I had a rabbit once. Her name was Britney Spears. She lived in a cage, except when I snuck her into my bedroom, but my mama hated it." She pauses and sighs before laughing again. "Tempest June, I don't want rabbit poop in my house." Her voice went high and pompous, obviously imitating her mother. "Such a fun killer."

"Is that a nickname or something?" she asks, forcing herself back up in the seat.

"Nope, just Cage."

"Just Cage," she repeats. "Where are you from?"

"Dallas."

When I stop at a corner, turning down her street, she gets more alert than she's been in a while. "Dallas?" I glance over to see her nose wrinkle. "Why'd you come here?"

"Change of pace," I offer, as honest as I wanted to be this time of night. Although, I realize I could probably tell her my entire life story and she probably wouldn't remember any of it come morning.

A few minutes later, I pull up in the driveway of a yellow house. The porch light is on, as well as a lamppost in the front yard. It's quaint and cute and it looks like a place where happy people live.

Turning the truck off, I look over to Tempest, but she's back to snoozing against the door. I wonder if she was happy … before. I bet she was. She seems like someone who is inherently happy, which pisses me off that she's been reduced to someone who drinks alone—at a strip club.

Once I ease her back out of the truck, holding her to me, making sure I got the key out before I got her, I make my way to her front door. Unlocking it, I hesitantly peek my head inside. It's weird being in someone else's space, especially not knowing her. Not really. And even though she's with me, I still feel like an intruder.

"Where's your bedroom?" I ask, just wanting to make sure she's safe and tucked in, so I can leave with a good conscience and not worry about her all night.

"Down the hall," she mumbles, snuggling into my chest.

I pause. She really shouldn't do that, because even though my brain wants to be a gentleman and take care of her, my dick has other things in mind.

"Not upstairs," she says. "That's where …" She drifts off, her hand grabbing onto the fabric of my t-shirt. She doesn't finish the statement, but if I had to guess, that's where she used to sleep … before her husband dipped his dick somewhere it didn't belong.

Flipping on a light switch, a kitchen is illuminated and it looks like a baker's dream—large counters, big mixer, a stainless steel island with shelves that hold every kind of baking sheet imaginable. When I start to feel like a creeper, I turn toward the hall and walk until I get to an open door.

It's a nice room, small, obviously a guest room. Walking over to the bed, covered in a fluffy comforter, I set her down and she groans.

Once my arms are free, I look around, wondering what I should do now. This is definitely unchartered territory for me. As she wiggles around, trying to get comfortable, I bend down and slip the red heels off, smiling at them before setting them on the floor beside the bed.

They're not fuck-me stilettos that most women would wear on a night out, but they're still fucking sexy as hell.

Pulling the comforter out from under her, I cover her up with it and she turns over, her hair a wild mess around her beautiful face. When I brush a few strands away, she angles her face into my hand and I have to force myself to step back.

I know she'll need some water and something for her head, so I walk quietly back to the kitchen and snoop around until I find a glass and some Advil. After I get some water from the fridge, I walk back down the hall and pause for a second in the doorway.

What the hell is it about her?

I'm never like this.

The last seven years, my life has been a series of dry spells and one-night stands. I don't ever get attached. It's never hard for me to walk away. Even after an amazing night of sex, I don't wonder what the girl is doing the next day. I'm never tempted to call them or text. So, why am I finding it difficult to walk away from her.

Tempest Cassidy.

Recently divorced.

Cheating husband.

Been in trouble with the law.

That's usually enough baggage to send me running for the hills, but all I really want to do is pull up a chair and watch her sleep, making sure she's okay.

Setting the water and pills beside the bed, I can't help but reach out and stroke her cheek … just one last touch … something she won't remember, but I have a feeling I will.

CHAPTER 5

TEMPEST

The incessant banging in my head reminds me of why I don't drink tequila.

Please God, I'll never drink again if you'll just make the banging stop!

God must still be talking to me, because suddenly, the banging goes away, only to be replaced with a high-pitch yell that sounds a lot like Anna Cassidy.

Hell.

That's it, I must be in hell.

"Tempest Cassidy!"

No, not Anna. *Please, God, no.* I would rather my mama be here right now, giving me a lecture about being responsible, instead of Anna. She's mean and bossy, and thanks to her alcoholic father, she hates drunk people. And as I shift around in bed, I still feel drunk. *Is that even possible?*

Two seconds later, the blinds of my bedroom windows are yanked open and I peek out of one eye to see perfectly-coiffed blonde hair sitting on top of a sasquatch that looks like it swallowed a basketball.

"What the hell, Anna?" I whine, my voice coming out rough, like I swallowed gravel and washed it down with motor oil. Somehow it sounds exactly like it tastes—thick and gritty. I need to brush my teeth and scrape the fur off my tongue.

"Language!" Anna exclaims, holding both sides of her protruding stomach, like her unborn child just heard me say *hell*, which is in the Bible, so it doesn't even count.

"Fuck!" I moan, rolling over and covering my eyes.

"Tempest! Are you trying to send me into early labor?" she gasps, clutching her stomach even tighter. "What has gotten into you?"

"Nobody, lately," I answer. I'm not this crass to everyone, basically just Anna, because it's fun.

"Lord, she does not mean the things she says," Anna prays, looking up at my ceiling and then back at me. "Tell Him you don't mean the things you say!"

"No," I tell her, hating her for even making me speak. "I don't feel like it."

She huffs, crossing her arms on top of her belly. "You've always been so stubborn and pig-headed, but it's one of the things I've always admired about you."

I sit straight up in bed and manage to open both eyes. "Did you just say *you* admired something about *me*?" Anna doesn't envy anyone; it's a sin. However, she's the envy *of* everyone. If it weren't for her being in so tight with the Big Guy, she'd probably flaunt that fact a lot more, but pride comes before the fall and all that.

"Oh, hush. There are many things I admire about you," she admonishes, swatting at me and making contact because I'm too slow to move away from her. I'm definitely still drunk.

"Do tell," I say, as eagerly as I can manage, fixing the pillows behind me. Drunk or not, I've gotta hear this.

She makes her pouty lips even poutier and slides her big brown eyes across the room, refusing to even look at me. "No, I'm still mad at you. Cole told me about taking you to the… *strip club*," she hisses, obviously thinking that God, as omniscient as He is, might not hear her if she whispers. "He also said he never got a call from you last night and I've been worried sick."

"I'm sorry, Anna," I say with all sincerity, because I am. Even though she's a pain in my ass, I love her and she's one of the few people still on my team, so I can't afford to lose her. "How can I make it up to you?" I know it's better to pay my penance now than to have her mad at me for the next month.

Turning her gaze back to me, her face is glowing, as she smiles from ear to ear. "Come to the church picnic with me next week."

What a player.

She was just waiting for me to fall into her traps so she could con me into a church activity.

"Not the church picnic! Anything besides that. Please," I beg. The only thing worse would've been her bi-weekly prayer meeting. So I add, "except prayer meeting. I'm not doing that again."

"You would deny a pregnant woman this one simple wish?" she asks, an eyebrow going up to her hairline. "You just asked how you can make things up to me and that's my answer—church picnic." Her arms cross over her belly again and her face goes rigid.

Damn, she's good.

"Fine."

She squeals and hugs me so tightly that I'm afraid I'm going to throw up all over her pretty pink dress.

"Okay," she says, standing up, "So, I'll save you a seat at church." She barely makes it out of my bedroom, before she pops her head back in. "Your mama will love to see you there."

I roll my eyes and feel it in the back of my head… my still pounding head.

I said I'd go to the church picnic, but not church. The last time I beckoned the doors, I ran smack dab into Asher and Mindy. I barely made it through the sermon, anxiously twitching the entire time, kind of hoping God would smite them on the third pew in front of the entire congregation.

When the final amen was said, I couldn't get out of there fast enough.

The next day, I let the air out of Asher's tires.

That's one thing I didn't get caught doing… and didn't go to jail for.

I feel like God knew I deserved that one and gave me a pass.

"Oh, and wear that green dress," she yells back, as she's heading out the front door. "It really makes your eyes pop!"

Even though it kills my head, I roll those eyes, because why do I need them to pop? Who are my eyes popping for these days? No one.

She and my mama have this crazy notion that my divorce is a phase. Asher is going to come to his senses and realize the error of his ways and I'm going to take him back and we're going to *fix this*, as my mama would say.

I hate to break it to them, but that is not happening.

As angry as I am about the demise of my marriage and all of my hopes and dreams that went down the drain with it, I know me. I'm loyal to a fault and I thought Asher was too, that's what made our marriage work. I trusted him. He'd been my boyfriend since I was sixteen. He was the only man I've ever been with. When I walked in that morning and found him in bed… *my bed*… with Mindy, everything changed.

I can't say I immediately fell out of love with him. I don't even know if that's possible. Logically, I know there is a fine line between love and hate. A professional might say all of my actions lately have been misplaced feelings, lines getting blurred. Since I can't love Asher anymore, I channel those emotions into other… *things*… like driving a truck into a pond and burning clothes and yelling at windows in the middle of the night.

Maybe Judge Carson's punishment of anger management isn't the worst idea. Someone to talk to, who isn't closely connected to my life, would be nice. I really do need to get a grip and get on with my life. I might no longer have a husband or a vehicle, and soon, I won't have this house, but I still have myself and my job, which I love, and my family. They may be pushy and overbearing, but they mean well.

Looking down, I take inventory of myself since last night is a big drunken, fuzzy blur. My shoes are off, but other than that, my clothes are still intact, which is always good after a night at the bar. I scan back in my memory, trying to piece the previous night together.

There was tequila.

And a few margaritas.

And singing.

And dancing… on the bar.

How did I get back here?

It physically hurts my brain to try and recollect the past however many hours. I don't remember calling Cole to take me home. Grabbing my phone off the nightstand and scrolling my call history proves I didn't. The last call on here is when I called him for a ride to the bar.

Well, I'm not in jail, so that's a plus.

There's no way I walked.

I wouldn't have made it past the first block.

Wait—wait a damn minute.

There was a guy… big muscles and very, very blue eyes.

And blond hair.

And a beard, not like a scraggly, unkempt one, but just a little… more scruff than beard… one that accentuated his strong jaw.

Weird how I was obviously very drunk, but remember all of that.

What was his name? Cain? Cade?

There were some words exchanged and then everything went fuzzy.

Shit.

CHAPTER 6

CAGE

"I really like what you've done with the place," Hank says, his eyes scanning the open space.

Laughing, I shake my head. "You made it out like this place was a dump."

"Well, it's not luxury, that's for sure."

No, it's not, but it's great and it's the perfect place for me right now. "I was actually going to ask you something."

"Shoot," Hanks says, taking a few steps closer to the stainless steel island.

"Well, I'm still rehabbing the shoulder, but I'd like to start doing some upper body workouts and I was thinking those steel beams downstairs would be perfect for some kickboxing bags."

It's been too long. Even if I don't get to punch the shit out of them, I can still get a nice leg workout in. I've been running every morning and doing crunches and some light weight workouts, but there's still something missing. That *it factor* I get from pouring all my power into another object—follow through.

I miss the cage, the fight, the rush of adrenaline. And I know I can't do that anymore, but I think I can find a new way to reach that place of Zen.

"Yeah," Hank says, nodding his head thoughtfully. "I think that'd be great. Whatever you need, man."

I let out a deep breath, not that I thought he'd say no, but just because it feels right. "Thanks. I think I'll start out with just a bag and a few mats. Maybe I'll add to it down the road."

"Maybe you're onto something here," Hank adds and I can see his wheels turning, always thinking. "You know, Green Valley doesn't have anything like what you're used to… gyms dedicated to training elite athletes." Pausing, he raises his eyebrows. "There's a chance a kickboxing class could turn into more. You could add equipment as you go. Maybe one day, build your own ring … put up a cage." His brows rise up to his hairline and then a wide smile breaks across his face. "I know it won't be the same… you'd have to stay on the other side, but it could be good for you. *You* could be good for someone else … someone like you."

Scratching my head, I huff a laugh. That's a little more than I'd let myself daydream about, but I'm not going to lie, what Hank's saying doesn't feel too bad either. "Huh," I finally say, still mulling it over, because now *my* wheels are turning.

"Don't think too long and hard about it right now," he says, hands braced on the shiny surface. "But do think about it. Start small and see where it goes."

As we walk back down the stairs and into the large, open room, I start to look at it as a blank slate—a new beginning—and for the first time since I rolled into Green Valley, I try to see myself staying indefinitely.

What does that look like?

Could I permanently live in a small town?

I didn't come here with a plan, but in the back of my mind I thought I'd get lost for a while, let the news of my early retirement die down, and then go back to Dallas.

"It's already seeping in," Hank says matter-of-factly, drawing me out of my thoughts.

"What?"

"Green Valley," he says, stuffing his hands in his pockets as he scuffs his feet against the concrete floor, the sound echoing off the bare walls. "It does that to people. Kinda sneaks up on you and the next thing you know, you find yourself liking it … and then one day you wake up and realize you never want to leave."

I scoff. "Not sure about that, but…"

"You're thinking about it." His smile is contagious and I can't help giving him one in return. "Heard you took Tempest Cassidy home last night," he says, effectively changing the subject and making me swallow my tongue. "Don't look so surprised. Small town… plus, I swung by while you were gone. Floyd filled me in."

"Oh, right." I let out a deep breath, trying to release the pent-up tension in my shoulders. I need a run. No, scratch that. What I really need is a good bout. I need to go nose-to-nose, toe-to-toe, glove-to-glove with someone. I need to feel the exhaustion that only comes with exerting every ounce of energy and adrenaline in my body… and then some—pushing myself to the limit.

But that's not going to happen, not today, anyway. So, I'll settle for a run.

"Yeah, she had a little too much to drink. Floyd tried to get in touch with her cousin …"

"Cole," Hank offered.

"That's right," I say with a nod, trying to not sound as interested or invested as I feel. "So, I drove her home. Made sure she got in okay."

Hank laughs. "That girl has really been stirring things up around here."

I've heard, but I don't tell Hank that. I wait and see what information he has to offer.

"I can't say I blame her, though," he adds, sighing.

For a second, I'm afraid he's going to stop there and leave me hanging, but then he continues. "She walked in on her husband and his … *mistress*," Hank informs, choosing his words carefully. "Guess she didn't handle that too well. First she ransacked the bedroom, and then one night, she set his shit on fire in the driveway." This garners a full-on belly laugh from my old friend. "And I don't just mean a few old shirts. She practically had a bonfire going. The fire department was called out and everything. I mean, I've heard of scorned women, but she seems to be taking it to a whole new level. Disturbing the peace, breaking and entering, destruction of property…"

Huh. Can't say I really pegged her for one to break the law, but it also doesn't surprise me. There was fire behind those green eyes… like an angry, sleeping dragon.

"So, it's good you took her home. She's a good girl, just had a lot of shit thrown her way lately and she hasn't been handling it so well."

I nod, trying for a non-committal response. Although, I'm not sure why. I doubt Hank would care if I told him I was into her, but that's my business, not his. Besides all that, she seems like she has a lot on her plate and a shit ton of baggage, so I think I'll keep my distance—do my job, work on this space, and figure out what I want to do with my life.

A clothes-burning, peace-disturbing, property-destroying, fiery redhead would only complicate things.

"You should come to the church picnic next Sunday."

I turn to look at him with what I'm sure is a confused expression. "Me?"

"Of course you," he says, laughing. "It's not a church house… you're not gonna get struck by lightning. It's a picnic… there'll be some good food and a pie auction. Well, cakes and all sorts of desserts. It's a great place to meet some locals. Who knows? Tempest Cassidy might even be there."

My mouth gapes at his insinuating tone and I pull my brows together. "I just took her home… and I didn't say anything about wanting to see her again."

"Didn't have to," Hank says, walking toward the door and opening it. "It's written all over that pretty face of yours."

I scowl.

First of all, my face is not *pretty*.

Second of all, I hate when people act like they know what I'm thinking… especially when they know what I'm thinking.

And third, because if there's a first and a second, there has to be a third… I might be seriously fucking attracted to Tempest Cassidy, but that doesn't mean I'll be acting on it.

"Yes, your face is *pretty*," he drawls. "I've seen the way women look at you… all dangerous fighter with Hollywood good looks." He laughs and I flip him the bird. "And yes, you're coming to the picnic." Pausing, with his hand on the edge of the door—one foot out, one foot in, he adds, "I just made it mandatory for all employees."

Oh, fuck me… and fuck him and his pink pony he rode in on.

Without waiting for a response, he gives me a shit-eating grin and waves, closing the door behind him. I watch him walk down the sidewalk through the large windows and glare at him, hoping he can feel the weight of it like most people, but I doubt it. Hank's always been immune to my brooding and intimidation.

The two of us are unlikely friends. Ever since we met at Harvard, we've been polar opposites, yet connected in a way I could never explain. It's been a long time since we spent late nights talking about what we wanted to do with our lives. Years have passed since we both dropped out and went our separate ways, but he's always been a great friend… one of the best.

So, I'll give him this one. I'll go to the fucking church picnic. But for now, I'm going to go for a run, because if I don't burn off some of this excess energy, I might go crazy, and tomorrow, I'm ordering a bag and seeing what I can make out of this place.

Maybe it'll just be for me.

Maybe it'll turn into something more.

I'm not sure, but I do know that for the first time in a few months, I feel like purpose is just around the corner. And I need that. Beyond the fight and the challenge of the ring, it's waking up with purpose every day that I miss the most.

This morning's run takes me down the sidewalk that runs in front of the building I'm living in, out of downtown Green Valley, past older, well-kept houses, and finally to the highway that leads to the Pink Pony. When I reach the gravel parking lot of the club, I turn around and head back.

I love the way my legs strain as I make the climb up a few hills.

I love the way my lungs burn as I push a little harder on my way back.

I love the way my mind clears, with my only thoughts being focused on my next breath, my next step.

Once the familiar buildings of downtown come into view, I slow my pace and begin my cool down. Wanting a change of scenery, I cross the street and continue my way up the opposite sidewalk. When I see several people coming in and out of one of the buildings, I slow my pace to a walk.

As I get closer, I notice a sign that read's *Donner Bakery — Home of the Banana Cake*. One lady carrying a box seems a little startled when she sees me, but quickly smiles and offers a polite hello.

"Good morning," I say, returning her smile.

"Best muffins in a hundred mile radius," she says, nodding behind her to the storefront. "I recommend the Folsom Prison Blues."

Folsom Prison... what?

Instead of asking questions, I just say, "Thanks."

I had plans of drinking a smoothie this morning, but now that I'm within smelling distance and caught a whiff of the lady's purchase, my mouth is now watering for carbs. A good run deserves to be rewarded with carbs—that's always been my philosophy.

One of the reasons I love working out so hard is because I can eat anything I want and never have to worry about packing on pounds.

Holding the door for another lady walking out with what looks like a bag full of deliciousness, hints of cinnamon and sugar and baked bread bowl me over.

"Welcome to the Donner Bakery," a cheerful voice calls out. "Picking up an order?"

Glancing up and down the glass case, I get lost in the selections. "No, no order… but I am hungry."

"Another batch of Ring of Fires," a familiar voice says, making my head snap up and my dick twitch.

Tempest Cassidy.

Her gorgeous red hair is pulled back in a ponytail, showing off the long lines of her neck, and I swallow, licking my bottom lip. Maybe I'll take her… if she were on the menu.

Which she is not.

Get your mind out of the gutter.

When she notices me, she stops and tilts her head, like she's examining me, and I realize that she's having trouble placing me, which is crazy. Usually, people meet me once and never forget. I'm not being cocky. It's just the truth. My dad is full-blooded Scandinavian and he passed on his pale blue eyes and blond hair, as well as a very defined jawline.

In the UFC, I was known as *The Fighting Viking*.

"Can I help you?" she asks, her eyes still scanning my face, but I don't miss the way they fall to my chest, which I'm sure is covered in sweat. I just ran at least six miles.

"Uh," I start, trying to get my bearings and not make a complete fool of myself. "I heard the Folsom Prison Blues is—"

"Out," she says, sliding in a fresh tray of muffins that are twice the size of any I've ever seen. "But we have a fresh supply of Ring of Fire… cinnamon, cloves, oats, and raisins… and a hint of cayenne pepper." Her eyes light up as she's describing the muffin and my traitorous heart hammers in my chest. "Sounds crazy, but I promise… they're delicious."

"I'll take two."

I watch as her creamy complexion turns a lovely shade of pink. "You, uh… you were," she swallows. "You were at the…" Now she's completely flustered and it's fucking adorable. Somehow, she's even more tempting and I wonder how far that blush goes… down to her chest? Tits? Are they just as creamy and delicious as what's visible?

"Pink Pony," I offer. "Cage Erickson." When I reach my hand across the counter for her to shake, she hesitates for a moment and I wonder if she's going to bolt or get sick, and that takes me back to putting her to bed the other night.

Finally, she takes my hand and I swear, heat travels from her hand to mine like a sizzling spark of electricity. "Tempest Cassidy."

"I know," I tell her with a smile. "I, uh…" I wonder if she has any recollection of me taking her home… or if I should tell her?

"You took me home." The color now drains from her face.

I nod.

"Thank you," she says quickly, tossing my two muffins in a bag and handing them to the girl at the register. When I see that she's getting ready to run off to the back, I stop her, not ready for this conversation to be over.

"Were you alright… I mean, did you feel okay?" I ask, unsure of what to say.

"Fine," she says, now unable to look me in the eye and I hate it.

Fucking look at me, Tempest.

Give me those gorgeous green eyes.

"Good," I tell her. "I was worried about leaving you, but you went right to sleep."

It's then I realize the other girl's eyes are as big as saucers.

"Uh, yeah…" She gives me an uncomfortable smile, side eyeing the girl. "Sometimes tequila makes me…"

Dance on bars, I want to tease, but I don't.

"Sleepy," she says, swallowing again.

"Five twenty-seven," the girl at the register says and I realize I don't have my wallet.

"Shit," I murmur. "Uh, can you hold these for me? I just realized I didn't bring any money… I was out for a run and—"

"It's on the house," Tempest says, taking the bag from the girl and handing it over to me. "Well, on me… I owe you one."

I smile at her, wanting to say so much more… things like: *I have ideas on how you can pay me back… I can make it good for both of us… let's work out some of that obvious pent-up aggression…* but I don't say any of that. Instead, I opt for, "thank you" and then I walk out the door, leaving Tempest Cassidy and all the temptation that pertains to her behind.

She's not on the menu, Cage.

End of story.

But these fucking muffins… I take a moment while out on the sidewalk to sniff the bag. When the aroma of cinnamon and sugar with a hint of spice hits my nose, I can't wait any longer. Opening the bag, I take one of them out, observing its size once more. My hands are huge and it literally takes up the entire span of my palm.

As I take my first bite, the second the baked perfection touches my tongue, I groan.

Not only is Tempest Cassidy going to be a temptation, so are her muffins.

CHAPTER 7

TEMPEST

Stepping out of the truck, a warm breeze catches the bottom of my dress and I stop it just before it soars over my head. My daddy is letting me borrow his old pick-up until I can figure out something of my own. It's not that I can't get a loan or anything, but until the house is sold, I don't want to make any large purchases. As I turn around, I make sure no one saw what just happened and quietly curse the blasted wind and Anna for making me wear a dress in the first place.

Trucks and cars are lined up in rows out in the pasture, just a half mile from the church. I spot my daddy's truck, surprised Mama didn't make him drive the sedan. That's their church car.

Everyone is congregating under a big white tent, but there are blankets scattered out in the deep green grass surrounding it where some have staked their claim for the afternoon. As I walk closer, I can hear the reverend greeting everyone and asking them to bow their heads in prayer.

Stopping just short of the crowd, I do as he asks and listen to him thank the Lord for good health and the rain we got last week, and asking Him to bless the food we're about to eat.

"Amen."

"Nice to see you still remember how to pray." I hear the easy voice of my father in my right ear, a little mirth behind his words.

"Stop it, Daddy," I say, swatting blindly behind me and making contact with his arm.

"Don't make me have to get the sheriff after you for assaulting an old man," he jokes, but then pauses for a second as we both take in the crowd of familiar faces. "It really is good to see you, Tempest. And you sure do look pretty in that dress. You're gonna make your mama one happy lady today."

I glance beside me to see his mustache twitch as he smiles underneath it.

"Well, it's far too nice of a day to be cooped up inside," I tell him, smoothing my dress down in the front.

"Uh, huh. I hear you also had some smoothing over to do with Anna, who looks like she's coming this way," he says, turning my shoulders to see the reason I'm here making a beeline for us. "Now, if you'll excuse me, I hear some fried chicken calling my name."

"Chicken shit," I whisper, just before he gets out of earshot.

"What was that?" Anna asks, saddling up beside me and winding her arm through mine.

"Uh, I was just saying that chicken smells good!"

"Well, good, because I fried up plenty! Cole found us a nice shady spot over by the tree. Let's hurry, before he eats it all!"

We say hello to people as we make our way through the tent and over to the large oak. I don't miss the side-eyes and whispers directed my way. Thankfully, I remembered my big girl panties, so I just smile and nod, not letting them get to me.

Anna wasn't lying when she said she made plenty. Cole already has three chicken legs on his plate eaten clean down to the bone by the time we walk up.

"Tempest," he greets, wiping his hands on a pretty, paisley napkin, before standing up to hug me. "Fancy meeting you here." When he pulls back, he winks and I smile.

Anna and I fix our plates, making ourselves comfortable on the blanket. The fried chicken is heaven. I could've used a few pieces of this last weekend when I had my hangover. Anything fried is great hangover food. Fortunately, I've managed to stay sober this past week. No trips to the bar or even to the liquor cabinet at my house.

My first anger management session was this past Tuesday, and as much as I didn't want to go… and I really hate to admit it… I think it helped. It was awkward, at first, and I felt completely out of place, but the longer I sat and listened, the more I started identifying with the people around me and realizing they were all there for the same reason —to get help, to figure out a better way to express themselves and find a solution to their impulsive behaviors.

Impulse control was on the agenda for this week's session and I felt it down to my toes. Control over my impulses has definitely been missing from my life lately and the session came with good timing. I'm sure, at some point today, I'm going to have to put a few of the coping strategies to use.

Be mindful of the impulse.

Be aware of your feelings.

Recognize the negative behavior, but channel it into something positive.

I haven't seen Asher and Mindy yet, but I'm sure they're here somewhere. They don't seem to pass up an opportunity to pretend like they're Green Valley's Couple of the Year.

After we eat, the three of us fall into comfortable conversation, reminiscing about old times and talking about the future, like we typically do when we're together. The newest topic of conversation is the baby. I can't wait to become an aunt. Cole may be my cousin, but he's like a brother to me, and I fully intend on spoiling their baby as if it were my own.

Anna looks at me with sad eyes from time to time. She knows about me and Asher trying for a baby, and I know she probably feels bad she's the one who ended up pregnant, but it's not her fault. None of us know how life will go.

A year ago, if someone would've asked me where I'd be today, I'd have said right where Anna is. But I'm not. I'm sitting here on the flip side—divorced and not with child.

"Hey, baby girl," my mama coos, leaning down for a hug. "It's so good to see you here today. I was just telling your daddy how pretty you look." As she gushes, I zone out a bit—nodding my head and smiling. When she gets going, there's no stopping her. I just hope she doesn't say anything too embarrassing. Cole loves to use things she says against me at later dates.

As my mama starts visiting with the Tanners, my eyes drift to a pair of long legs in faded blue jeans. I look a little further up and see a taut chest squeezed into a gray T-shirt and a familiar head of blond hair.

What is he doing here?

I mean, it's a church gathering and the pastor always makes it clear everyone is welcome, but *damn him*. The run-in at the bakery the other day was enough to fluster me to no end. Seeing him face-to-face filled in the missing pieces from my drunken memory and I was mortified when I thought about him driving me home and putting me to bed, and also a little smitten. No one had ever done anything like that for me, besides Cole, and that was only once, right after my first night in jail.

But being attracted to someone is completely out of the question right now. There is no way I'm going to be the woman who jumps right into someone else's bed. I've seen that time and time again—women who think they can't be alone or that they need a man to feel complete. That's not me. Sure, one of these days, after I work on me and making myself happy, I'll consider the possibilities, but not right now. And not with someone like Cage. He's… well, he's big and strong and kind of scary beautiful. He's the polar opposite of Asher and I have no idea why I'm attracted to him, which must mean it's a fluke.

I'm still trying to rebound from the shock of Asher's betrayal and suddenly being divorced. That's it. It has to be. There's no other logical explanation. Just like my irrational behavior, my emotions are following suit.

He's laughing at something Mrs. Tanner is telling him, and I see her hand reach out and rest on his strong forearm. With his short sleeves, all the muscles and tendons are on full display. I love a good strong forearm. I don't think I realized that about myself until right this very moment. The visual causes my mouth to go dry and I swallow hard, trying to ignore the pull I feel toward him.

Oh. My. God. Tempest June Cassidy, get ahold of yourself.

Yeah, I just first, middle, and last named myself, because I really need to get my shit together. I also need to stop cursing in my head at a church picnic. *I know, God, You're still listening.*

"Lemonade?" Anna asks, as if she could read my mind and knows I need to take it down a notch.

Dear Lord, please don't let her be able to read my mind. She really would go into early labor.

I nod and accept the glass she's offering, tilting it back and draining half of it before I come up for air.

She cocks one of her perfectly groomed eyebrows at me. "Thirsty?"

"Yeah," I say on an exhale. "I think it was all that chicken I ate. I'm sure it's loaded with sodium… makes you thirsty." I try to smile, but it feels more like a grimace and I can feel her interrogating stare.

"Uh huh," she says, as she eyeballs me and then looks back over to where Cage and Mrs. Tanner were standing just a few moments ago. I'm not disappointed when I see he's no longer there.

Maybe he's gone.

Maybe he just came for some food and left.

"Uh, I'm gonna go bid on one of the pies over at the silent auction," I tell Cole and Anna as I stand up quickly. "I'll be right back!"

"Oh, Tempest," Anna calls. "Be a dear and put my name down on your mama's Mississippi mud pie!"

"Anna, you know you're not supposed to eat all that sugar!" Cole admonishes.

"Excuse me, but are you the one carrying around a Butterball turkey?" Anna starts. I've heard this rant before and I scurry off before I get caught in the crossfire. If the pregnant lady wants a Mississippi mud pie, a Mississippi mud pie is what she'll get.

As I'm leaning over the table inspecting the pies and cakes and other desserts that are up for auction, I feel someone come up beside me. Looking up, I'm greeted with blue eyes and a smirk.

"Hello, Tempest." His deep voice feels like warm honey, but I quickly shut that shit down.

"Hey," I say, as cool as I can manage, meeting his gaze only briefly because his blue eyes are entirely too close for comfort. Turning back around to the pies, I start to write my bids down on the sheets in front of them.

"We should be friends," he proclaims, his hand brushing against mine as he grabs a pen from beside me and starts writing down his own bids.

"What?"

"Friends," he repeats, coming right in behind me and jotting down a higher bid on the Mississippi mud and the lemon meringue.

I look at him like he's grown three heads. "Well, *friend…*" I start. If he wants to go there, we can go there. I can do friends. Friends is safe. And after the past few months I've had, I could use an extra person in my corner. I'd damn sure rather be his ally than his enemy. I mean, he looks like he could do some damage, which is no wonder he's the new bouncer at the Pink Pony. After he showed up at the bakery, I started putting two and two together, remembering things about that night much clearer than I'd like.

Cage pulling me off the bar.

Cage carrying me to his truck.

Cage helping me out of his truck.

Cage tucking me in bed.

And then the next morning, after Anna had left, I found a glass of water with some Advil lying beside the bed. My heart did this weird flip. I refuse to give it any thought, because again, I'm not interested.

But friends. I can do that.

"Maybe you should reconsider trying to outbid me," I finally finish, scratching out his name beneath mine.

"Oh, huh uh," he says, taking the pen from my hand. "These pies are fair game!" he declares. "I may be new to town, but I know how these things work." As he rewrites his name and bid, he hums to himself and I have to close my eyes to keep from feeling it through my body. "Tempest Cassidy," he says quietly. "Such a pretty name for such a pretty girl. And, it's so sad that I'm going to have to outbid you," he continues, leaning across me to write his name on a couple more sheets.

"Well," I say, straightening up and collecting my wits. "This isn't over yet!"

Wait, did he call me pretty?

"I'll remember that," he chuckles. "So, are we just going to stand here and continue to outbid each other for the rest of the picnic, or should we go mingle or something?" he asks, looking around.

"Uh, I guess mingle?" I question him back.

"You're the local. You're supposed to tell me," he says, smiling.

"Yeah, well, I've been avoiding mingling lately," I mutter, partly to myself, but I feel him watching me. We both casually walk out from the tent together. I still feel people's eyes on me, but I don't notice it as much with Cage next to me. It's like he's sharing some of the attention and it calms the anxiousness I feel these days when I'm out in public.

"So, if we're going to be friends," he says. "Tell me something about yourself." Walking toward an empty blanket, I realize he expects me to sit, but I can't. I mean, what would people say? And then I see Hank Weller.

"Wait. You're friends with Hank?" I ask, starting to put it all together. Hank owns the Pink Pony and Cage, new to town, works there.

He nods, stopping short of the blanket. "We're old friends," Cage offers. "Hank and I go way back."

"Makes sense," I say, my eyes darting around to see who's watching. It's then I see Asher and Mindy walking into the opposite side of the tent.

"What's up?" Cage asks. "Did someone steal your pie?"

Be mindful, I tell myself. I knew they'd be here. I knew they'd be together. I can handle this.

I laugh. "Well, I've never heard it put that way, but I guess you could say that."

He must have followed my line of sight because he then asks, "Who's that?"

"That would be Asher... and Mindy, the most perfect couple in Green Valley." The fakeness in my tone is oozing all over the lush green grass at my feet. I want to puke when I see him put his hand on her back and walk her toward a group of people. "Also, my ex-husband."

I'm aware... boy am I fucking aware.

I watch as they talk to a few of our friends… or, I guess they're technically Asher's friends, but people I've known all my life, nonetheless. Asher is being his usual charismatic self, fully engaging people as he tells his story, and Mindy is being the picture-perfect companion, smiling sweetly and laughing at all the right places.

Recognize the negative thoughts…

I can't help but stare at them like they're some kind of exhibit in a museum. It's so strange seeing someone I've loved, and spent the last twelve years of my life being committed to, with someone else.

It hits deep.

I feel the lump in my throat before the familiar wave of heat creeps up.

When she laughs again and her left hand comes up to her cover her mouth, I see it.

A large, sparkling diamond on her fourth finger.

The way she flashes it seems intentional and when her eyes cut over to me, I flinch.

"You've got to be fucking kidding me," I mutter under my breath, biting down on my lip so hard it hurts and then I taste blood. Before I do something crazy—something the entire town is probably expecting out of me at this point—I turn on my heel and practically run toward where all the vehicles are parked.

When I finally reach it, I see my truck is completely blocked in by other vehicles, meaning I won't be driving out of here any time soon.

A second later, I hear the thud of heavy feet as Cage catches up to me. "Going somewhere?" he asks.

I ignore him, not ready to talk just yet, and start pacing, my fists clenching and unclenching at my sides. So many hateful thoughts, so many hurtful ideas are floating through my mind, but I'm trying really hard to ignore them. I don't *want* to be this person. I don't *want* to be the pitiful, angry woman. I just want to... *be*. But I can't when everywhere I turn, Asher and Mindy are there to remind me of everything that's messed up in my life.

A fucking engagement ring?

Are you kidding me?

How could he do that?

"Do what?" I hear Cage ask from behind me and I realize I was speaking my thoughts out loud.

Turning slowly, I swallow, unable to wrap my head around it and needing to talk it out, regardless of who's listening. "She was wearing a ring… on her fourth finger… a fucking big ass diamond." I look down at my hand where my wedding band once resided, the tan line from years of wear still visible. I thought about covering it up with a new ring, but I haven't yet. Mine was never that big. Asher bought it for me when he was still in college. I hadn't even started yet because I was working to save up money. It was small, but I'd loved it, because it was a symbol of his love for me… or so I thought.

Now, I don't know what to think.

I'm not even sure *I* make sense anymore without him and that kills me.

The truth is I never felt pretty or worthy or significant until Asher Williams noticed me.

Before then, I was an awkward teenager trying to make it through high school. I spent lunch hours in the library, hiding away behind cookbooks. Julia Child was my companion.

One day, Asher came into the library to do some research for a history paper. He sat down at the table across from me and started talking to me like we were old friends.

We were.

Once upon a time, I'd been good friends with the majority of the people in my class, but the older we all got, the more we parted ways, each of us finding our own niche. Mine just happened to be in the back corner of the library or in my mama's kitchen, whipping up my newest concoction of baked goods.

Before Asher, I hadn't even been to a high school football game.

After we were an item, everything changed.

I was *noticed.*

I was *invited.*

I was *liked.*

But now, with him removed from my life, I'm left wondering who I am without him.

"Do you want to be alone?" Cage finally asks, pulling me out of my thoughts, and it's only then I realize my cheeks are wet with tears. Wiping at them, I force myself to look up at him.

"I just want to go home," I croak. "Before I do something to end up in jail… again."

He points over my shoulder. "Hank's truck is over there. I can drive you home and come back and get him."

Biting down on my lip, I close my eyes, willing myself to hold it together, just a little while longer. "You don't have to do that… you've already helped me out once."

"We're friends, right?" he asks and there's sincerity in his words I didn't expect. "Let me take you home. I'd much rather do that than have to bail you out of jail."

That gets him a laugh, but then I stop, frowning. "You just met me. Why are you being so nice?" I ask, immediately wary of his intentions. Also, he needs to know I'm not good company these days. "I'm crazy, you know? That's what they all say about me. If you're seen with me, people will probably think you're crazy too."

He shrugs. "I like to form my own opinions," he says, crossing his large arms over his chest. "And you let me worry about what people think about me."

There's nothing but pure honesty in his eyes, so I take him at his word and up on his offer. When I turn in the direction he'd pointed earlier, he slowly begins to follow me. "Want to talk about it?"

I shake my head, still feeling on the verge of tears and not trusting my voice.

"Okay." He sighs and I realize this isn't going to be a quiet trip home. Cage is going to make me pay in conversation. "Well, I did want to tell you that the muffins you gave me the other day were… well," he pauses, letting out a breath. "By far the best fucking muffins I've ever eaten."

I fight back the smile as it works its way to the surface, replacing the tears.

"Glad you liked them," I mumble.

"What's with the names?" he asks as we approach a truck and he jumps in front of me to open the passenger door. When I climb into the seat, a sudden rush of recognition hits me. This is the same truck he drove me home in. The smell of the cab is familiar and I remember leaning my head over onto the window, soaking in the coolness of the glass.

"I like old country western music," I tell him when he gets in on the driver's side. "Patsy Cline, George Jones, Merle Haggard, Loretta Lynn, Conway Twitty—if it's got a steel guitar and a sad story, I'm a fan."

Cage chuckles, and for a second I think he's making fun of me, which would be nothing new and I really don't care. I've been defending my taste of music for twenty years. I remember on my eighth birthday, I invited a few girls from my third grade class over for a slumber party and when I put a Loretta Lynn album on my turntable, they all thought I was weird.

That label stuck for a while, basically until I started dating Asher in the tenth grade.

"I love it," Cage says, setting me at ease. "Hope you'll make some Folsom Prison Blues again sometime," he says, turning out of the field onto the road. "I've heard those are a hit."

Smirking, I turn in the seat to face him. "Do you even know any country western music?"

He shrugs. "I guess I probably don't know much, but doesn't mean I don't like it. I'm a fan of whatever music fits my mood. Doesn't matter if it's rap or heavy metal or country. It's about how it makes me feel."

I nod, considering his reply. "I can respect that."

The smile he throws me over his shoulder is… well, it's a good thing I'm sitting, that's all I've got to say. If Cage Erickson and I are going to be friends, I'm going to have to work really hard at keeping my feelings in check.

As we drive down the road, I try to not look at him, keeping my eyes straight ahead.

Friends.

Yeah, I could do this.

I need one right now.

And look at me, driving away before I let Asher and Mindy get the best of me… being the bigger person, removing myself from the situation. *Go, Tempest.* I mentally fist bump myself and steal another glance at Cage… my new friend. Having someone to talk to that isn't close to me or my family or Asher might be exactly what I need. If Cage is willing to fill that role, I'll take him up on it.

CHAPTER 8

CAGE

I have no idea what it is about Tempest that makes me want to talk, but being in her presence has turned me into a fucking Chatty Cathy. Normally, I'm very tight-lipped. Unless I'm around people I know well, I don't have a lot to say. My actions have always spoken louder than my words, giving me a reprieve from small talk.

Maybe it's because there's this crazy connection I can't ignore that makes her feel like she's an old friend. When I told her we should be friends at the picnic, I don't even know where that came from. It's like I opened my mouth and the words just tumbled out. Now, here we are, in the same truck I drove her home in the other night and I'm trying to keep my eyes on the road instead of that fucking green dress she's wearing.

It brings out her eyes, making them greener than the pine trees.

"My grandpa used to play with Lester Flatt and Earl Scruggs," she says. "They were the Foggy Mountain Boys… not that you'd know who they are, but they were a bluegrass group that played on the Grand Ole Opry. He didn't play with them officially, but they'd have jam sessions." I glance over to see her soft smile. "He loved bluegrass and country western… all the old stuff, which I guess wasn't old to him. I can remember sitting on the center console of his truck… you know, before they enforced seatbelts… driving down the road. Just me, him, and George Jones or Patsy Cline."

I could listen to her talk all damn day. She has a soft lilt to her voice, but there's also a raspiness I noticed from the first night. It's a little grittier than you'd expect, given her exterior, which makes it even more intriguing… it makes *her* even more intriguing.

"You, uh… turn," she starts and stops when she realizes I already know how to get to her house. "Right." She's quiet for a minute as we drive down the road leading to her house. "Thanks again… for the other night. I don't usually… do that."

I didn't figure.

Even from the moment I saw her sitting in my spot, I knew she was somewhat out of her element.

"Don't mention it," I tell her, not wanting her to feel bad about it. "We all need to blow off a little steam from time to time."

This time when she laughs, it's lost all humor. "I've done my fair share of that lately."

"I've heard," I say before thinking.

"I'm sure you have." Her tone is resolved, maybe even a bit defeated, and I hate it.

"Hey," I say, getting her attention. "I form my own opinions, remember?" The smile she gives me is weak, not the one I'm looking for. "So, why don't you tell me your story… set the record straight."

She looks at me like *I'm* crazy. "Why? Why do you want to know? Why do you care?"

I see the distrust in her eyes. She's guarded and I don't blame her.

"Maybe I'm just… bored," I say with a shrug, trying to blow it off like it's no big deal whether she tells me or not—feigning disinterest. "Besides, if we're going to be friends, I think I should know your story."

Under that load of shit, the truth is buried—*you're an enigma, Tempest Cassidy… help me understand you better.* She smiles again, still guarded, but a little less so. When she swallows and brushes a strand of her red hair behind her ear, I know she's going to at least give me something.

"It's simple, really," she starts, shifting in her seat as we pull into her drive. With her eyes trained on the yellow house, she continues, "I walked in on my husband in bed with someone else… that was almost four months ago. Since then, I've destroyed our bedroom, burned his clothes, broke into his house, stole a football, and parked his truck in Mr. Miller's pond." Sighing, I think she's going to stop there, but she doesn't. Turning toward me, she says, "I've spent two nights in jail, paid over a thousand dollars in fines, and been sentenced to twenty-four hours of anger management."

Our eyes lock and I feel the load she's been carrying.

"The night you drove me home, I was celebrating my divorce being final. I thought once the ink was dry and I was officially Tempest Cassidy again I'd be able to move on and get over it, but I was wrong. Today, seeing that ring on Mindy's finger, it was a reminder that my marriage is over and the man I loved for over a decade has moved on. He's giving someone else the life I once had. He took my truck and soon I'll have to move out of my house… and he took away my chances of having a baby," she says, her voice dropping to a near whisper as she turns back to the house. "I think, deep down, that's what I'm the saddest about."

The cab of the truck is silent as we both sit, me processing the information she just gave me and her probably reliving the heartache she's faced over the past few months.

"I'm sorry," I tell her, not knowing what else to say. The smile she gives me this time is sad and I want to remove it from her beautiful face.

Sighing, she reaches for the door handle. "Thanks for the ride and for listening. I'm sorry I just dumped my drama on you."

"That's what friends are for, right?"

As I stand in the open door of the truck, I get a hint of the real smile I've been wanting. "Yeah… friends."

"Hey, Tempest," I say, an idea popping into my head. "Tell me about the anger management. What's that all about?"

Her shoulders go up to her ears and she lets out a deep breath. "It's just a group thing… I go once a week… everyone talks about their anger." When she laughs, I see a little more of the tension leave her shoulders. "I've only been once, but I think it's helping… maybe a little…" She hesitates, chewing on her lip for a second. "Except, seeing Asher and Mindy today, I was able to use the coping mechanisms I've been learning … until I saw that ring."

Her eyes go straight to mine, vulnerable and transparent.

"Then what happened?" I ask, wanting her whole story—the whole truth.

"I wanted to hit something, or someone. I wanted to physically do damage." She huffs and shakes her head, stepping back and then bracing her hands on her thighs. "That's when the crazy sets in… that's why people talk about me. And maybe I am… crazy," she says, swallowing and fighting back emotions. "Maybe he made me crazy."

"You're not," I tell her, wanting to get out of the truck and walk around to her, but I've got to keep my distance if we're going to make this whole *friends* thing work. "It's totally understandable. You've been through a lot and you need an outlet for your feelings." I pause, really thinking through what I'm getting ready to offer, but knowing it's the right thing to do… the right thing for her. "I could teach you kickboxing, possibly throw in some jujitsu. I think it would really help you channel the negative thoughts and feelings you're having."

I don't mention that it'll also give her confidence and discipline, but those would be great residual effects. I've seen it time and time again, even in myself. It'll also reduce her stress, which I think she could definitely use.

"Kickboxing?" she asks, finally standing up straight to look at me. "Do you… is that why… you're a kickboxer?" The way she stumbles over her words is adorable and I have to fight back a smile.

Friends, Erickson. You're just friends.

"Yeah, I dabble," I say with a smirk. "And I just ordered a new bag that should be delivered this week. I'm staying in one of the buildings downtown, just down the street from the bakery, and I'm turning the downstairs into a studio of sorts." Pausing, I catch a vision of what the place could be and I store it away for later. *Possibilities*. "Maybe next Wednesday?" I ask.

She thinks for a minute, obviously trying to decide if it's a good decision. Does she trust me? Could she trust me? "Okay," she finally agrees. "Maybe after noon? That's when I get off work on Wednesdays."

"Noon." I almost add "it's a date", but think better of it. "You know where Hank Weller's building is? It's the red brick one."

Slowly, she nods. "Yeah, I know the one."

"Okay, I'll see you Wednesday."

CHAPTER 9

TEMPEST

I woke up this morning with a lead weight in my stomach.

The realtor is coming today to start the process of putting our house... *the* house... up on the market. She thinks it will sell fast, which means I have to finish getting things packed up and figure out what I'm going to do when it sells.

Asher moved his things out months ago, right after the day I walked in on him and Mindy. Except for the things in the garage and a few stragglers, which I took care of in what is now known as the driveway bonfire.

Over the past few months, I've slowly thrown out anything that reminded me of Asher or our marriage or anything remotely sentimental. So, basically, all that is left to pack up is the kitchen and the spare bedroom I've been sleeping in. As far as the living room furniture is concerned, I don't want it. Asher picked it out and it can either stay with the house or go down in flames... or the Goodwill.

I guess that's the safer choice.

As I'm purging the mail holder, my phone rings.

I don't even have to look at the screen to know it's my mama. Merle Haggard's *Mama Tried* plays on loop a few times before I finally swipe my thumb across the screen and place the phone between my cheek and shoulder. "Hey, Mama."

"Hey, darlin. Look, I know you have a lot on your plate today but your daddy was telling me he saw that scary looking man take you home from the picnic and I knew that couldn't be true, so I'm calling to get some answers."

My mother has never been one to beat around the bush and once she gets going with her twenty questions, it's hard to stop her.

"Because," she continues, "I know I raised my girl right and she'd never accept a ride home from a stranger. Let's be real here, Tempest, your self-preservation skills have been somewhat lacking here lately, but to willingly put yourself in harm's way, I just don't know what to think."

A dramatic sob forces her to take a breath, so I use the opportunity to defend myself. "Mama, calm down." I have so many things to say, I'm not sure where to start. Closing my eyes tightly while rubbing my forehead, I will myself to bite my tongue and not say anything that will only aggravate the situation.

"First of all, Cage is not scary looking." I'm not sure why I started there but at least I stopped myself before admitting just how "not scary" I think he looks.

"Well, he's built like a brick wall, if I ever did see one. The man is huge!"

She's not wrong, but where my mama may see Cage's size as a threat, I see it as a safe fortress. I mean, not for myself but just in general, of course.

"Just because the men around here walk hunched over, dragging their knuckles like their Neanderthal forefathers, doesn't mean it's wrong to be tall. He can't help it. Also, he's not a stranger, not to me anyway."

"Oh, my heavens, Tempest. Did you meet him when you were *in jail*?" She whispers *in jail* even though it's just the two of us talking *on the phone*. "And, now he knows where you live? It's a good thing you're selling that house. He might've been… you know, casing the joint. Isn't that what they call it?"

"Mama, stop! He wasn't casing the joint and even if he was, I wouldn't care. He can have everything in this damn house, if he wants."

"Tempest June, you don't mean that!"

"I do, Mama, I really do. Asher and I are over and as much as I love this house, I'm tired of being surrounded by memories of us. This place, and everything in it, only reminds me of how we failed and I don't want to be here anymore." I deflate against the counter, feeling unwelcome emotions coming to the surface as the truth spills out of me.

"Oh, honey," my mama sighs.

I swallow the lump that's formed in my throat before speaking, the fire in my voice now put out. "I saw Mindy's ring at the picnic. I know they're engaged."

"It's worse than that. The truth is, they're already married." I appreciate how my mother delivers this news. Her words are precise and her voice is steady, but I can hear the underlying tone of disgust. It gives me hope she's finally seeing Asher for who he really is.

As for what she's just told me, I'm going to have to reexamine that later. I can't think about it right now. Compartmentalize. I think that's what they call it, when you can't process something, so you tuck it away into a box until your mind is ready to tackle the problem. Instead, I go back to my mama's comment about self-preservation and my lack of it.

"Mama, I don't want to talk about them. I want to talk about you questioning my, as you called it, preservation skills. Do you really think I want to hurt myself?"

"No, I don't mean that. I just don't think you realize the consequences of your actions when you do these crazy things."

After hearing it so often over the past four months, it's easy to ignore the "crazy" remark but, coming from my mother, it still stings.

"I'm well aware of the consequences, thank you very much, and I don't want to hurt myself or anyone else when I do those things. But," I pause, sighing and attempting to mentally pull myself up by the bootstraps. "I'm working on it, Mama… I'm working on *myself*, and I'd really like your support." It's physically and mentally exhausting when I feel like it's me against the whole damn world. I never realized how alone I feel until she starts in on me like this. The one person who should always have my back. "Lastly, stop judging Cage. He's a nice guy and was helping me out by taking me home. That's all."

"Okay, baby," she finally says, but I can still hear the hesitance in her tone. "Okay, just promise me you won't get tangled up with someone like him. Do you even know who he is… really? I mean, he's new to town, so you obviously just met him."

I want to spill all the beans and make her head spin.

Yeah, Mama, he's the bouncer at the Pink Pony and he knows kick-boxing and he's going to teach me. Oh, also, the first night we met, he drove me home when I was trashed on tequila and put me to bed.

Instead, I tell her, "He's friends with Hank Weller and he's from Dallas and he's been a good friend to me, which I can't say for anyone else in this town over the past few months, outside of Cole and Anna, but they have to because they're family."

"I don't think you realize the impression," she says, pausing for dramatic effect, "you're giving people when you're seen with him."

My eyes can't roll any further into the back of my head without falling out.

"Oh, good Lord, Mama—"

"He is good, Tempest. And He is watching." When she starts in with her holier than thou speech, I know the conversation is over.

"Goodbye, Mama."

"I expect to see you at church on Sunday," she says, right before I give her a final "I love you, Mama" and hang up the phone.

Pressing it to my forehead, I hold my breath for a count of ten, hoping it will help center me and keep me from doing what I want to do, which is rage and scream and cry.

Don't do it, Tempest.

Don't destroy everything in this kitchen.

That's just more work for you.

Because you're alone... and divorced... and being forced to leave the house you love.

And Asher and Mindy are married. MARRIED.

I feel the tears slip under my palms that are pressed into my eyes, and it immediately makes me even more angry. He doesn't deserve my tears. Our marriage doesn't deserve my tears. So, why am I crying? Why do I care?

Those are questions I don't have an answer to.

After a few more tears and some deep, cleansing breaths, I'm finally able to open my eyes and step away from the counter, turning in place as I look around.

This is just a house. It doesn't define me.

Asher doesn't define me.

I've been trying to convince myself of that, but failing.

Looking at the screen of my phone, I see I have half an hour until the realtor is supposed to be here and an hour before I need to leave for Knoxville. My anger management session is this afternoon and I need it. If nothing else, I'll sit and listen to other people's problems until I feel better about mine. Regardless, the drive alone will be a welcome reprieve. The awesome thing about going to Knoxville once a week is no one knows me there. I can walk down the sidewalk and no one stares or whispers after I walk by.

To keep my mind off the phone call with my mama and the news about Asher and Mindy, I dive back into the pile of mail and start purging. If I can't burn shit, I'll throw it away.

It takes the edge off, until I come across an envelope that's been tucked down in here since it came in the mail a few months ago.

Green Valley High Class of 2009

My knee-jerk reaction is to throw it in the trash with the rest of the junk mail, but I can't help reading through the invitation.

Join us for two days full of friends, family, and fun!

Our ten year class reunion will kick off with some good ol' Green Valley pride at the football game on Friday night. Come join us and cheer GVHS on to victory. Class of 2009 will have a dedicated section and we'll be recognizing some of our classmates who made history at Green Valley High.

On Saturday, join us for a fun day at the park. Bring your spouses, significant others, and kids!

Saturday night, we'll go out with a bang! Taking it back to the good days. Dinner, Dancing and this time around, we'll be serving alcohol... legally. Your 2009 Homecoming King and Queen will be the guests of honor and emcees for the evening.

Don't miss your chance to reconnect and rekindle old friendships and flames.

Cost: $25 for one/$40 for couple

RSVP to Mindy Mitchell...

Mindy Mitchell.

Something inside me snaps, similar to what I've experienced lately —heart pumping wildly, blood rushing, logic fleeing—and I'm left with the rawest, most basic needs. And right now, I need to go to this reunion. I can't explain it. But I don't want to do what they all expect me to do—throw this invitation away and hide away like the guilty party.

Hell no.

I'm not.

I'm going to do exactly the opposite. I'm going to show up and hold my head up high, knowing I'm not the one who is wrong in this situation. I didn't sleep around on my wife. That was Asher. I didn't sleep with someone else's husband. That was Mindy. And I'll be damned if I'm going to let them flaunt themselves around for two days like they're the king and queen of the goddamned world.

Walking over to the refrigerator, I take off one of the magnets and place the invitation there, holding it in place. Nodding to myself, I pick up my phone and open up my email, sending a brief, non-threatening, email to Mindy Mitchell.

Class president.

Husband stealer.

Miss Mitchell...

Scratch that.

Mrs. Williams.

I'm sure the invitations were made before she accepted Asher's proposal, but I'm extremely too petty these days to let this opportunity pass me by.

Please add me to the list of attendees for the Class of 2009 reunion.

Tempest Cassidy.

Wait…

Please put me and a plus one down for the Class of 2009 reunion.

Tempest Cassidy.

I have no idea who that plus one will be, but I'll be damned if I'm going alone. My thoughts immediately turn to Cole, but that would just be weird, taking my cousin, and would only further their opinions of me. But I've got a few weeks to figure it out.

I'm a smart girl and I'm not entirely unfortunate looking.

I can find a date.

At least, in theory, but the truth is that I've never actually approached a guy before. Before Asher, I hadn't really had a boyfriend. There was this one guy, Tim, who took me to the movies my freshman year, but it was awkward and my mama drove us.

Before I can chicken out, I hit send.

As I'm driving to Knoxville, I think about the email, the invite, the marriage. I let it all sink in.

When I walk through the doors of the church, where the anger management group sessions are held, I take a deep breath. Somehow, I made it. I made it here without losing my grip, my temper, or my mind.

"Welcome," the group leader says, when she sees me. "Tempest, right?"

I nod and give her a small smile, my eyes darting around the room, noticing a few familiar faces from last week. Most of the people stand around talking in groups of two or three. Since I've only been to one session, I don't feel comfortable enough to approach any of them. So, after I sign in, I take a seat in the semi-circle of chairs, opting for one closest to the exit.

And my mama thinks I don't have any self-preservation.

"Hello everyone," the leader says as she walks to the front of the room. "As most of you know, I'm Lana. Pretty sure everyone has been here at least once, so I won't force any awkward introductions." She smiles and claps her hands, pacing for a moment as she waits for everyone to find a seat.

Once everyone is seated, she starts. "Something we haven't done in a while is speaking individually about why we're all here. A few of you spoke about isolated incidents last week, but this week, I'd like us to all share… at least a brief synopsis of what brought you here." Pausing, she smiles and lets her eyes travel around the circle. "I know this might be hard for some of you, but the thing we need to realize the most is that we're not alone. Everyone here is dealing with something."

A guy to my left holds a hand up, getting her attention and she nods at him. "Go ahead, Steve."

"My wife and I were having issues at home," he starts. "She's…" he stops, "*I'm* not very good at keeping my cool. When we argue, things get heated."

At his confession, my heart beats a little faster.

"I've never hit her," he clarifies, clearing his throat. "But I have broken things at our house… tables, lamps, doors. And I know it's wrong. Our marriage counselor suggested these sessions and they've really helped."

When he's finished, I notice that he wipes his palms down the legs of his jeans. And I realize my palms are sweaty too.

"I'm here because a judge sentenced me to anger management sessions instead of jail time," a guy across the room says, and I look up at him. He seems like an average guy—probably in his early thirties, dress shirt and slacks. "I was in a bar one night and a guy made a pass at my girlfriend. I let it go the first time, but when she told me he followed her to the bathroom," he pauses, running a hand through this hair and letting out a deep breath. "Well, I lost it… body shakes, blood boiling… you name it, I felt it. One minute I was standing toe-to-toe with the guy and the next minute I was in handcuffs in the back of a cop car."

The personal stories continue and with each one, I start to feel less and less alone. Sure, I'm flying solo these days, but something about hearing other people—normal, everyday people—who've been through similar things, dealt with similar things, makes me feel… less crazy, more normal.

"I'm Tempest," I say, when I'm the last one left who hasn't talked. "Like you," I say, pointing across the circle to the guy in the dress shirt, "I was sentenced to anger management after my fourth… *episode*, as my mama likes to call them." I smile, shaking my head. "I walked in on my husband and his… well, wife, now… he just recently married his mistress." A few people shift in their seat and I glance up to see their disapproval, making me feel like they're on my side, and it makes all of this easier. "About four months ago, I walked in on them together in bed. My first time in jail was for disturbing the peace. I stood outside his new house and yelled… everything… I can't even remember. I'd been drinking that night and then I had a bad dream, and I figured if I couldn't sleep, he shouldn't either. Then, I burned all of his stuff he left at our house. Apparently, it's against the law to start a bonfire in your driveway."

The guy beside me laughs a little, but it's not at me, it's different—it's understanding, solidarity.

"I also broke into his new house and stole a football… and hocked it to pay for some fines. Then I put his truck in a pond. So, after I had a few strikes against me, the judge decided this would be a good place for me, and—" I pause, looking around the room. "I think he was right."

Everyone nods in agreement and Lana gives me an encouraging smile.

The weight from the day is lifted off my shoulders. Just like when I shared some of this with Cage. It's like I'm not carrying the full load of the burden any more.

"For the next thirty minutes," she says, looking down at her watch, "I'd like us to talk about other ways we can release stress."

The talk ranges from yoga to meditation to journaling to physical activity.

Listening to them talk about how karate or swimming or running have helped makes me think that Cage's offer to teach me kickboxing might not be too far off from what I need.

When I leave the anger management session, I stop by for a coffee at a local coffee shop, sneakily judge their muffin choices—deciding they're nowhere near as good as mine—and enjoy a few more moments of the anonymity before heading back to Green Valley.

An hour later, as I turn down my street, a familiar truck in my driveway catches my eye and I nearly stop in the middle of the road. Creeping the rest of the way, I slowly turn in and feel my heart begin to race as I put the truck into park and turn off the ignition.

Asher is standing in the driveway, leaning against the side of his own truck. I haven't seen my old truck since the day I drove it into the pond. I'm assuming he did as he said he was going to and sold it.

Deep breaths, Tempest.

You didn't need that truck. It was just a mode of transportation. And you have another one to drive until you can buy your own... in your *name... one no one can take back.*

"Tempest," Asher greets when I step out of the truck.

"Asher," I reply, trying to keep my voice as even and calm as possible. I want to ask him what he's doing here… and tell him to leave… and make some snide comment about his nuptials, but instead, I try something new and hold my tongue.

It's strange, seeing him like this. The last time we were actually face-to-face, just the two of us, was the night before I walked in on him and Mindy. Since then, we've always had a window or a person between us… someone or something acting as a buffer. I'll give it to him, this is actually a pretty ballsy move, something totally un-Asher-like. He's normally a play-it-safe kind of guy… well, until he decided to have an affair.

I guess he's been doing a lot of un-Asher-like things lately, or maybe I didn't know him to begin with?

What does he want?

Why is he here?

Those questions are on the tip of my tongue, before he finally speaks.

"Did the realtor show up today?" he asks, and I breathe a little easier. Of course he wants to know about the realtor and the sale of the house. He seems overly anxious to be done with us… everything that was ours… me.

"She did," I tell him, swallowing down the edge of emotion, the bitter taste of anger on the tip of my tongue. *Keep it together, Tempest.* "She already has a few people who are interested."

He nods, his eyes down, focused on the driveway at his feet. "Good."

"Yeah," I agree. *Good.*

Good.

I'm sure you need your portion of the sale to fund your second honeymoon or something.

Internally, I roll my eyes, but manage to keep my calm facade.

"Who is your plus one?" he asks and for a second I stop breathing.

Are you kidding me?

"What?" he asks, his eyes snapping up to meet mine, and that's the moment I realize I said that one out loud.

"You don't get to ask me that," I inform him, feeling my spine straighten and my heart pound in my chest. "You don't get to know anything about me." *Deep breaths.* "Outside of this house selling, we're done… over."

I don't miss the minute squint of his eyes. He doesn't like me denying him this information. Asher's never been good at handling being told no.

"I hear congratulations are in order," I add, walking past him to the front door. As I pass him, I notice him stiffen. Maybe he thought I wasn't privy to that bit of information. Before I walk into the house, I add, "I hope the two of you will be very happy."

CHAPTER 10

CAGE

I've been giving myself a talk all morning.

Actually, I take that back. I've been giving myself a talk since the day, excuse me, night, Tempest Cassidy walked into my life.

Friends.

I don't have many of them, not just in Green Valley, but in life period.

Tempest needs a friend.

I need a friend.

So, we'll be friends. I can do that. I can ignore my crazy, ridiculous, instant attraction to her and be what she needs. Starting today, I'm going to teach her how to kickbox. And what she doesn't know is that this isn't just for her. I need this too.

Looking around the downstairs, I smile to myself. Where there was once stark, white walls and gray concrete floors, blue mats now cover a large portion of the floor and half of the walls are covered in mirrors. Not to mention the two bags that are hanging from the steel beams. I plan on adding a few more, eventually. And I need some speed bags, but it's a work in progress.

What a difference a week makes.

What a difference a few months makes.

The day I rolled into Green Valley, which doesn't seem that long ago, I was searching and pretty fucking lost. Over the past seven days, as I've worked all my nights at the Pink Pony, spent my mornings running, and every afternoon working on this place, I've found a sense of peace and purpose.

Yesterday, I popped into Donner Bakery after my run, looking for a muffin… and the Duchess of Muffins, but she'd already left for the day. The consolation prize was the last two Muffins of the Day —*Mama Tried.* They were peanut butter and banana… and fucking delicious. I had to go run a few extra miles just to make up for them, but they were well worth it.

Tempest and her muffins—and the names—are quickly becoming my favorite things in Green Valley.

Checking the clock I hung on the wall, I see it's almost time for her first lesson—if she shows.

She'll show, right?

I mean, no big deal if she doesn't. I was planning on doing all of this before I offered to teach her, so it's no loss, but I really hope she shows up.

What the fuck is wrong with me?

Who am I these days?

Worried about whether or not a woman will show up?

This is so not me and I'm worried that along with blowing out my shoulder, I might've also grown a vagina. Glancing down my abs that are covered in a tight black T-shirt, I give my dick a nod.

Still there.

Not like it doesn't give me a reminder every fucking time Tempest is around—or I think of her—or catch a whiff of something sweet.

Turning on the radio I brought down from upstairs, I amp up the volume to fill the space and drown out my thoughts. I don't think it's a coincidence that the only two channels I can pick up on it are an old, classic rock station and a country western one. I smirk at the thought of Tempest—red hair, perfect little nose, big green eyes… full lips and—

Fucking stop.

Growling out my frustration, I turn to one of the bags, pull on some gloves, and go to town. The tightness in my right shoulder keeps me from unleashing the beast. The *Fighting Viking* isn't as intimidating as he once was, but I still let the punches fly and every kick makes contact, giving my lower body the workout it's been craving.

When the front door opens, my eyes slide over to the mirrors, seeing Tempest's reflection. Just before she sees me looking at her, I'm pretty sure I catch her ogling me. Those green eyes go wide before zeroing in on my back... and if I'm not mistaken, her teeth bite down on her bottom lip.

"Hey," she says, scanning the room, nerves replacing whatever it was she was just feeling and the wall she usually has up seems to reinforce. "Am I too early?" While she's looking down at her phone, obviously checking the time, I take a split second to do inventory: tight black yoga pants, loose tank top, sports bra peeking out under her arms. Her hair is pulled up on top of her head, no makeup.

Perfect.

"You're right on time," I tell her, pulling one of the gloves off with my teeth, and then the other, tossing them to the side. "You can put your bag over there."

She walks to the corner I'm pointing to and I try to not look at her ass as she bends over to deposit her bag on the floor.

Try and fail.

Miserably.

"We should, uh," I begin, clearing my throat. "We should stretch first."

Turning toward me, she nods slowly. "I'm not very… athletic." She makes the statement like it's a warning or maybe an apology. "I like to go running and sometimes I do work-out videos at home, but I've never really tried a sport… I mean, if I had one, it'd be baking, and that doesn't really burn calories." Her awkward, uncomfortable laugh is enough to pull me out of my head and get my dick in line. It's adorable, and a turn on, but it's also a reality check.

She's nervous and out of her element and she's expecting me to be her guide.

This is what I'm good at.

I can do this.

"We'll start simple, so don't worry about it. Don't even think of it like a sport. The awesome thing about kickboxing is that you don't have to involve another person until you're comfortable. For the time being, we'll work on basic punches and kicks. Today we'll just do some shadowboxing and then next week, or whenever you want to come back for a class, we'll start on the bags."

Her eyes go around the room again, taking it all in. "I really like what you've done with the place."

"It's a start," I tell her, shrugging.

"You're going to add to it?"

Walking over to the mats, I nod. "Yeah, I don't really know what I'm going to do with it, but I needed a place to work out… and it felt like a waste letting a big, open space like this stay empty. Hank was cool with it. The rent is cheap. So, even if I only ever use it for myself… and the occasional class… it's worth it."

"I can pay you," she says. "I don't feel right taking up your time and not paying."

I immediately shake my head. "No way," I tell her. "I'm the one who offered. And besides that… we're friends." She smiles at the term we keep throwing back and forth between us, but the more I say it, the more it sinks in and starts to feel real. "I'd never charge my friends… haven't ever in the past, don't plan to start now."

"So you've taught before?"

"Oh, yeah. I've been taking it since I was a kid, along with other martial arts. When I'd graduate to a black belt, my instructors would usually put me to work and have me earning my keep."

The slow smile and the way her shoulders relax tell me she's feeling more comfortable and it puts me at ease as well. "Ready to stretch?"

"Yeah," she says, shaking her head. "I've had quite the last couple of days. I've actually been looking forward to this."

"Well, let's do it."

Leading Tempest through stretches isn't as hard—all fucking puns intended—as I thought it would be, but only because I made her stand beside me and follow my motions in the mirror. From there, I forced myself to keep my eyes to myself. But what I did see from her was promising. She's limber and has very fluid movements. Those are all good qualities in a kickboxer… amongst other things… which I'll not be thinking about today, at least not right now.

"Ready to learn some punches?"

She scrunches her nose, making it even cuter, if that's possible. "Are we sure this is a good idea?" she asks, her words stretching out as she worries her bottom lip. "I mean, with my track record and all, is it a good idea to teach me how to punch?"

"The best idea," I tell her in all seriousness. "With that temper you've been working with, you really need to know how to defend yourself." I'm being serious, but I laugh to make light of the situation. "But more than that, getting out the frustration and anger you've been feeling in a constructive, controlled environment will help you manage it… it's like defusing a bomb."

Taking a deep breath, she nods. "Right… that's basically what Lana was saying."

"Who's Lana?"

"My anger management… person," she says, her cheeks blushing a little. "Part of our talk this week was about ways we can release stress and tension, clear our heads… that kind of thing."

I nod, hoping she knows there is zero judgment here. "She's right."

"Okay, then… show me what to do."

We stand in front of the mirrors again and I have her do some basic punches—jab, cross, uppercut, hook—which she picks up fast. She might not be an athlete, but she's a really fast learner and seems to be in good shape. I've turned a lot less capable people into great kickboxers. My guess is that Tempest is probably one of those people who's good at whatever she puts her mind to, but what holds her back is her lack of confidence.

"How about some kicks?" I ask, walking over to take a drink of water. "Did you bring some water?"

"Yeah, it's in my bag." She walks over and bends down to open her bag and I let myself have a quick second to admire her. I shouldn't, but

I do. "So, you're from Dallas," she says, coming up with a water bottle and forcing me to avert my gaze. "That's really all I know about you, outside of you being friends with Hank and working at the Pink Pony. What did you do before you came here?"

"I was a fighter, most recently in the UFC circuit," I tell her, realizing it's the first time I've talked about it in a while. The only person I've even skirted the topic with is Hank.

Her eyes go wide again. "Wow, like one of those guys who fights in the cage?" She smiles. It's small at first and then goes wider. "Like a cage fighter? Cage the cage fighter?" Her laugh is contagious and I can't help but join in, even though I've heard this joke. It's different coming from her. I don't mind it. Anything that brings a smile to her face like this, I'm good with, even if it is at my expense.

But I can't let her get her jab in without one in return. "Okay, Sundance Kid."

She tips her chin up in a challenge, eyes narrowing. "Did you really just go there?"

"Oh, yeah," I confirm, nodding my head. "I mean, that's what friends are for, right? Just keepin' it real." We enter into a minute-long staring contest before I go in for the kill. "It's rather fitting, you know? What with your run-ins with the law."

When her jaw goes tight and her full lips pull together, I'm afraid I've overstepped my boundaries, but then she quirks an eyebrow. "Oh, it's go time."

She starts punching the air around me, putting to use the forms I've been teaching her and doing a pretty damn good job, but the way she's zipping around me like a little hummingbird makes me laugh. I try to hold it back, but I can't.

When her jab misses the air and makes contact with my arm, it shocks us both. She stops, her hand flying up to her mouth, eyes going wide. "Oh, my God. I'm sorry," she laughs. "I was… I mean, I'd never…" Her laughs overtake her and before I know it, I have my arms wrapped around her, holding her arms down to her side and tossing her over my shoulder.

The melodic tone of her laugh continues to fill the air, bouncing off the concrete walls and it's fucking music to my ears. When I finally set her back down on her own two feet, her hair is wild, falling haphazardly out of her ponytail, and our breaths are coming out in short spurts. We share the same air for a second, maybe more, and our eyes connect.

My body tells me to kiss her.

And for a moment, I think she wants me to.

It feels like minutes or centuries pass between us as we stare into each other's eyes, but it's probably only mere seconds. Tilting my head even closer, I lick my lips, swearing I can already taste her on them before we even make contact, but I don't get the chance. She goes rigid in my arms—eyes going wide with the realization of how close we are, bodies touching—and surprises me by pushing hard on my chest, creating distance between us.

Smoothing her hair back out of her face, she straightens. "I, um… I've gotta go. I just remembered that I have a… meeting… with the, uh, realtor. I'm selling my house. We're selling the house. Asher…" She pauses her rambling to look at me, bending down to retrieve her bag. "I've gotta go."

One second she's here, and everything is great—fucking amazing—and the next second she's gone, walking so fast, she's disappeared far enough down the sidewalk that I can't see her any longer. Poof. Gone. And I want to punch myself in the face.

What the fuck was that, Cage?

Running a hand down my face, I turn and begin to pace the room.

Yeah, I fucked that up.

Shit.

CHAPTER 11

TEMPEST

Walking into the pantry, I peruse the shelves, looking for the necessary ingredients and then trying to decide on what I'm throwing in with them to make today's Muffin of the Day.

I've already decided on my song—*The Fightin' Side of Me*—so now I just need to think the recipe through. Sometimes, I get an inspiration for a muffin and match it up to a favorite song, but sometimes, like this morning, I have a song in mind and work with it to come up with something delicious. I've had failures, sure. But most of the time, they're a hit.

Letting my mind wander and my taste buds do the talking, I decide it will be a dark chocolate muffin with bacon crumbles. Those are literally the two things I couldn't go through life without, and they're always fighting for dominance.

Chocolate or bacon?

Sweet or savory?

I mean, it's really cruel to make anyone choose between them, so the beauty of this recipe is that you don't have to.

Initially, I had the song on my mind because, even though last night's kickboxing lesson ended abruptly and, albeit, awkwardly—well, at least on my part, it was awkward—it was still a great outlet. I felt like learning how to throw a proper punch and using my body in a new way, I found the fighting side of Tempest Cassidy.

Showing up and agreeing to him teaching me was a good decision.

Everything was fine until Cage and I started joking around, and then it went topsy-turvy, literally. One minute, I was bouncing around, trying out my new moves, and the next, he had me tossed over his shoulder, caveman style.

I felt the rush of adrenaline.

I felt the release of tension.

I felt the increase in confidence.

And then, I felt something foreign, something I haven't felt in a long time—lust, desire, butterflies.

I swear, he was going to kiss me.

Or maybe I was going to kiss him.

That's when I ran home like a yellow-bellied chicken.

The more I've thought about it, the more I want to kick my own ass. I battled myself the entire class—forcing myself not to look at Cage like he's a piece of meat, berating myself for taking his instructions in a sexual manner.

Put your body into it. A simple request. But after my sex-deprived, attention-lacking psyche got ahold of it, it sounded a lot more perverse. I found myself shaking my head, trying to clear out the dirty thoughts and focus on the task at hand, not the man who was spending his free time to teach me.

I'm just glad I left before I did something I couldn't take back and that I'd be seriously regretting this morning.

But it's fine.

Nothing happened.

I'll make him some muffins… as a thank you… and at the next class, I'll keep my hands to myself and keep my mind out of the gutter.

Merle Haggard's lyrics—*if you don't love it, leave it*—are striking a chord with me this morning. Humming to myself, I walk back into the kitchen with my ingredients. A month or so ago, this song might've made me sad— or mad. I probably would've internalized these lyrics. I would've thought about how Asher didn't love me, so he left me. And I'm sure that's true, but it doesn't affect me like it did.

The feeling that's taking precedence over all the others this morning is *fight.* Maybe it's the empowering feeling still lingering from yesterday. Even though things didn't end on a good note, the rest of the class was awesome. I've never felt so alive and in control of my body as I did punching my way across those mats. It was a rush, and it made me feel like fighting.

Not the kind that will land me in jail, but the kind that says *I'm Tempest Cassidy and I'm still here... I'm not going anywhere... and you're not going to win.*

"That's right, Merle," I mutter to myself as I measure out the exact amount of flour, leveling it off with a knife. The key to great muffins is precise measuring and not over-mixing. "You know, we're kind of two peas in a pod…" I continue, speaking to one of the few men who truly gets me—Merle Haggard. "You hear people talking about you…" I mutter as I begin to fold in ingredients. "I hear people talking about me."

If The Hag was still alive, I think we could be great friends.

I chuckle to the muffin mixture taking shape in front of me. If anyone caught me holding a conversation with a dead man, they really would think I'm crazy. But what's a girl to do at four in the morning when she has things on her mind and no one around to talk to. Besides, I do my best thinking while I'm creating. This is my time to process and recollect without interruption.

Lana suggested mediation. Well, this is my form of meditation—me, Merle, and muffins.

"If you don't fucking love it… leave it," I agree as the song plays on loop. Whatever song I'm using for inspiration becomes my morning soundtrack. Sometimes, I'll listen to the same song a dozen times. As I sing along to the chorus, folding in some dark chocolate chips, I start to feel a twinge in my bicep, reminding me of the burn I felt during my lesson with Cage.

As my mind wanders from the muffins back to the lyrics, I have a thought: I wish Asher would've taken advice from Merle and left me *before* he decided to fuck Mindy Mitchell.

On more than one occasion, I've asked Asher how long… How long was he with her before I walked in on them? How long did he know he no longer loved me? Was it before or after the miscarriage? Was that the deciding factor… Did it make him feel like as much of a failure as it did me? Those are some of the burning questions he's yet to answer.

Maybe I'm a masochist for wanting to know, but I do.

After the whole bedroom incident and that first trip to jail, one of the first things I did—after changing the locks to the house and burning the sheets and my fluffy, white comforter—was go to my doctor and order an entire panel of tests. I knew I wasn't pregnant, so that was never a concern, seeing as I never got a chance to find out if that little window of fertility was working. But more than anything, I was freaked out. I know Mindy's past and her reputation. I needed to make sure Asher, and Mindy by proxy, hadn't given me any STDs.

I shiver at the thought.

Fortunately, everything came back fine. But it still didn't set my mind at ease.

For the first couple months, the mere idea of sex made my stomach roll. And I briefly thought he'd ruined it for me forever, but thanks to Cage and his ridiculous amounts of pheromones and testosterone, I know that's not the truth. He makes me feel things I thought were dead and gone, kind of like Merle.

Just friends, I remind myself.

Don't screw this up, Tempest.

When my mind finally shut up last night, and I quit second-guessing and over-analyzing, I eventually fell into the best sleep I've had in months. My body was deliciously spent and I didn't feel like punching anyone or burning anything. It was the most peaceful I've felt in the last five months, since my life got turned upside down.

After I have a few batches of On the Fightin' Side of Me done, I start on some Ring of Fires. Those sold really well last week. We also have some late-season cherries that need to be used up, so I pull those out.

As I go about the kitchen—measuring, mixing, pouring, baking—I let my mind be free, dreaming up something creative to use the cherries for, when an idea comes to mind. Running to the pantry, I pull out all the ingredients I'll need.

I've always thought a nice addition to a traditional Texas Sheet Cake are cherries.

The flavors are very complimentary.

Going Through the Big D also comes to mind. It's perfect—the story of my life mixed with where Cage is from. I smirk to myself as I think about it a little more. In an odd way, Cage and I are a good fit. He seems to get me and I like myself when I'm around him. Even if he does ruffle my feathers, he makes me feel confident. I like it. It's so much better than feeling sorry for myself.

Mark Chesnutt isn't as old school as I normally go, but it'll fit this recipe well and look great on the menu board.

When the muffins are cooled, I pour ganache over each one and top them with cherries. Setting four of them off to the side and putting them in a box, I make up my mind to visit Cage later. They'll be my *I'm-sorry-I-almost-kissed-you-and-ran-away-like-a-loon* and *thank-you-for-teaching-me-kickboxing* muffins. Thankfully, I don't need to fit all of that on the chalkboard sign.

By mid-morning, most of the muffins are gone, making me glad I set some aside for Cage. I'm placing the last dozen into the display case when the bell above the door chimes and a familiar face walks in, making me cringe.

Stella Wilson.

She's Mindy Mitchell's right-hand girl, always has been. Everywhere Mindy went, and I do mean everywhere, there Stella would be as well. It was like it'd been sent down to Moses on the Mount, along with the Ten Commandments. So, her showing up here this morning, although a public place and the most popular bakery in a fifty-mile radius, it still puts me on edge.

"Welcome to Donner Bakery," I greet, wishing I wasn't up here all alone and I could hide away in the back, but everyone else is busy with other customers or doing something else, so it's just me… and Stella. "What can I get you?"

Her sugary sweet smile makes me swallow hard, grateful I haven't had a chance to eat today, because it might be making a reappearance. Back in high school, that smile was a precursor to evil. Right before her sharp tongue would dart out and slash you, she'd smile.

"Tempest," she says, my name sounding condescending and patronizing and making me want to hurl… all the remaining muffins in her face. But that would be a waste of very delicious muffins, if I do say so myself.

And I do.

I made them.

I may not be confident in many things, but muffin making is my domain. I kill it. Own it.

I am the Duchess of Muffins.

After my brief mental pep talk and envisioning her with layers of crumbs and chocolate and cream all over her, I give her a smile in return. "Stella," I offer, hoping it comes out sounding just as ugly as I intend it.

"So," she says, taking a few more steps toward the counter. "I hear you'll be joining us at the reunion."

Oh, God.

"Mmm hmm," I manage, unable to open my mouth for fear I'll say something I'll truly regret.

"And you're bringing a date?"

Oh, God.

"Uh, yeah…" Cutting my eyes across the bakery, I look for help, anyone.

She places her expensive bag on the counter, leveling me with her stare. "Is it someone I know? Someone we went to school with?" Her questions come out inquisitive, like we're two old friends and she's interested in my life. "It's a shame about you and… Asher," she says, whispering his name behind her hand. "I mean, you know me and Mindy are tight, but that's just not the way to go about things."

For a second, I almost fall into her trap, a false sense of security creeping up on me before I give it a good kick, along with myself. *Wake up, Tempest. Do not fall for her tricks. You are older and wiser… this is not high school.*

Back then, I would've assumed she was genuinely trying to be my friend, but now, I see her for what she truly is—a snake in the grass, scoping out the latest gossip. A full-time employee for the enemy.

"A friend," I tell her, hoping my face expresses the mock confidence I'm going for. "You wouldn't know him."

Why are they so concerned about who I'm bringing? Is it not enough that Asher and I are divorced? I assumed they'd lose all interest in my life once I was no longer a part of his. So, is this morbid curiosity or is my life so pathetic they assume I'm lying? I am, but she doesn't have to know that.

Her lashes bat quickly. "Oh… is he from… out of town?"

"Yep."

I only put plus one on my email because I didn't want to sound pathetic. I have no clue who I'd take with me, my choice of friends is limited.

And that's when a plan starts to take shape.

Glancing back over my shoulder, I eye the box of muffins I set aside earlier. "Yeah, he's from out of state, actually. No one you'd know."

The look of confusion and obvious skepticism is blatant. She wants to call me out on the lie, right here in front of God and everyone, but instead, she gives me that same smile. "Well, I can't wait to meet him."

As she turns, walking back toward the door, I call out after her. "Did you want some muffins?"

"Oh, God, no," she says, pausing long enough to put a pair of expensive-looking sunglasses over her fake ass eyelashes. "I'm trying to drop another five before the reunion… gotta look good for my prom dress. We're all wearing them. You should too." Smiling, she waves, tossing her bag over her shoulder and walking out of the bakery.

The urge to puke or punch something is so strong, I have to walk away from the counter.

"Mikey, cover for me?" I ask, passing him on my way to the back. "Please," I add, tossing my apron on the counter and not waiting for his reply as I push my way through the back door.

Once I'm alone, I hide my face in my hands and let out a muffled scream.

When that doesn't work, I start punching the air, putting into practice the moves Cage taught me yesterday—right jab, left hook, uppercut.

That's it, nice and smooth. The memory of Cage's voice in my ear washes over me like a soothing balm. *Breathe.* I continue with the movements, over and over until a sheen of sweat breaks out on my forehead and I feel a slight burn in the muscles of my arms and legs. *Release the pent up anger, pour it all into the movements.*

After a few more minutes, the urges have passed. Taking a deep breath, I close my eyes and appreciate the burn in my lungs that matches my muscles.

I'm in control.

I'm calm.

I own the feelings… the feelings do not own me.

When I walk back into the back door of the bakery, I feel a change… it's subtle, but it's there. I'm the same Tempest Cassidy I've always been, but I'm learning how to handle the emotions that have plagued me and I'm a becoming a better version of myself. Slowly, but surely.

Something else I just realized: I don't care about Asher the way I used to… not even a month ago, or a week ago… not even a few hours ago. I no longer want him.

All I want is to move on with my life.

CHAPTER 12

CAGE

I've spent the last two days beating myself up over the almost kiss.

Yesterday, after my morning run, which I doubled in length because I needed the extra time to clear my head, I almost stopped by the bakery, but it was packed. There was a line of people out the door. Peering inside, I saw her, and I immediately felt the spike in my pulse, which was crazy after the kind of run I'd been on.

How can a petite redhead have this kind of effect on me?

I knew then that I needed to walk away and put some space between us, let her come to me. If that ever happens. The way she pushed me away and ran out of the building like it was on fire, makes me think I won't be seeing Tempest Cassidy for a while. At least not up close and personal.

Which is where I want her.

And all the more reason I should lay low.

Candy and Fuchsia are on stage doing their thing when I catch a whiff of sweetness—vanilla and sugar mixed with homemade goodness. It's not your typical store-bought perfume. Those are too sweet and honestly make my stomach turn. This is the scent of a woman who spends her days in a bakery, surrounded by baked goods and decadence.

It's the scent of Tempest Cassidy, the very same woman I was just thinking I needed to keep my distance from, walking into my bar. Well, not mine… but I have to be here, she doesn't. However, I can't say I mind that she is, as long as she doesn't have a repeat of her last visit.

Now that I know her a little better and know my feelings for her run deeper than an instant attraction, I couldn't be held responsible for my actions. Especially, if she decided to make her own stage on the bar again. The way those men were looking at her that night still makes me want to wipe the floor with them.

Maybe I'm the one who needs some anger management.

Her eyes are everywhere but on me as she walks closer.

My first thought is that maybe something happened—Asher showed up at the bakery or she saw Mindy at the bank. Maybe he's being an asshole about the house? Her comment about them selling it has stuck with me. I want to ask her what she plans on doing after the house sells. Not only has she had her entire life turned upside down, but she's also being displaced. I know what the life being turned upside down part is like, but unlike Tempest, I chose to leave my old life behind. And unlike her, I still own it and can go back there anytime I want.

She's lost her husband, future plans, hopes, dreams… and now her house?

It seems like too much—too much for one person to deal with—and worry for her settles in my gut.

Be a friend, Cage.

Make this right.

Smooth the waters.

Give her an outlet.

When she finally makes eye contact with me, it's like looking in a mirror—a tinge of guilt, a hint of reluctance, and a glimmer of hope that maybe all is not lost. I'm not sure why she'd feel guilty. She's not the one who almost kissed her *friend.*

"Tempest," I say in greeting as she saddles up to the bar.

"Cage," she returns, sliding her eyes over to me and then turning them to Floyd. "Hello, Floyd." Her smile is genuine and gorgeous. I want that smile. I want all of them.

Fuck.

"What can I get you, Em?" he asks. And there's that nickname again. I want to know all about it. Who gets to call her that? Are we close enough for me to use it? Would I even want to?

With a name like Cage, I've never really had a nickname, at least not a shortened version of my name. I've never been a big fan of them. But maybe I want to use hers.

"I'll just have a Coke," she says. "Straight-up with a lime." When she laughs, Floyd winks at her and goes about pouring her drink. And I breathe a little easier. If she's not drinking tequila tonight, maybe she's here for other reasons that have nothing to do with her asshole ex.

I watch from the corner of my eye as Tempest drinks her Coke and tries not to look at me. She glances my way then quickly looks in another direction while biting down on her bottom lip. It's completely adorable, but I force myself not to react. It's obvious she has something on her mind but is stalling, so I'll wait until she's ready to share, enjoying just being near her in the meantime.

She's on her second *Coke, straight-up with a lime* when she finally turns to face me.

"Yes, Tempest?" I ask, managing to keep my eyes on the patrons in hopes that she'll work up the confidence to say whatever she came to say. All the while praying it has nothing to do with the fact I almost kissed her the other night. I'm hoping we can just let that slide. Honest mistake. Beautiful girl. Close contact. These things happen. "Something you'd like to say?"

"I'm sorry for the other night," she spits out and my heart drops.

This catches me off guard. If anyone needs to apologize for that night, it's me.

"Sorry for what?" I ask.

"For leaving so... abruptly. It was very rude of me to walk out like that. I didn't even say goodbye… or thank you. After you took time out of your day to help me. I swear, I have better manners than that. And I promise I'll be better next time."

"It's fine, really," I assure her. Turning to see the earnest look in her eyes. She means it. "I'm just glad to hear there'll be a next time. I was afraid I'd scared you off."

"Definitely not," she says with a nervous smile that she covers quickly by taking another sip of her Coke. "I really enjoyed it and I slept like a freaking baby that night. Who knew spending the day with you, getting all worked up and sweaty, would end up being so relaxing?"

Her blush is immediate and the laugh I bark out serves a multitude of purposes. One, I need to diffuse the situation before she runs off again. Two, it was funny as shit. And three, if I don't distract myself right now, I'll only be thinking of other ways to make Tempest sweaty.

Meanwhile, she now has her head in her hands and is mumbling about not going out in public ever again. "Relax," I whisper, placing my hand on her shoulder, I give her what I hope is a comforting, albeit *friendly* squeeze, while trying to control my laughter. "You can't stay locked inside forever, Tempest. Life would be too boring."

She picks up her head and looks at me but doesn't look convinced. "You're really too nice, Cage. Thank you for being such a good friend."

There's that damn word again. *Friends*.

"We *are* friends, right?" she continues.

"Of course," I reply.

"Okay, then I have a favor to ask."

The nervous look is back and I don't like it, so I sit next to her on one of the barstools, hoping my closeness helps her relax. "What's up?"

She takes a deep breath, pushing some hair behind her ear. "You can say no," she starts, worry creasing her forehead.

"Just tell me… spit it out."

"Okay, here goes… this year is my ten year class reunion. I don't know if you know what it's like living in a small town, I'm guessing you don't, but see, here's the deal, if I don't go, everyone is going to talk about me… well, they're going to talk about me regardless, but if I don't go, they'll assume I'm weak and pathetic and that Asher ruined me. And he'll get to walk around like the king he was back in high school, with his brand new wife on his arm. And well, I can't let that happen. Which means, I have to go, but I can't go alone… that would be even more pathetic than if I didn't go at all. So, I need you to pretend to be my date… or well, you know, go as my friend, but if anyone asks, maybe we could pretend like we're more than friends?"

Her words flood out in a nervous, jumbled mess. But I think I get the gist—Tempest has a class reunion and she needs to go to save face and she wants me to be her date. I try not to let a smug smile creep onto my face, but I fail. Instead, I turn my head to look out at the club, making it look like I'm just doing my job.

"Uh, I guess I could do that… I mean, we're friends," I tell her, keeping my tone casual. *Nothing to see here, move along.* "And friends don't let friends go to ten year class reunions alone."

I turn back to her just in time to see a wide smile split her beautiful face, reaching all the way to her eyes. I think for a split second she's going to leap off her barstool and hug me, or better yet, kiss me. But instead, she bounces in her seat and claps her hands. "Thank you. Seriously, I'll owe you an entire batch of whatever muffins you want for the next year." I could go for being paid in Tempest's muffin… *muffins*. I mean muffins, like the baked variety… sweet and delicious.

Cut it the fuck out, Cage.

"Well, I definitely can't pass up a deal like that."

She reaches into a bag that she'd set down at her feet and pulls out a box I recognize from the bakery. "I was hoping you'd say yes. Consider these a down payment."

Cracking the box open, the smell of chocolate and cherries practically knocks me off the barstool. "Fuck," I groan, immediately picking one up and lifting it to my mouth. Most of the time, I'm not an instant gratification kind of guy. I typically take my time, knowing the best things in life take hard work and patience. Being a fighter taught me that. But right now, sitting on this barstool in a strip club in Green Valley, Tennessee, all of that goes flying out the window.

I want this delicious looking muffin… that appears to be more of a mini cake than a muffin… and I want it now… almost as much as I want the woman who made it. Taking one bite makes my eyes roll into the back of my damn head.

Heaven.

Fucking gooey, delicious heaven.

"It's uh, *Going Through the Big D…* and I don't mean Dallas," Tempest says hesitantly, adding on a nervous chuckle at the end. "It's like, if a Texas Sheet Cake had a baby with a Black Forest Cake… but in a muffin… with chocolate drizzled over the top… I mean, go big or go home, right?"

That nervous, jumbled mess is back and I'd like nothing more than to shut her up with my mouth on hers, tasting her. I bet she tastes even better than her muffins.

Is Dallas in reference to me? I almost ask, but hesitate. That sounds a little conceited, even in my head. Speaking it out loud would definitely make me come off as an egotistical prick. But then Tempest sets the record straight.

"A little you… a little me."

The gorgeous blush on her cheeks steals any words I might have, so instead of comments, I just take another bite and swallow down my desire… for now.

CHAPTER 13

TEMPEST

Milk

Cereal

Bread

I mentally run through my grocery list because, of course, I forgot to bring my notepad with my actual list on it. I swear, I can't focus on shit these days. I'd blame the divorce or the ongoing stress of selling the house, but I'd be lying.

It's Cage.

It's always fucking Cage.

Actually, *not* fucking Cage, to be exact.

I don't remember ever having this many naughty thoughts about Asher or anyone before, not even when my teenage hormones were supposedly running rampant, but I cannot get Cage Erickson out of my head.

Our midday kickboxing classes are really the culprit but there's no way I can quit. I don't want to, for one. For two, they're fun and exciting. And best of all, they're working. I've changed in so many ways over the last few weeks—positive changes… confidence, better sleep, less stress—that any lady blue balls I'm suffering are worth it.

Who can blame me, though?

Being that close to Cage—with his perfect, sweaty muscles and his ice-blue eyes—for any amount of time would bring most sane women to the brink. And although my sanity has been questioned a lot recently, no one could fault me for lusting after Green Valley's newest, hottest bachelor.

The thing is, I think Cage likes me, too.

I mean, *likes me*-likes me. At least, I think he's attracted to me, much in the same way I am him, which honestly blows my mind. On most days, I convince myself I'm delusional, but then he'll look at me a certain way—those blue eyes full of heat—or he'll find a way to touch me without seeming forward or like he's coming onto me. Maybe he doesn't want to get mixed up with someone like me, and I don't blame him for that. I wouldn't want to get mixed up with me either, if I could help it.

The way he looks at me, though… there are times when it seems as if he can see into my soul and there's no judgment, just acceptance. Then, there are the times, like yesterday, where he looks at me like he's on death row and I'm his last meal.

The more I think about it, the more I'm certain I felt a bulge against my ass as he came up behind me and pressed his body to mine, in an effort to correct my punching form. It was brief, but I felt it, and now, I can't stop daydreaming about it.

"Is that cucumber firm enough for you, Miss Cassidy?"

"Huh, what?" I turn to see sweet, little Johnny Baker watching me for some reason. Of course, Johnny isn't little anymore. I believe he's now a senior in high school and is having one hell of a football season, but he'll always be the same little boy I used to teach in Sunday School.

"That cucumber," he says, pointing to my hands. "You've been squeezing it for a few minutes now. If it's not firm enough, I can maybe go to the back and see if we have any fresh off the truck."

It's then I realize Johnny works here at the grocery store and I have a large cucumber in my hands… stroking it.

When did I get to the produce section?

And when did the produce section get so erotic?

Is it hot in here?

"Oh, um, no," I stutter, grabbing a plastic bag from the dispenser. "This one is fine. Thank you, Johnny." I give him an apologetic smile and put my one stupid cucumber in the bag, tossing it in my buggy and heading for the back of the store.

Too bad I wasn't groping an eggplant. At least I like to eat those, unlike the cuke I'm now stuck with.

What am I here for again?

I run through my list again, eliminating items like sausage, because I obviously can't be trusted right now with phallic-shaped food items, and end up in the canned goods aisle. While I'm scanning the many soups available, trying to make a decision, because this is what cooking for one looks like—cans of soup, frozen dinners, and boxes of cereal—I catch a glimpse of someone out of the corner of my eye. Glancing over, what I see before me nearly makes me drop the can of tomato soup in my hand.

Well, not *what*, but *who*.

Fucking Mindy.

Of course, I'd run into her here, at the Piggly Wiggly. I've put this task off for weeks, scrounging around in my cupboards for random things to sustain me, for fear of this exact thing. The last time I broke down and came grocery shopping, I did it right before closing time, in hopes I'd miss all the busybodies, but ran smackdab into Mrs. Mitchell, Mindy's mother. It seems I can't even grocery shop in peace.

I make a mental note to start picking up the things I need while I'm in Knoxville… maybe I should just move to Knoxville. No, that would be stupid. I'd have to drive an hour to work at o'dark-thirty, because I love my job… it's the one bright spot in my life… besides Cage and kickboxing.

As I inspect the adulteress to my left, the petty side of me can't help but grin when I notice Mindy has put on a few pounds. Maybe she's a stress eater. Maybe I should send her a dozen muffins… you know, be the bigger person… like an olive branch.

Muffins laced with arsenic.

Get it together, Tempest.

Murder is a federal offense.

Thankfully, she hasn't spotted me yet, so I quietly move to put a few more cans into my buggy, hoping I can sneak off before being spotted. This is me using the tips I've learned in my anger management classes—*identify pitfalls, seek out solutions, think before you speak.* Rather than looking for an opportunity to confront Mindy, I'm taking the high road and leaving before things get nasty. We don't need to be throwing down at the grocery store, that's for damn sure.

Because I'm apparently a glutton for punishment and a freaking idiot, I give her one last look over my shoulder before I push my buggy in the opposite direction.

That's when I see it.

She hasn't just put on a few pounds, she's gained a considerable amount of weight. Her new tummy, though, isn't flabby, it's very round and pronounced and it makes my own stomach churn with acid.

Fuck my life, Mindy is pregnant.

Very, very pregnant, by the looks of things.

An odd sound pulls me out of my thoughts and it takes me a moment to realize it's coming from me. I'm making the sound. It's part whine and part growl and it's obviously caught Mindy's attention because she's walking right toward me.

Shit.

What do I do? I don't want to talk to her, but I'll be damned if I run away from her. Why couldn't Lana or Cage, or even Cole, be with me? Don't they know I can't be trusted in public alone?

Just don't get arrested, Tempest.

For the love of eggplant and sausage, keep your cool.

As Mindy gets closer, she begins rubbing her hand over her belly, ensuring I know she's with spawn, I mean, child. *How far along is she anyway?* The picnic wasn't that long ago and she didn't look pregnant then, did she? Maybe she did, but I was too shocked by the ring on her finger to notice? Also, my mother would've said something to me when she broke the news about Mindy and Asher being married, so she must not have noticed either.

Maybe she just carries big… and early. Maybe she's pregnant with multiples. That would be rich—I can't even get pregnant with one, but Mindy Mitchell, husband stealer extraordinaire, can have my husband and all the babies.

All I know is I have to stop gawking because Mindy is enjoying this way too much.

"Hey, Tempest. Soup for one, I presume?" Her smile is large and condescending as she glances at the contents of my shopping cart.

Bitch.

"You know, I've been so busy lately that canned soup is all I have time for some nights. It's not always the healthiest option, with all that sodium, but I'm fortunate to not retain water, like you obviously do."

Really, Tempest? Is that the best put-down you can think of?

"I'm not bloated, silly." She laughs, swatting the air in front of her face. "I'm pregnant! Of course, I don't expect *you* to notice the difference."

It's illegal to hit a pregnant lady, Tempest.

She's not worth the jail time.

Deep, cleansing breaths.

You don't look good in orange.

"How far along are you?" I ask, willing myself to stay calm. "Elephants are pregnant, for what, two years?" I know I'm being immature, but I'm using my words and not my fists, so I'm calling it a win.

"Gah, you're such a bitch. No wonder Asher wanted to leave you. At least I was able to give him what he wanted," she brags, rubbing her belly even faster than before.

Maybe if she rubs a little more, a fucking genie will pop out, and I can at least get three wishes out of this deal. *Wish one: Asher and Mindy disappear off the face of the planet.*

"And," she continues, "because I know it's driving you crazy, I'll let you in on the secret. I'm in my third trimester." She smiles and squeals, like we're BFFs and she just told me the *best* news. "Just a couple more months to go and this precious bundle of joy will be in the world… gah, Asher is going to be *such* a great daddy."

The blood drains from my face as I do the math in my head. Asher and I have been divorced almost two months. I found them in bed together three months before that. Two plus three does not equal the amount of months it takes to be in the third trimester. I know my pregnancy facts.

Mindy just answered one of my many burning questions: that sack of shit was cheating on me months before I busted him.

And now, he's having a baby with someone else.

Honestly, I don't know how to feel right now… numb, blind-sided, furious, hurt?

All I know is I'm trying my damnedest not to lose my shit.

Deep breaths.

"Believe me," Mindy says, breaking through the haze I'm in. "I tried and tried to get Asher to leave you before you found out about us on your own, but he didn't listen." She sighs, like she's disappointed for me… like she's on my side and she was trying to do me a favor. "Oh, well, life goes on, right?"

We enter into a bit of a staring competition for a brief moment, her bright, smiling eyes against my crazy, sadistic glare. I feel the crazy oozing out of me. When she finally starts to back her buggy up to make a U-turn in the aisle, she has the audacity to smile... and wink at me.

She's the incarnation of Satan.

Asher and Mindy aren't going to have a bouncing bundle of joy, they're going to have a devil love child. I should alert the media. This has a horror movie written all over it.

"See you around, Tempest," she says over her shoulder, before stopping and turning. "Oh, I guess I'll see you at the reunion, if not before… and you're bringing a date, right?"

Deep breaths, Tempest.

I don't answer her with words, only with my glare, hoping it burns a hole in her skull.

You can do this.

Don't let that cow win.

After she makes a turn onto another aisle, I take a few more deep breaths, willing my nerves to calm, and when that doesn't work, I close my eyes and try harder. With my hands on my knees, I suck in air like it's going extinct. My breathing becomes routine and I automatically start swaying my body in preparation for the Tai Chi moves that come next.

Cage has been teaching me a little bit of Tai Chi to further help channel my anger and anxiety and I have to admit, I love it. Completely forgetting where I am, I begin to perform my favorite combination of steps. If people see me, I don't care. I'd rather them talk about me doing Tai Chi in the canned goods aisle than losing my shit at the Piggly Wiggly.

I'm finally feeling relaxed and in control of my emotions, so to celebrate my victory, I decide to throw a few punches to the air, similar to what Rocky Balboa did after running up all those stairs in the movie.

I am Tempest Cassidy, master of my emotions.

Thoroughly enjoying myself, I decide to end my impromptu workout with a killer roundhouse kick… right into a tower of Pork N Beans.

At first, it's only a few cans. I lurch out, containing them in a lunge, looking around to see who might've witnessed my performance. Only a lady down at the other end of the aisle seems to be in the know. I breathe out a sigh of relief, feeling uncharacteristically lucky as I try to balance the cans and myself.

Just as I decide it's safe to stand up, I lose my balance and the cans in my hands take a tumble… and then the entire end cap begins to fall.

Cans.

Cans of Pork N Beans are rolling everywhere.

When everything finally comes to a rest, I'm sprawled out on the glossy tile of the Piggly Wiggly in aisle six, using my body as a dam to stop them from getting too far. I'm afraid to move… afraid to breathe… and just about that time, Mr. Henderson, the store manager comes jogging—well, more like waddling—down the aisle, sweat obvious on his pudgy brow.

"Tempest Cassidy," he exclaims. "What on earth is going on here? What have you done?"

Swallowing, I try to use my arms to scoop up as many cans as I can, hoping it doesn't look as bad as it is. "I can explain," I begin. "It was an accident."

His annoyed expression tells me he's not interested in my excuses, so I just get straight to the point. "I'm really sorry," I tell him, still spread out on the floor. "I'll clean it all up… it'll be good as new. Promise."

He huffs out an exasperated sigh, hands on his round waist. "Is this another one of your stunts? I'm in the right mind to call your daddy and let him deal with this."

"No… no," I begin, working my way to a kneeling position and starting to restack the few cans I have in my arms, in good faith. "No, please don't do that… I promise, this was an accident. I was backing out of the aisle… and I… I slipped… actually, I don't know what happened. One minute I was going for a can of, uh, cream of mushroom… and the next thing I know, everything is crashing down. Are you sure this is display is safe?"

His expression begins to change as my phone begins to ring.

"I'll send Johnny over to help you," he mutters, rubbing his bald head.

Looking at the screen of my phone, I see a local number but no identification.

"Not necessary," I tell him, swiping my thumb across the screen to answer. "I'll have this cleaned up in a jiffy."

After another wordless grumble, he walks away and I place the phone to my ear, watching Mr. Henderson retreat down the aisle and breathe a sigh of relief. "Hello?"

"Tempest?"

It's Cage. Glancing at the screen again, I don't recognize the number, but it's local, so maybe he's at work. Letting out an exasperated sigh, I finally reply, "Hey."

"Where are you?"

"Piggly Wiggly," I tell him, looking around at the mess. "Aisle six, to be exact."

His laugh helps ease the tightness in my chest. And I start to laugh too, because now that I know Mr. Henderson isn't going to call my daddy… or Sheriff James… I have to admit, this is pretty damn funny.

"What exactly are you *cleaning up in a jiffy*?"

"Oh, God," I groan, turning to examine the extent of the work ahead of me. "Well… I sort of knocked over an entire display of Pork N Beans."

"What the fuck?"

He laughs again and I roll my eyes at this ridiculous predicament.

"Exactly."

"I was actually calling to see if we're still on for a session today. I'm just getting ready to leave the Pink Pony, had to swing by and help Floyd with a food delivery. But I could come over and help you, if you want."

My mouth is hanging open with my typical, knee-jerk response on the tip of my tongue—*no, no need... I'm fine... I'm sure you have better things to do.* But instead, I tell him, "Sure."

"Aisle six?"

The smile that spreads across my face makes my cheeks ache, and it helps weaken the lingering hurt and anger from Mindy's revelation. "Yeah, me and about two-hundred-and-fifty cans of Pork N Beans, you can't miss us."

After I hang up, I slowly begin stacking the cans, trying to remember how they looked before everything came tumbling down and just as I'm placing the sixth one onto the bottom of the pile, a wave of emotion hits me.

Me and this pile of cans have something in common.

I might not be starting from the bottom, but I am starting over in so many areas of my life.

Sitting back on my haunches, in the middle of aisle six, I begin to cry… no, not just cry… sob. It's disturbing, even to myself. So, when Cage shows up about ten minutes later, it's a relief, because even though I didn't think I needed help, I do. I can't do this on my own and I don't think I'm just talking about the cans.

It's not a sign of weakness to ask for help.

Lana's words come rushing to my mind and it makes me crumble a little, right into a sobbing heap over the pile of cans.

"Hey," Cage says, kneeling down beside me, his mouth right next to my ear so only I can hear. "You're fine… better than fine… you're

Tempest Cassidy and you're one of the strongest people I know, okay?" He doesn't wait for me to reply, just continues telling me everything I need to hear. "Whatever happened here today… you're more than that… more than however you feel… and whoever made you feel that way."

Part of me wonders if he's somehow creeped into my mind and stolen my thoughts, because how does he know? I haven't even had a chance to tell him about Mindy and her ginormous revelation. "She's pregnant," I whisper, licking tears off my lip. "Like really, really pregnant…"

Cage's arm wraps around my shoulder and he squeezes, letting me have my moment.

When someone walks by and makes a remark under their breath, I feel him tense and then tell them to keep walking, like only Cage Erickson can… with authority and effectiveness. He shields me until I can get myself under control and get on with it—life, my day, cleaning up these cans.

After a few more minutes, I'm able to dry my cheeks and take a deep breath.

"Let's get this cleaned up and then we can go back to my place for a session," he says, his ice-blue eyes darker than usual. "Okay?"

"Okay," I agree.

CHAPTER 14

CAGE

"What's been going on with you, man?" my brother asks, huffing. Knowing him, he's beating a speed bag while talking with me. I swear, he's never doing just one thing.

Conducting a board meeting while trading stocks on his phone.

Watching a football game while negotiating a deal.

Out on a date while hitting on the chick at the next table over.

You know, you've got to keep your options open.

"Just working at the Pink Pony for Hank," I start. "Living in this great, old building… just started turning the downstairs into a studio—"

"Whoa, whoa, whoa," Viggo cuts me off and I hear his activity die in the background. "You said this was temporary… going to Bumfuck, Tennessee, getting your shit together, getting back. I thought that was the plan."

Pacing the downstairs, which is quickly becoming my favorite place, I let out a huff. "Look, I don't know what my plans are anymore."

"I can't believe you're just giving up this easy," he says, disappointment thick in his tone. "Oz said you were done, but I figured you, of all people, would find a loophole… some way out of this."

Pinching the bridge of my nose, I reply, "It's an injury, Viggo... a career-ending injury… it's not like I got my wrist slapped for using supplements… or I failed a drug test. Y'all act like I'm just on hiatus. I don't know how to make it any more clear… it's over."

Dead silence is all I get as a reply.

Quiet, uncharacteristic silence.

"Does Dad know this?" he asks and I feel the familiar lead weight that appears every time I think of our dad and the look of disappointment on his face when the doctor gave me my verdict.

Sighing, I take a deep, steadying breath… similar to the ones I've been coaching Tempest in lately. Tempest. God. I cannot start thinking about her right now, because there is no way I'm telling Viggo, the Mouth of the South, about Tempest Cassidy. The next thing you know, my mother would be calling, planning a visit.

The thought of her drives an imaginary stake into my chest.

"Yes," I finally reply. "Of course Dad knows…"

He lets out a defeated breath. "This isn't good," he sighs. "This thing we've got going… it's like a machine… me, you, Val, Oz… it takes all of us contributing to make it work." Now, I feel like I'm one of his employees or minions who's not quite performing up to snuff. "Without you, things just don't work as well as they should."

"Vig," I start, but stop while I try to wrap my head around all of this and try not to lose my cool with him, because what he's basically saying is that without me fighting, I'm killing the family business, which is a well-known gym in the Dallas area. We thrive off of word-of-mouth and the publicity that fights bring. Without me fighting, we lose a key component of our marketing strategy.

Over the years, starting with our father who was a boxer, we've turned the Erickson name into more of a brand. Erickson MMA houses some of the best fighters in the world.

I was their anchorman.

I was what brought people in.

Every time I stepped inside the cage, I was a walking billboard.

Come to Erickson, be a champion.

"Vig," I start again, "it's not like I planned on getting injured… I didn't plan on leaving until I was good and ready. You know what my plan was," I tell him, reminding him. "We've talked about it hundreds of times over the years."

He sighs. "I know… fight until your forty-five… beat all the greats… your final fight, a KO."

"I didn't get a chance to fight half the people I wanted to fight," I tell him, hoping he realizes I'm just as disappointed as everyone else. This is not how I saw my life going. But here I am—twenty-eight, retired, no college degree, and no clue what I'm going to do for the rest of my life. But I'm starting to see glimpses of a vision, and since I have the luxury of exploring my options, I'm going to take my time and figure it out.

That's the beauty of Green Valley.

Yeah, it's a slow town, but in the relaxed atmosphere, I've found a different part of myself. I never thought I had the patience for teaching, but my sessions with Tempest are easily the best parts of my week. I count the days between our time together. And yes, some—a lot—of that may be due to my student, but some of it's not. Some of it is feeling like I'm getting the chance to pass on something I love to someone else, and seeing it enrich their life.

"You know," Viggo says after a few moments, "Vali has a fight set up… he wants you in the ring. The payout is pretty good… all you'd have to do is show up. Step into the octagon. Walk away with no less than a hundred grand." He pauses and I begin to get pissed the fuck off. "I'm sure you could use the money… and we could use the publicity—"

"Listen to yourself, Viggo," I growl. "You want me to walk into a ring, knowing I'll lose, just so I can get a little cash and the gym can get some publicity? Are you fucking kidding me?" I run a hand down my face and then back up to grip at my hair, which is longer than it's ever been. "What does that say about us? How the fuck does that help?" I ask, fuming. "We're bigger than that… better. Integrity, Strength, and Excellence, remember? Huh?"

When he still doesn't reply, I continue. "Have things changed that much since I've been gone? Have you all forgotten who we are and what we stand for?" I ask, hoping I'm wrong.

"We all know you could beat anyone with one arm tied behind your back," he finally says. "Vali has put a lot into this fight… really went out on a limb with this one and if we don't find some talent to fill out the ticket, it'll be a bust. You know how much money that'll be? Down the fucking drain?"

He asks me this like it's my problem, and I guess, in a way, it is. We're family. We're always in it together, but I really hate that he's trying to make me feel guilty for something that's out of my control and something I never asked to be in the middle of in the first place.

Val is always taking risks.

"I can make some calls," I tell him, thinking of a few people that might be interested, a few favors I can maybe call in.

"Thanks," Viggo says. "When are you coming home?"

Shaking my head, I look around. "I don't know, man. I'm just playing it all by ear right now."

After I hang up with Viggo, I think about calling Vali, but decide to wait until I have a chance to make a few other phone calls first. I'd rather call him when I have an alternative plan for him, rather than to just tell him there's no fucking chance of me stepping in that ring.

Looking at the clock on the wall, I see it's almost time for Tempest's kickboxing lesson, so I put my phone over on the stairs and grab some tape.

Tempest has really taken to the bags. For someone so small, she really makes an impact and has nice control over her movements. Today, I plan on getting her started on one bag while I get in a workout on the other. It's better if I keep myself occupied while she's here, because if I don't, my mind stays in the fucking gutter and I'm constantly having to put myself in place— literally and figuratively.

A few days ago, right after the Pork N Beans incident, I was helping her with the roundhouse kick that landed her in a pile of canned goods when I felt something. It wasn't my stiff dick. I'm used to that… and used to telling him to forget it. There is no way I'm messing this up… this friendship, something we both need. But that day, there was this intensity flowing between us and I know she felt it too. The way her eyes widened when my hand was on her thigh, even though it wasn't in a sexual manner, I could see that her mind went there.

I wanted to ask her about it, force the issue, but like I said, I'm not going to ruin what we've got going.

Besides, between this upcoming reunion and the impending birth of Asher and Mindy's baby… as well as her cousin Cole and his wife Anna, who are also expecting, she has a lot on her plate. So, for now, I'll keep my semi in my pants and my thoughts to myself.

One of these days, I'll come clean about how I feel about her and I'll put the ball in her court, but that day is not today.

"Hey."

Whirling around, I school my expression and give her a warm, *friendly* smile. "Hey, yourself."

CHAPTER 15

TEMPEST

"So, your mama tells me you've been getting acquainted with that scary guy who's working for Hank," Anna says quietly, with her hand daintily placed on her basketball-sized tummy as we watch the older ladies of the church mingle. Every once in a while, one of them looks our way, but as of yet, none of them has said a word to me.

Maybe they think my bad juju will rub off on them?

Good. Because I don't want to talk to them anyway. All they ever want to discuss is my lack of attendance at church and how sad it is that that Asher and I are no longer married.

Fuck that.

Like she can hear my thoughts, Anna cuts her eyes at me. Maybe I said that out loud?

Lord, forgive me for my profanity... actually, if you could cover me for the next two hours, I would appreciate it. I'm barely hanging on here and could really use the help.

Amen.

"He's not scary," I tell her, keeping my voice low, because I don't need any busybodies in my business... or Cage's. "He's a friend... a really good one, and his name is Cage." I knew she'd bring this up, but I'd rather not discuss it in the middle of the church fellowship hall during her baby shower.

"The last thing you need is more gossip," she says on an exhale, keeping her eyes moving around the room.

"Can we please drop this?" I ask with sugary sweetness and a fake-ass smile, because Sister Anguiano is looking straight at us.

"You know what I mean, Tempest." She tsks, and I don't have to see her to know she just rolled her eyes. It's all in the inflection of her voice. "They're all gonna think you're some kind of hussy who sleeps around."

"So, if a woman… *me*," I say, pausing for a second while the pastor's wife walks by. "If a woman is seen being friends with a man, she's automatically screwing him? That's so backwards and twisted I can't even think of a good retort. And don't worry, Mindy already has a corner on hussy."

"Tempest Cassidy!"

"Oh, Anna, loosen up!" I hiss. "She is and you know it. She's been sleeping around with every Tom, Dick, and Harry since we were in high school. Asher isn't special. He's just the one who finally knocked her up," I seethe, still not okay with that piece of information, but I'm coming to terms with it. In the last day or so, I've decided they deserve each other and I deserve better. "I hope his dick shrivels up and her boobs sag to her knees."

"Tempest!" Anna's shriek draws the attention of every eye in the room, including Mindy's.

Yeah, she's here.

Practically every female Green Valley resident between the ages of twenty and seventy is here.

Anna turns her back to the women and whispers, "You can't say stuff like that in church!" She looks like she's afraid lightning is fixing to strike.

"Well, I'm also not going to *lie*—in church or anywhere else. Now, can we focus on something else? Like, the reason we're here," I tell her, patting her leg in hopes it will calm her down. The last thing I need is her going into labor. "You're going to be a mama. Isn't that exciting?"

I know better than to poke the bear, or a hormonal pregnant lady—verbal or otherwise.

Uh oh. I see tears forming in her eyes, and these aren't the usual Anna crocodile tears. "What?" I ask nervously, shifting in my seat to face her—blue eyes glistening with unshed tears. "What did I say? If it's about cussing in church… I already prayed about that."

She shakes her head and swallows thickly, turning away. "It's not fair," she whispers.

"What?"

"You want a baby," she says quietly, dabbing at the corners of her eyes. "And that… *woman,*" she says, anger lacing her words, the first I've heard from her in a long time. During her pregnancy, she's tried to keep her emotions as even as possible. *The baby feels everything I feel,* she says. "She stole your husband… and got pregnant. It's a sin… all of it." Anna's tone is indignant. She's sorely offended on my behalf. "It's not right."

Resting my hand on her arm, I give it a gentle squeeze. I love Anna, always have. But I think I just fell for her a little harder, right here in the middle of the church fellowship hall… surrounded by balloons and crepe paper. "It's okay," I soothe. "It just wasn't meant to be." Swallowing down my own emotions, I take a second to be sad.

It's my right.

Through my anger management sessions, I've learned I'm allowed to feel any emotion I want. It's what I do about them that makes the difference.

But what I told her is the same thing I've been telling myself the past few weeks… or more like the past six months. As much as I didn't want to acknowledge it, I know it's true: Asher and I weren't meant to be.

I loved him, that's true. And if he hadn't cheated on me, I'd still be married to him. But what I've realized is that everything happens for a reason. It might take a while, but eventually things get clearer. One day, I'll be able to look back and see how one thing led to another and another… until I'm happy again.

Actually, I'm already getting there.

"You're right." Anna sniffles and turns her bright smile toward me. "I'd been praying for Asher to have a change of heart and for the two of you to reconcile, but I'm done with that."

Now I'm the one to roll my eyes, because she sounds just like my mama.

"I'm going to be praying you find a new husband… someone good and *Godly*, of course," she says thoughtfully. "With good swimmers."

"Good Lord," I groan, leaning my head back and looking toward to the ceiling, searching for a way out of this madness.

"He is good," she muses. Again, sounding just like my mama. "You're a big hit in my prayer circle, you know. So I guess it's a good thing you're set on keeping us busy on our knees."

My mouth is hanging open as I stare at her, not believing what just came out of her mouth. Anna never makes off-colored jokes or gives sexual innuendos, so you can imagine my shock as I sit there. I'm doubly shocked when she quirks an eyebrow at me, daring me for a response.

"Obviously, I need as many prayers as possible," I tell her, refusing to fall for her tricks. "Who am I to deprive you and your nosy friends from your true calling?"

My semi-acquiescence catches her off-guard, which is exactly what I was going for. Anna eventually smiles, slipping an arm around my shoulders and hugging me to her as she laughs. "I love you, you big ol' heathen."

"I love you, too, you Amazonian holy roller."

After everyone has had their cake, punch, and mingle time, Anna takes her place in the designated chair, ready to receive gifts. Of course, I draw the short straw and have to sit next to her, writing down who gives her what so she can personalize thank-you cards later.

Everything is going just peachy. I'm avoiding Mindy's stares and

Anna is getting some adorable gifts, when a loud gasp gets my attention.

Turning to Anna, I see her big blue eyes are as round as saucers. With her mouth hanging open, like she's shocked or surprised, I look around for some audacious gift, but see nothing out of the ordinary—diapers, bibs, and bottles.

Then, I see the panic. With a fake smile frozen on her face, she speaks to me, slowly but deliberately, through her clenched teeth. "Tempest, I think I just *tee-teed* on myself."

Giggles bubble out of my mouth before I can stop them. "What?"

"Tee-tee. You know…*pee*." She rolls her eyes before admitting, exasperated, "I just *peed* myself, Tempest!" She implores me with a desperate look to understand.

"What would you like me to do?" I ask, setting the notepad I've been writing on down on the table. "Do you want me to walk you to the bathroom and block everyone from seeing your wet dress?" She's twice my size, but I could at least cover her ass while she walks.

"I don't know!" She's starting to lose it. I see it all over her face and I desperately search the crowd of women for my mama. She always has a solution for any problem. "Maybe I should stay here until everyone leaves…" she drifts off as her eyes go to the floor, taking mine with them.

"Um, Anna, I don't think that's pee."

"What do you mean? Of course it is. What else could it be?"

I answer her by discreetly pointing to the pink liquid running down her leg.

"No, Tempest, just…*no*." She starts to stand, but then her hand goes to her belly and I think she's having a contraction. "My… my water cannot break during my baby shower... at church. This is not in my birth plan!"

"Uh, sweetie," I tell her as calmly as possible, "I really don't think that's up to you. I'll go call Cole and the hospital to let them know you're on your way."

A throat clears next to me. "Girls, is everything okay? I don't want to be pushy, but everyone is waiting for your private conversation to end so Anna can finish opening her presents." The Lord really is listening… He knows I needed my mama.

"Mama, her water broke… the shower is officially over."

Thankfully, her alarmed expression morphs to one of calmness before she turns and begins addressing everyone. "Ladies, I'm afraid Anna will have to open her remaining gifts later. It appears as though Baby Cassidy will be joining us soon, so if you'll please excuse us, we need to get to the hospital."

A mild hysteria hits as the women jump into action, squealing in excitement and offering to help, just as Anna has her next contraction.

"Son of a bitch, that hurt!" Every eye in the room flies to Anna, bringing the room to an absolute halt. Anna doesn't show any signs of embarrassment as she continues. "Oh, don't look at me like that. You know this hurts… why didn't any of you warn me about this?" Her question is followed up by an anguished cry and Anna Cassidy has officially lost all decorum.

Anna's mother takes over by escorting her daughter outside to her car while I call Cole and tell him to meet us at the hospital. After the shock of Anna's outburst wears off, the guests begin cleaning up the room and packing the gifts for me to take.

As I'm loading up the last gift bag into the truck, I see Mindy waddle out of the church and notice Asher's truck parked in the front. When he hops out to help her in, I stand there, watching. I'm waiting for the longing to kick in… sadness, desire… but nothing.

When he looks my way, I give him a smile… not a friendly one or an I-miss-you smile, but a knowing smile. One that says *I know…* and *you don't win*, because *congratulations, Asher, you're stuck with her for at least the next eighteen years*.

I can see his jaw muscles tense before he gives me a fake smile and an awkward nod of his head as he rounds the truck and climbs inside. When they drive away, I swear I feel Mindy's glare until they've turned out on the main highway.

On my way to the hospital, I think about calling Cage and letting him know Anna is in labor and I won't be by for our Sunday kickboxing session, but I don't have his phone number. So instead, I call the Pink Pony and leave a message for him with Floyd.

"There you are!" Cole says as he rounds the corner of the tiny hospital waiting room. "I thought you deserted me." The look on his face is pure panic. His skin is a little pale, and there's a bead of sweat rolling down his forehead. He's a mess.

"Are you okay?" Normally, Cole is the calm one, always having every situation under control.

"Uh, yeah. Anna's a little, uh . . . How do I put this?" He paces back and forth as he rests his hands on his gun belt. "Well, she's already threatened to kill me twice, and my balls have been threatened repeatedly. She's so scary," he whispers.

"It's gonna be alright," I tell him, putting an arm around his shoulder and pulling him into a two-person huddle. We've always been a team and that doesn't stop today. "Here's the game plan. You and I will take shifts. It's gonna take a team effort, but I think we'll make it, if we stick together."

"Sounds good," he agrees, looking relieved I'm not abandoning him in his time of need. "Thanks for being here."

Unfortunately for us... and Anna, she labors long and hard for the remainder of the day, but between me and Cole, all she has to do is ask and it's hers—water, ice chips, cold rags, her bible, a hand to hold, someone to yell at. The grandmas-to-be left to go to Anna and Cole's house and wash all of the new baby clothes and make sure the nursery is ready for the baby.

Cowards.

Around midnight, Anna finally makes it to ten centimeters, and the doctor comes in to clear the room so she can start pushing. As I'm making my way out the door, Anna yells at me to come back.

"You can't leave me now!" Her voice is desperate, and her eyes are pleading.

"You've got Cole, Anna. He's not going anywhere," I soothe,

wiping her forehead with a cool cloth, trying to talk some sense into her, because she's obviously out of her mind… I'm not staying in here. As much as I want a baby of my own, I don't think I'm ready to watch one be born. Ignorance is bliss… right?

"Yeah, but he's a jackass, and I need you! Please stay with me!" she begs, tears forming in her eyes.

Damn tears!

"OK, I'll stay. I'll stay." I pat her arm and try to calm the full-on panic attack that's going on inside me. *Holy shit! No, no, no. Getting ice chips is one thing, but I can't watch this! I can't watch them pull a coconut through a hole the size of a pea!*

As Anna starts to push, she squeezes the shit out of my hand. I look across at Cole. He's so white he's starting to blend into the wall behind him, and his eyes are glazed over.

I know this look. I saw it once in the woods when I cut my leg on a big stick. There was so much blood and he nearly passed out on me.

"He's going down!" I yell out, just in time for the nurse to push a chair under him before he hits the ground.

"Cole! You big wuss! Ahhhhhhhh," Anna screams as she pushes through a hard contraction. "I'm the one pushing a baby out of my vagina, and *you're* passing out?"

"Thi—this is why I needed you to stay. I knew he wouldn't be able to handle it," Anna pants.

I can't help but laugh at the chaos around me—Cole trying to stay with us, Anna screaming as she pushes—but the second she bears down for the final push, everything seems to stand still.

The wail of a baby fills the room and a nurse quickly wipes him off, swaddles him, and lays him on Anna's chest.

I take this as my cue to make my exit. Cole gives me a confident smile when I look over at him before he takes the scissors from the nurse and cuts the umbilical cord. I lean over and kiss Anna's head, telling her "congratulations" and get a good look at Cole, Jr. Well, his name is Matthew, but I can already tell he looks just like his daddy.

Walking out into the hall, I slowly slide down the wall and sit on the floor.

Damn, that was intense.

Looking at my phone, I see the time and it's time for me to head to the bakery to make some muffins.

I'm thinking an espresso-infused triple chocolate with a cherry filling… *Back in Baby's Arms*.

CHAPTER 16

CAGE

The bell over the front door to the studio rings and my mouth instinctively begins to water. It's not only because of the Pavlovian response I seem to have now when Tempest walks through the door but also, because of the delicious aroma that enters with her.

My payment.

My very own specially made muffins from the Duchess of Muffins herself.

I'm trying really hard to remain casual, so I glance at the entryway over my shoulder and try not to swallow my tongue.

Delicious. Both the muffins and their maker. I mean, I can only assume Tempest tastes as amazing as her muffins because I haven't had the pleasure. Yet.

Shit. It's getting harder and harder to keep my feelings platonic, but I know I have to try.

Her smile is bright and beautiful as she holds up the package of baked goods for me to see and I smile in return before turning back around and briefly adjusting my dick. When I've collected myself and feel somewhat in control of my body, I walk over to the set of chairs where she's standing.

"What flavor do we have today?" I ask, opening the box to take a peek.

"These are called *Hello, Darlins*—salted caramel with white chocolate chips." The way her green eyes grow with excitement makes me excited too. I love the passion she has for her baking. "Today is the first day I've made them, so you're my guinea pig."

I smirk, taking another look inside the box and practically drooling over the freshly-baked muffins. "I will gladly be your guinea pig, even if I have to add extra workouts to my regimen." I allow myself a big whiff of the sweet scent coming from the box and moan. "Oh, yeah, these will be totally worth the extra gym time."

She laughs and I catch a hint of something other than humor in her chuckle. Nerves? Her own desire, perhaps? When I glance up at her, I catch the heat in her stare.

Do my eyes deceive me or did Miss Cassidy just give me a quick once-over?

She most certainly was checking out the goods.

I'm not blind and I know when a woman wants me.

The tricky part with Tempest is that she's obviously denying herself for one reason or another. If I had to guess, she's probably sworn off romantic relationships, which is why I've been put in the *friend zone.*

I turn back around and walk over to the small table in the corner, placing my muffins there for safekeeping and giving her a chance to look all she wants. I'm an open buffet, Tempest… feel free to have a taste.

Looking up into the mirror, I see the way she's biting on her bottom lip and I'd say she likes what she sees, too. *Oh, Tempest... we should just give into this…* I want to tell her I could rock her world, change her perspective, give her the release that would take away every care in the world. If only we were more than friends, but we're not… right?

"Ready to get started?" I ask her, picking up some tape and wrapping my hands. I already know I'm going to need to pour some of this pent-up energy into a bag. If I don't, I'm liable to explode… leaving tiny bits of myself all over these mats.

"Yeah," she finally says, pulling herself from whatever trance she was in, making me laugh to myself. "I've gotta leave a little early today, so we should get started."

My head pops up at that, not liking the idea of our time being cut short. "Where are you going?" I ask the question before I can catch myself. *It's none of your fucking business, Cage. Geez.* "I mean… is everything okay?" I ask, hoping it'll cover up my need to know and come off as more of a casual conversation, but Tempest doesn't seem to be any the wiser.

She finished placing her bag by the wall and then walks to the middle of the mats, already stretching out her legs and arms. "Oh, my anger management session got moved up today… Lana, the lady who runs the group has to fly out for her cousin's wedding."

Again, before I think it through, I ask, "Mind if I tag along?"

Her eyes snap up to the mirror, catching mine. I watch as she traps her full bottom lip in her teeth and then darts her eyes down to the floor. "Uh…" she starts, hesitantly, and I'm getting ready to tell her to forget it… or that I was just kidding, but then she recovers and says, "Sure."

There was a small battle going on in Tempest's mind for a split second, but the way her shoulders relax and she replaces the slight worry with a smile tells me she's okay with it.

"You sure?" I ask, not wanting to put her in an uncomfortable situation.

"Yeah," she replies, giving me an even bigger smile. "It'd be great to have the company, but my sessions last at least an hour."

I join her on the mats and begin to stretch my arms over my head, walking in a circle around the perimeter to get my body warmed up. "No problem," I tell her. "I've got a new bag I ordered that I need to pick up… and I wanted to shop around for a speed bag."

"What's that?" she asks, giving me an adorable scrunched-up nose of confusion.

I laugh to keep myself from telling her how adorable she is. "You'll know it when you see it," I tell her. "Everyone in the gym back home always wants to start on it first. It's small, hangs from the ceiling and you punch it… *fast.*" When I emphasize that last part and raise my eyebrows, she giggles and I feel it down in my chest.

"I like to go fast," she says, beginning her shadow boxing—lead hook, rear uppercut, jab with the left, duck and block… she's getting really good. But it's her words that put extra speed in my steps as I make my way around the mats.

"Oh, really?" I ask, keeping my head forward and my breaths steady.

"Yeah… well, you know… I mean." Her fluster is something I've come to love. Not that she's uncomfortable, but Tempest loves putting her foot in her mouth. Well, she must, because she does it quite often and it's hilarious.

I laugh before saying, "I kinda picture you as a take-it-slow kind of girl."

"Don't make this dirty," she huffs, still punching the air and ducking her imaginary opponent.

"Move your feet, speedy," I command, turning my head so she can't see my ridiculous smile.

We continue on with the workout, switching from shadow-boxing to some Tai Chi. I've found it's a crucial part of the class for Tempest. Once we're finished with the Tai Chi she always looks so calm and at peace with herself.

I love it.

Helping her find her inner strength is empowering. I've always loved teaching people, but teaching Tempest is opening my mind up to a whole new realm of possibilities.

"I need to shower," Tempest says, smoothing her hand over her sweaty ponytail. Have I mentioned how tempting she is when she's all hot and sweaty? And dare I say she smells even better, which makes my mind go to filthy, dirty places… all involving Tempest and sweat… and being naked.

"You can shower upstairs if you want."

What the fuck, Cage?

I have no idea why I just said that, but then again, I have no idea why I say half the things I do when she's around. They just fucking fly out of my mouth without permission.

We're friends and I'd offer that to any of my other friends, even if they weren't gorgeous and funny and fun to be around. But the look she's giving me isn't friendly. It's not unfriendly. But it's definitely more. I feel it all the way down to my cock.

Clearing my throat, I try to fix the situation. "Or I can just swing by and pick you up, or you can drive. Whatever… I'm just along for the ride." Now I'm the one rambling on like a fool. Tempest's lips curve slightly up and then she licks them, making them stand out even more.

"How about you pick me up… since I'm on the way out of town," she offers.

"Sounds good." I nod, stopping myself from saying "it's a date." How fucking stupid can I be in one day? I guess we're getting ready to find out.

CHAPTER 17

TEMPEST

Opening the front door of my house, I exhale and close my eyes.

"Holy shit," I mutter to the empty quiet. "That was a close one."

Maintaining that friend status between Cage and I has been a struggle. I hate to admit it, even to myself, and of course I'd never admit it to anyone else… especially him. But there's just this… I don't know, a pull? Electricity? Heat? Something intangible, but it's there. I feel it every time I'm around him, and no matter how hard I try to ignore it or tune it out, I can't.

So, him asking to tag along to Knoxville, although I love the thought of spending more time with him, it's a horrible idea. But how could I say no? I mean, that's what friends are for. If I would've turned him down, it would've made all of this even worse.

"Suck it up, Tempest," I tell myself. "You can do this." Pushing off the door, I make my way to the downstairs bathroom and turn on the shower.

It's just one hour there and one hour back. I'll be in my session while he does his errands. No biggie. I can do this.

After a quick shower, I walk into the spare bedroom and pull out an old T-shirt and jeans, my most comfortable options, and hesitate, looking at a few of the nicer selections hanging in the closet. Nope. Not going to do that.

"You are not dressing for impressing," I mutter to myself, throwing on a basic set of bra and panties… white, virginal… I might not be a virgin, but I swear my hymen has probably reattached itself by this point, so I might as well roll with it. Besides, it'll be a good reminder to myself to not let my mind wander.

Because it will try.

It will try it's damndest to imagine Cage and myself in compromising positions. I already know this, because I have to shut that shit down every time we're around each other.

And I'm already anticipating how bad this is going to be. Having been in a truck cab with Cage a time or two, I know his scent—woodsy, manly, clean… confident and a bit mysterious—floods the small space. Up until now, I've only had to deal with it in small spurts, but two hours on the road will test the Jesus in me.

After I'm dressed, I pull my damp hair into a high bun and secure it with a few bobby pins. Pinching my cheeks for a little color, I give myself a look in the mirror and think about applying makeup, but again, I'm not trying to impress anyone. The people at the anger management session have seen me in all states. It's a come-as-you-are environment. So, if I made an effort today, it would only be for Cage's benefit.

Turning, I go to walk out of the bathroom, catching the light switch on my way out, but then pause and reach back over the counter for my lip gloss. Swiping it across my lips, I give them a smack and toss it back.

There. That's fine. I mean, I can't go with dry lips. That's more of a necessity than a frivolity.

A few minutes later, there's a knock at my door and my heart leaps up into my throat.

"Hey," I say, albeit a tad breathless, but I think I cover well as I reach around the door to grab my bag. "You didn't have to come to the door."

Cage's smile is slow and easy and it makes my insides turn to mush.

Dear, Lord, give me strength.

"It's rude to honk," he says, stepping aside and waiting while I lock the door.

"I give you permission to honk next time," I tell him with a laugh, tossing my keys in my bag and following him to the truck. When he opens my door for me, I get a ridiculous flutter in my stomach.

He smirks, quirking an eyebrow at me, as if to challenge me.

Say something about opening your door, Tempest. I dare you.

So, I don't. I smile and say thank you as I climb inside. Being a little on the shorter side, it's a bit of work getting into big trucks like this, but I make it. Besides, all of this kickboxing I've been doing paired with my occasional runs, I've never felt better. Hanging around Cage makes me a better version of myself. He makes me feel things I haven't felt in a long time, and I'm not just talking about the butterflies and tingles. It's more than that. I feel stronger and more confident.

And I swear he looks at me sometimes like I'm appetizing.

I've tried to convince myself it's my imagination, my own desires being projected onto him, but every once in a while, there's heat in his stare and if I were to meet it for too long, I'd be burned alive from the inside out. Which is why I don't. I never allow myself to hold his gaze when he looks at me like that. I shut it down and walk away.

It's actually one of the coping mechanisms Lana has been teaching us.

When all else fails, walk away. Remove yourself from the situation.

"So, we turn left at the stop sign?" Cage asks and I realize I've been deep in my thoughts for a couple minutes.

"Sorry," I say, reaching over and buckling up. "Yeah, just make a left." Guiding him out of town, we make small talk about the weather and how beautiful it is this time of year, until we hit the highway.

When Cage sets the cruise, I relax back into my seat, trying to not let the intensity of his scent and closeness get to me. Needing something to focus on, I decide now is a good time to get to know Cage

Erickson a little better. I mean, if he's going to be my date to the reunion in a few weeks, we need to cover some basics, right?

"How do you know Hank?" I ask, starting with something I've wondered since I met him and never got a chance to ask.

I hear him sigh, but it's not in annoyance, it's more of a *where-do-I-start* kind of sigh.

"That good, huh?" I tease, chancing a glance his way and seeing his lips pull up in a smile.

"Well, it's pretty cut and dry," he starts. "We were both enrolled at Harvard—"

"What?" I ask, cutting him off, thinking he's pulling my leg. He and Hank are the last two people I'd picture going to Harvard.

Cage's laugh fills the truck and I almost regret thinking conversation would be a good distraction. His laugh is almost as intoxicating as his smell. "It's true," he continues. "We were both just starting our freshman year when we met and hit it off... found some sort of common ground between the two of us, even though we're as different as night and day. I think Hank enjoyed the business side of fighting as much as I enjoyed the fighting."

This time, his chuckle is reminiscent and maybe even a little sad.

"You miss fighting," I tell him. It's not a question. I can hear it in his voice.

He sighs again, shifting in his seat, hands gripping the steering wheel, eyes straight ahead. "Yeah, I miss it."

That's obviously still a sore subject, so I go back to the Harvard thing. "So, are you a Harvard graduate?"

"No," he says with another laugh. "Let's just say me and college didn't really agree."

"But you must be smart... and you had to have some amazing grades, not to mention test scores," I ramble. "I went to culinary school, so I wouldn't know too much about that. But my cousin, Cole, he got into The University of Tennessee and he had to have a twenty-four on his ACT. I can't imagine what you had to have to get accepted to Harvard..." I drift off, my mind whirling with this piece of information and my eyes drift back to Cage, mesmerized by his strong jawline.

Since he's been in Green Valley, he's started to grow a beard, but you can still make out the lines. On some men, a beard ends up being camouflage, covering up their features, but on Cage, it sets them off, making his full lips look fuller and his blue eyes bluer.

Damn it, Tempest.

When Cage takes his eyes off the road for a split second and catches me ogling, I snap my head back around and avert my gaze out the window, waiting for him to say something… anything to distract me.

Deep breaths.

Distract me, please.

"I scored a thirty-six on my ACT, four-point-two GPA, Valedictorian, and I wowed them with my extracurriculars. I was a first-degree black belt in Taekwondo by the time I was fifteen and was teaching at the dojo by the time I was a senior. Add on top of that countless hours of community service and a self-defense course at my local high school… and you've got yourself a Harvard acceptance letter."

I chuckle, partly because he just wowed the pants off of me… literally and figuratively… and partly because what do I say to that? "So, you're not just a pretty face?"

"Pretty?" he scoffs and it's not just because he's trying to be modest. I can tell there's genuine disbelief in his tone and I'm shocked. Surely he knows. Surely women throw themselves at him. Which brings me to my next question.

"Is there someone special… back in Dallas?"

He laughs lightly, following it up with a sigh as he runs a hand over his face and through this dark-blond hair… which has also grown since I first met him. And for the second time since we started this journey, I wonder if I've touched on a sore subject… or maybe there is a someone?

That thought makes my stomach tighten, but not in the delicious way it does when Cage looks at me with his blue eyes ablaze. This feeling resembles jealousy.

What the…?

"No," Cage finally says. "No one special… unless you consider my four brothers special," he adds. "Some people do." This time when he laughs, it's back to the deep rumble that goes straight to my core. "And my parents… but the closest I had to a girlfriend or a wife was the ring. I was married to it—ate, slept, drank, and breathed it."

Interesting. "So, fighting wasn't just a hobby for you?"

"No." He clears his throat. "No, not just a hobby… it's what I left Harvard for… all I ever wanted to do. I knew I was born to be a fighter the second I stepped into a ring at the age of seven. My dad put an old pair of gloves on me and I was at home." He looks over at me and our eyes meet briefly and it's one of those exchanges where the information is on a cellular level and it goes straight to your soul. "My dad said it was equally his worst mistake and proudest moment. He saw it too… told my mom I'd be better than him."

"He was a fighter too?"

Cage nods, licking his lips and making me do the same. "He was a professional boxer… fought WBA bouts back in the 80's and went up against some of the greats."

"Wow."

I see his shrug out of the corner of my eye and smile. He doesn't think he's pretty and obviously doesn't want me to think any different about him due to his intelligence or success… or the success of his father.

As we drive down the road, I decide that his modesty is my new favorite trait. After we sit in silence for a few moments, I can't help but continue to ask more questions. "Four brothers, huh?"

"Yeah," he replies.

"Are you the oldest?"

He shakes his head. "No, Viggo is a year-and-a-half older than me… then me, Vali, Ozzi, and Gunnar."

"Interesting names," I say, liking that they're different.

"Scandinavian," he says. "My dad's grandparents immigrated here from Finland."

"Vikings," I say, fighting back a smile, because now that I think about it, that's exactly what Cage reminds me of. "A few years ago, I was obsessed with that HBO show." Cage grunts and I look over to see him… blushing? Is he…? "Are you blushing?"

"No," Cage says incredulously.

I laugh, turning in my seat. "You're totally blushing."

"I am not," he argues, sounding more like a petulant child than a big, bad Viking and it makes me laugh. "What's wrong with me calling you a Viking?"

"Nothing… and I'm not blushing."

Biting back another laugh, I watch his profile for a few moments before pulling my eyes off him and turning back around in my seat. But I can't stop thinking about him… and eventually ask another question. "How did they all get cool Viking names and you got Cage?"

He cuts his eyes at me and I'm afraid I've offended him, so I backtrack. "Not that Cage isn't a cool name… I love it, but it's not Viggo… or Vali."

"Cage is my middle name," he mutters, barely audible.

I get that this isn't something he wants to talk about, but I can't help prying. "So, what's your first name? I mean, you're talking to Tempest Cassidy… the Sundance Kid," I offer, hoping my own cross to bear will make him comfortable enough to share his.

"Leif," he says and I'm confused.

"That's an awesome name… I love it," I tell him.

"Leif Erickson," he says and then it finally clicks.

I bite back the laugh and clear my throat. "So you're… named after a famous explorer… that's… really… cool." I stumble over my words, but I mean them. It's also funny as shit, and I mean that in the nicest way possible. Coming from the daughter of Butch Cassidy, I know what it's like to be teased about a name. So, I can only imagine the jokes Cage… I mean, Leif… got when he was younger.

"I've always gone by Cage," he says, a bit of hardness to his tone. "My brothers and the neighborhood kids had already made fun of me for it before I ever made it to first grade. I'd already decided I was going to be Cage… and that was that. But," he continues, taking a deep breath and blowing it out. "Once I started fighting bigger bouts and earning a name for myself, everyone started referring to me as The

Fighting Viking." He huffs a laugh and shakes his head. "My brothers always tease me that they're going to let it slip one of these days, but so far, it's been kept under wraps."

The Fighting Viking.

Is it wrong that I want him to conquer me?

Yes, Tempest. It's wrong. He's your friend... *let's keep it together.*

"You'll take a right up here… and then the church is on the right," I tell him.

When he pulls up at the curb, he goes to turn the truck off, but I stop him. "You don't have to stay… just go ahead and do your errands. I'll be done in an hour."

"You sure?"

I nod, reaching for the handle. "Positive." Opening the door, I can't help myself as I climb out and turn back to him. "Don't get lost, Leif."

The smile that splits my face makes my cheeks hurt. Cage rolls his eyes and shakes his head, already regretting confiding in me, I'm sure. But I wear the smile all the way into the church and into the session, earning a few looks from everyone around the circle.

CHAPTER 18

CAGE

Watching Tempest walk into the church has me reflecting about the saying that goes "I hate to see you leave but I love to watch you go." I'd never given it much thought before but I get it now. And the view I have makes me want to *get it now* with Tempest.

Being surrounded by her sweet scent on the drive to Knoxville was killing me in the best way. I'm becoming addicted to being close to Tempest and I'm not sure how much longer I can resist. I would never force myself on her or make her feel obligated in any way; I just want to tell her how I feel and see what happens. Of course, I want more than that, but she can't play the game if she doesn't even know the ball's in her court.

Damn, why do all sports make me think of having sex with Tempest?

Maybe I just have too much time on my hands. Now that I'm not training full-time and fighting, I have more time to think of other things, namely The Duchess of Muffins.

Maybe I've never met anyone like her before and it's totally natural for her to take up so much space in my brain. I mean, she's fucking fascinating. I don't understand how no one else can see that but, at the same time, I'm glad because that means I get her all to myself.

If she'll have me, of course.

This trip to Knoxville came at the perfect time. Not only do I get to spend extra time with Tempest, but I can pick up some more supplies for the studio. Some things, such as wrapping tape and protective equipment, I don't mind ordering online, but for others, I prefer a more hands-on approach.

For example, the speed bags I'm looking at right now. I have a couple already but I need a few more in different sizes. Being so close to a bag, I can't help but tap it a couple of times with my fist. It's like breathing to me and it feels so damn good.

I continue to move around the area, testing out the different bags, before deciding on a few I plan to buy. After I tell the sales guy which ones to set aside for me, I check out some boxing gloves. I'd really like to surprise Tempest with her own set of gloves, but I want them to be perfect. They need to be tough, obviously, but also flexible, just like she is. They also can't be pink or anything too girly looking. Not that there's anything wrong with pink; I just don't think that color suits her.

A pair catches my eye and I immediately know they're perfect for her. Black with bright red flames covering where her fingers and knuckles will be. I can't help but laugh at the multiple meanings behind my choice. They obviously match her name and red hair but they also remind me of the story of when she burned all of her ex's belongings in the driveway. Lastly, the flames represent how freaking hot I think she is.

I make my purchases and drive back to the church to wait for Tempest. I'm a few minutes early, so I roll down the windows and cut the engine, enjoying the nice breeze as it blows through the cab of the truck. It's such a nice day and with her faint scent lingering around me, I find myself somewhere between dreaming and awake, my mind wandering and contemplating life, as you do—where I'm at, where I'm going… what I want, and of course, *who* I want. Images of Tempest easily flood my mind and my daydreams seem so real, I swear I hear her voice.

It takes me a moment to realize I really *am* hearing her voice and when I open my eyes, I see her walking toward my truck with a guy. I'm assuming she knows this man from her sessions but that doesn't make me feel any better, especially as I notice the way he's looking at her. He's not even trying to hide the fact that he's checking her out and it makes me sick to see him leer at her that way. Tempest doesn't seem to notice as she continues to talk, but I'm confident she'll put him in his place if he oversteps her boundaries.

She's a tough girl, but I can't help wanting to help her, be there for her.

I also can't help the slight twinge of jealousy flowing through me as this man stands close to her, breathing her in, appreciating what I'd like to be mine. So, maybe, it's a bit more than a slight twinge because the moment that jackass places his hand on her lower back, leaning in as if he's trying to hear her better, my muscles tense and I swear steam comes out of my ears. In fact, I'd like to take that arm of his, rip it off, and beat him with it, but I know I can't do that.

Tempest squirms a bit, moving away from him, and I instantly relax. I hate that he made her feel uncomfortable, though. I should kick his ass for that, too.

Shit, maybe I need to put the new bags I just bought to use tonight and blow off some of this pent-up aggression I'm feeling. Jacking off would probably help, too, if I'm being completely honest.

Anyone in their right mind would be able to tell Tempest is wanting her conversation with Mr. Handsy to be over based on her body language alone, but the guy just can't take a hint. She's being too nice and I'm about to lose my cool, I can feel it. She edges closer to the truck and I take that as my cue to do something.

Stepping out of the truck, I walk over to the passenger side and open her door like a fucking gentleman.

"Hey, T, you ready to get some dinner?"

Tempest looks a little surprised to see me but she plays it off well. "Oh, hey! Yeah, I'm definitely ready for food." Turning toward her escort, she thanks him for walking with her and tells him to have a good night. Her back is facing me as I help her into the cab of the truck, so I use the opportunity to look over my shoulder and glare at her buddy, daring him to try something with her again.

Fortunately for him, he's smart enough to concede and walk off.

Sorry, not sorry, dude.

Once Tempest is settled in her seat and buckled in, I hop back in the truck and start it up. Glancing at her, I'm about to ask where she wants to go eat when I notice the expression on her face. It's a new one for me, one I'm not sure how to decipher. She looks a little annoyed but also amused, perhaps? Either way, I should probably address it before driving anywhere.

"Everything okay?"

"Did you seriously call me 'T' out there?" Her body is turned fully in my direction and when I start to stutter a bit, she quirks an eyebrow at me, letting me know she's onto me.

"I, yeah, well… I mean—"

"Do you not think I can handle myself, take care of myself?"

Oh, shit. I should've known that would piss her off.

Is it wrong that I find her even more attractive right now?

She continues, "Are you not the person teaching me how to protect myself? Do you doubt your own skills as a teacher?"

"Now, wait a minute," I say, holding up a finger between us. "I may have jumped the gun a bit, but that's because I didn't like that guy putting his hands on you. It had nothing to do with me doubting you or *my* skills."

Tempest starts laughing, which only confuses me more.

"Cage, I'm just teasing you." She grabs my upheld fingers and pushes them down to the seat, and even though I'm relieved she's not angry with me, I'm struggling to concentrate thanks to the feel of her skin on mine. Jolts of electricity sear where she's touching me, making me wonder what would happen if she touched me in other places. She must feel it too, because her pupils have dilated and she seems to have lost her train of thought.

A moment later, she clears her throat, which breaks the tension a little bit. "I'll be honest. Normally, I hate all that 'pissing on my leg' business but it was actually kind of cute. That doesn't mean I need to be rescued all the time, though, got it?"

"I got it, I do. I didn't plan on overstepping any boundaries today and I'm sorry if I upset you, I just didn't like that guy. You were obviously trying to end the conversation, but he refused to take the hint. I see that shit and worse at the club all the time and it pisses me off."

"I can appreciate that and I'm grateful for your concern, but Andy is nice guy... from what I can tell. I don't think he meant any harm."

I don't tell her I disagree. Instead, I ask what I meant to ask a few minutes ago. "Where do you want to eat?"

Tempest tells me how to get to a Mexican restaurant that she swears is 'the real deal'. Being from Dallas, I'm pretty sure I know more about real Mexican food than she does, but I'll trust her opinion this time. Truth be told, I couldn't give two shits where we go as long as I get to spend more time with her.

We're seated quickly and are just about to dig into our chips and salsa when I see a guy coming our way. I can only assume he knows Tempest since I'm a nobody here, so I keep my guard up in case he's like the other troublemakers she has to deal with.

"Sorry for interrupting." Instead of looking at Tempest, he's looking at me… with what can only be described as anticipation. "Are you Cage Erickson… The Fighting Viking?" he asks, completely catching me off guard.

I quickly glance at Tempest and see she's sitting straight up in her chair, extremely interested in this interaction.

"Uh, yeah, that's me... but people don't really call me that anymore," I say as politely as I can. I've had people approach me in the past, mostly when I'm in a city hosting a fight… or in Dallas, where the Erickson name means something, but not in Knoxville, Tennessee. And not since I haven't fought a publicized fight in over eight months.

"I knew it!" the guy exclaims, slapping his leg and turning back around to gesture to the guy sitting at a table across the room. "I told my buddy it was you but he didn't believe me. My name is Tony." He sticks his hand out toward me and I shake it. "I'm a huge fan; I saw a couple of your fights in Nashville… Bridgestone Arena… you were awesome. Shame about your injury."

He shakes his head in disappointment and I feel eyes on me from around the restaurant. I don't want to be rude, but I'd really like to end this and get back to my date… not date… *meal* with Tempest.

"Yeah, it sucks, but I've kind of come to terms with it." I shrug my shoulders and am instantly reminded of how when doing that motion I still feel the twinge. Surgery helped and physical therapy got me to a pretty good spot, but I'll never be what I was.

"So… you're not training for that fight against Wilson?" he asks.

"No," I reply, not trying to be short, but between him interfering with my time with Tempest and asking stupid-ass questions that have no doubt surfaced through the rumor mill, it pisses me off.

He sighs, turning to Tempest and giving her an approving smile. "So, what brings you to these neck of the woods?"

None of your fucking business, buddy.

Clearing my throat, I look up at Tempest and then back to Tony. "Visiting."

He must finally get a clue, because he straightens and takes a step away from the table. "Oh, well, enjoy your stay… and the enchiladas here are the best."

"Thanks," I tell him, watching his back as he walks to his table to make sure he doesn't change his mind. "Fucking Chatty Cathy."

Tempest laughs, like a forced huff of laughter. "What was that?" Her green eyes are wide as they dart from me back to Tony across the restaurant, sitting at his table, obviously telling his buddy all about our talk. "Oh, my God… so you're like one of those guys who fights on the television?"

The way she phrases the question makes me laugh and it helps to diffuse the tension that'd built in my shoulders while I felt like everyone in the restaurant was staring at me. I obviously don't have a problem with people looking at me. I've fought in public since I was a kid, but when I'm not fighting, I don't really enjoy being the center of attention.

"Yeah, I'm one of those guys… was," I clarify, looking at my menu and immediately writing off the enchiladas. Fuck the enchiladas. I'm getting fajitas, just to spite Tony.

"I didn't realize," Tempest says, trying not to make a big deal out of it, but obviously wanting to know more.

Sighing, I set my menu to the side and lean over onto the table. "Remember how I told you my dad was a boxer?" She nods. "Well, me and my brothers started training in kickboxing and mixed martial arts from a young age. I happened to be the one that really took to the sport and started fighting in tournaments when I was about fifteen. I fought my first UFC bout when I was twenty… two months after I dropped out of Harvard."

Tempest is hanging on every word I'm saying, her adorable chin cupped in her hand and not an ounce of judgment in her jade green eyes. "Wow," she says. "The only other person I know who's been on television is Jenn… she's the Banana Cake Queen."

I can't help the laugh that bursts out of me. "Only in Tennessee."

"She's a big deal," Tempest says, nodding her head. "Not just a local celebrity, either… like, national. It's why the bakery is so popular. People drive from a hundred miles away just to buy our baked goods."

"I've noticed," I tell her, my focus going to her lips. I can't help it. When she talks, the way they move mesmerizes me. "And rightfully so… those muffins." Whistling under my breath earns me a smile from the Duchess of Muffins.

"What can I get for you?" our waiter asks as he walks up to the table.

Tempest and I order—me sticking with my decision on the fajitas and her going with the "world famous" enchiladas. After he comes back with our drinks and lets us know he turned our order in, she looks at me pointedly. "So, what do the other Vikings do, if they're not fighters?"

"Well, my older brother Viggo and my younger brother Vali own a gym. It was where I used to train and I worked there, conducting kickboxing classes. My other younger brother Osmond… Ozzi… he works there too, mostly training with young fighters. And my youngest brother, the baby of the family, Gunnar, is the one who will probably pick up the gloves."

She smiles and I feel it deep down in my chest… every time. "He wants to follow in your footsteps."

I shrug. "I'm not so sure it's me he's trying to emulate, but he definitely has the fighting gene… and he's good. He's got great potential."

"Do you miss them? Are y'all close?" she asks, dipping a chip into the salsa and popping it into her mouth, drawing my attention back to those damn lips.

"Sure," I say, forcing my attention to the chip basket. I usually don't eat carbs, but I think I'll make a concession. Needing the distraction, I dip a chip. "I talk to them almost daily… and things have been a little… stressed since the injury."

Tempest frowns. "Why?"

"Well, the gym really depended on the publicity it gained from my appearances and fights."

"So it was riding on your coattails?" she asks.

Cringing a little, I clear my throat, feeling a little uncomfortable talking about it. I never speak about the gym with other people, at least not like this. If I'm not discussing the business side of things with Viggo or Val, I'm promoting it to a camera or people in the industry. Never do I get a chance to just voice my opinions without fear of repercussions.

"It might sound that way, but it was mutual," I tell her, being completely honest. "I benefited from the gym just as much as it benefited from me. By being so connected to it, I had opponents to spar with at the drop of a hat, access to one of the most elite training facilities in the Dallas area, and the best support system."

"I bet they really miss you," she says thoughtfully, something in her gaze shifting.

I shrug. "I guess… yeah." Grabbing another chip, I dip it and shove it in my mouth to buy me a few seconds to think about my response. "They miss the notoriety and the opportunities… but things change.

It's not like I planned on getting injured, and regardless of my involvement, Erickson MMA is still an elite facility in the southwest."

"Impressive," Tempest says, nodding her head.

The waiter steps up to our table about that time, a sizzling plate of beef fajitas with my name on them and a plate oozing with gooey cheese for Tempest.

"Yum," she says, inhaling deeply as she closes her eyes.

Mexican food is like a religious experience for Tempest and I'm feeling so fortunate to be along for the ride. As we get down to business with our food, the conversation shifts to lighter topics… how amazing the side of guacamole is and how we both love sopapillas. And Tempest wasn't wrong, this is some of the best Mexican food I've ever had.

The surprises in Tennessee just keep coming.

On the drive home, I find myself wishing I could call in sick and find a way to spend the rest of the evening and night with Tempest. But duty calls. So, as we make our way back to Green Valley, I just enjoy the view, both inside and outside of the truck.

The scenery in this part of the country is hands-down some of the best views I've ever witnessed, and I've been everywhere. The Appalachian Mountains are quickly becoming my favorite thing, well second favorite.

"I bet it was great having siblings growing up, huh?" Tempest asks, her elbow resting on the window as she kicks back and enjoys the ride.

I laugh. "That's something an only child would say."

"Hey!" she protests. "I didn't have a choice in the matter and I honestly can say I spent the better part of my life wishing I had someone to share the burden of being a Cassidy with. I mean, I never had anyone to split the chores or commiserate with when my mom was being overbearing or my dad was being a hardass… which they still do," she mutters.

"Was it that bad?" I ask, glancing over at her and then back to the road. "Green Valley seems like a pretty good place to grow up."

She sighs, sitting up a little straighter. "Home life wasn't terrible. I always had food on the table and clean clothes to wear. My parents were involved in my schooling and activities… well, I didn't have many of those, but they were always present… I had a good childhood."

"But?" I ask, sensing there's a flip side.

"School was rough. Thankfully, I had Cole. He was the big brother I never had, which is probably why we're still so close. And then he started dating Anna and we became friends."

Now I'm sitting up a little straighter in my seat, not liking the sound of this. "So, let me get this right… Cole and Anna were your only friends?" That's how she's making it sound, but I hope I'm wrong. The thought of Tempest being alone or lonely doesn't settle well with me.

"I had friends, but they weren't great ones," she says. "They were the kind of friends who would turn on you at the drop of a hat, always swaying to play the side that benefited them the best." For a second, she's quiet—contemplative. "But," she continues, fortifying her voice, "after I started dating Asher, things got better… at least on the surface, but looking back, I'm not so sure he did me any favors. My friends were his friends and after the divorce, I realized their loyalties always resided with him."

That pisses me off.

"I think that's why I felt like I was fighting for air those first couple months… I didn't know what was up or down or sideways. When he was out of my life, I didn't know where I stood. It was scary and I constantly felt like lashing out at everyone and everything… like my fight-or-flight mechanism kicked into high gear, and I chose fight."

We sit in the quiet for a few miles, just the noises from the road filling the truck. It's not that I don't have anything to say, but I'm trying to think about how I want to reply without telling her what a dick her ex-husband is and that's she's better off without him… and that I'm grateful for his mistake, the worst mistake of his life, because due to his stupidity, I get to sit here… with her.

"You know he doesn't define you, right?" I start. "The only thing he did for you was provide life experience, which you've grown from and become a tougher person because of. That's it." When she doesn't reply, I turn my head to see her brows furrowed and her lip between her teeth. "What?"

She shakes her head, but doesn't look at me. "Nothing. It's just that I was either dating or married to Asher for twelve years... it's hard to move past that."

"Do you still love him?" I want to grab the question out of the air and swallow it back down, but I can't. It's out there now and I'm not sure I want to hear her answer, but then she huffs a laugh.

"No," she says with ferocity. "And I'm not just saying that because I'm hurt and pissed... actually, I'm neither of those anymore. I'm just... done... and definitely not in love with Asher."

I breathe a sigh of relief, but try to hide it with a cough.

"And just for the record," I add, needing to get one more thing out in the open. "You're better than all of those people who chose Asher's side after the divorce. They obviously don't know what they're missing out on by not having you in their lives... or they're too stupid to realize."

She laughs. "You have to say that."

"Why?" I ask, incredulously.

"Because you're my *friend*." The way she draws out friend makes it a stark reminder to what zone she's placed me in and also that she needs me to fill that role.

I want to be Tempest's friend.

I just want to be that and so much more.

"Thanks for that," she says after a few minutes as we make the turn onto the road that leads into Green Valley, which means our time together is almost up. "For being my friend," she adds and I can feel her gaze on me, so I keep my eyes on the road. "You came to town just in time... it's like the universe knew I needed someone."

When I turn down her road, I remember the gloves I bought for her, but decide to keep them for our next session.

"So, you're still on for the class reunion, right?" she asks. "Even after knowing that I went to school with a bunch of assholes."

"I wouldn't miss it," I tell her, turning into her drive. "There's no way in hell I'd let you go alone."

And that's the truth. If she's going to that damn reunion, I'm going with her, if for no other reason than to make sure Asher and his new wife don't make any trouble for Tempest. I get why she needs to go, but I wish she didn't feel like she had to. Most people claim that in ten years everyone changes and people who were enemies are friends… and the unpopular people are now part of the in crowd. But some people never change. Change only happens when a person wants something different. It sounds to me like all of these people are still stuck on being the same assholes they were ten years ago.

"Thank you," she says, unbuckling her seat belt and reaching for the door. "I'm not sure what I'd do without you."

This time when she turns to look at me, I meet her stare and those green eyes draw me in. When she darts her tongue out to wet her bottom lip, I can't help staring, wishing I could have a taste… just one.

Maybe there wouldn't be a spark. Maybe this connection I've felt since the night I drove her home from the bar is what Tempest keeps saying… friends. But maybe it's not. Maybe it's what I feel deep down in my gut. Maybe it's more.

Before I know what's happening, Tempest leans across the seat and her lips graze my cheek… like a friendly kiss, but not. So fucking not. The way her mouth hesitates over my skin, her breath eliciting a groan from the deepest parts of my soul, I can't help myself.

Just that small gesture has my entire body sparking to life. Letting my mind and any thoughts of just being friends fly out the window, I reach up and cup her face, pausing for the briefest of moments to drink her in, feeling her soft skin under my palm. *Sweet. Delicious. Fucking perfect.*

When my fingers slide into her hair, caressing the strands like I've wanted to on so many occasions, she leans into it, closing her eyes and giving me the non-verbal permission I'm looking for.

My lips brush hers.

Once.

Twice.

And then she's kissing me back.

At first, it's soft and slow—tentative. Then, she parts her lips and I deepen the kiss, slipping my tongue against hers. It's everything I ever wanted it to be and so much more. When her hands grip my shoulders, I wrap my arms around her waist, pulling her closer and loving the way her body feels pressed against mine… so good… so right.

Just as I'm getting ready to move her into my lap and devour her, a phone rings.

Tempest jerks back, her eyes going wide as her hand comes up to cover her mouth. She stares at me like a deer in headlights for a split second before she breaks the connection and answers her phone. A bit breathless, she says, "hello," without looking at the screen, like she'd talk to the devil if he'd give her an out.

When her shoulders go rigid, those fucking walls that I hate so much thud back into place.

Fucking Asher… I have a love-hate relationship with that prick. I love him for fucking things up because I want Tempest for myself. But I hate him for what he did to her and the distrust he planted in her heart. That's not going to be an easy thing to get past, but I'm not going to stop trying.

CHAPTER 19

TEMPEST

Standing in the middle of my empty living room, I'm not sure how to feel.

When Asher and I bought this house almost nine years ago, months before our wedding, I thought we'd live here forever. I remember the first time I sat on the front porch and envisioned our children playing in the yard and years of happiness… and one day, being old and gray and sitting with my husband on a quiet evening.

Part of me wants to write love off, letting go of those old dreams and wishes.

I want to say I tried and obviously failed horribly, so why even try again?

But another part of me still wants it and believes it might still be out there for me… *someone* might still be out there for me. Someone who will love me unconditionally and fight for a forever, instead of throwing it to the wayside the moment something, or *someone*, better —more appealing—comes along. I want to believe there's someone who brings out the best in me, instead of the worst. Someone who wants to be my best friend *and* do life together.

When Cage's face pops into my mind, I try to shake it off, like I've done for the past few days.

That kiss.

That damn kiss shook me to my core.

I've never been kissed like that. I've never felt that way. Not my first kiss with Asher or the last kiss or any of the kisses in between. He never made me feel like the world was tilting and everything around me was falling away, leaving only me and him. But that's how I felt when Cage kissed me… or did I kiss him?

Yeah, I definitely kissed him. I was so caught up in the moment and the feelings I was having—so grateful for him and his friendship. When I leaned in to kiss his cheek, something happened. I was overwhelmed by his closeness and his scent, everything was heightened and I just fell into it… into him. Then, his lips touched mine and once the threshold had been crossed, I was done for. There's a good chance I would've let that kiss carry me all the way to bed, and then my phone rang and popped the bubble, pulling me back to reality.

I'm Tempest Cassidy, recently divorced and not looking for a rebound.

I don't jump into things without thinking them through.

Recent events excluded.

Maybe that methodical, well-planned Tempest checked out the day she walked in on her husband and his mistress? Maybe that snap I felt inside my body was a switch?

Regardless, I can't let that kiss happen again, because I couldn't be held responsible for my actions. Cage Erickson holds great power over me. He has the potential to make me forget myself and my inhibitions. If my phone hadn't rang, there's no telling what would've happened and that scares me… and thrills me.

My body still tingles every time I think about how his lips felt as they were claiming mine—a residual electrical current attached to the memory.

"That's the last of it," my dad says, walking in the front door, his voice echoing off the empty walls, driving home the realization that this place holds nothing any longer—no furniture, no pictures… no love… only memories… and those aren't good ones. All of the good ones have been tainted and forgotten, replaced with betrayal and hurt.

I nod, turning to face him. "I'm ready to go."

"Maybe we should make one last sweep?" he asks, looking around the space.

"No, it's good… if anything gets left behind, the next couple can have it."

I don't want anything that reminds me of Asher, so most of the furniture was either sold or donated. My kitchen appliances are staying with the house. The rest of it—my baking supplies, stand mixer, pots and pans—has been packed up for over a week. The new bed and bedding I bought recently is already in my new apartment—a studio apartment half a block away from the bakery.

Two blocks from Cage, but who's counting?

I've been trying to ignore the fact we'll practically be neighbors. It's probably not the best location for me, given my weakness when it comes to him, but it's cheap and close to work. For now, I just need a place to call my own and regroup. At some point, I'll probably buy a house again, but it'll be mine and won't have anything to do with Asher Williams.

Now that the house is sold, there's nothing left between the two of us, and I honestly couldn't be happier. "Let's go," I tell my dad, walking past him and out the door, leaving the key on the counter in the kitchen and the last of my anger and resentment with it.

It's time to let all of it go and move on with my life.

My dad helps me get the boxes moved into the apartment above the old hardware store. After the kiss and the phone call from my realtor telling me the house sold and the buyers wanted to move in ASAP, Cage offered to help, but with all of the mixed feelings coursing through my body, I couldn't accept.

My internal walls crept up as I answered the phone and the realization of what I'd done hit me full force, along with Cage's intense stare. I felt them fortifying, protecting me from the inside out. And I think Cage saw it, because when I got out of the truck, there was disappointment and regret written all over his face.

"Your mama said she'd come over and help you get everything

settled," my dad says, setting the last box down on the counter. "She would've come tonight, but she had a prayer meeting."

I nod, stuffing my hands in the back pockets of my jeans as I look around at my new place. "It's fine. I'd really like to do it myself… you know, fresh start, all me," I say with a smile.

My dad meets my gaze and holds it. "You're gonna be just fine," he says, willing it to be so. My whole life, when things go topsy-turvy, he's always been there to remind me that it'll all work out—*this too shall pass*. Even through his tough love lessons over the past six months, he never failed to remind me that I was going to make it. Unlike my mama, my daddy never doubts me. He may not always understand me or my motives, but he always believes in me.

"Thanks, Dad," I tell him, walking over and wrapping my arms around him. "Not just for your vote of confidence, but for all your help… for always being there."

He sighs, his arms squeezing my shoulders. "You're my baby girl. That's my job."

"But you won't bail me out of jail anymore?" I ask, teasing.

He chuckles and releases my shoulders, pulling me back to look at me. "I don't think I'm gonna need to," he says, sincerity in his expression and tone. "I think that's behind us…don't you?"

It's like he wants to say more, something about Asher or the past, but he doesn't. My daddy is typically a man of few words, always practicing the belief that actions speak louder.

"Yeah," I tell him, walking over to the large window overlooking the main road that cuts through downtown. "I think my inmate days are over."

From here, I can see the bakery and the barber shop. I can't see the building Cage lives in, because it's on the same side of the road as mine, but it doesn't stop me from thinking about him and wondering what he's up to… probably already working his shift at the Pink Pony.

"Good," he says, making his way across the room. "That's what I like to hear."

"Tell mama I'll call her."

He nods, reaching for the door. "Call if you need anything… and lock this door."

"Daddy, this is Green Valley... what do you think is gonna happen?"

Turning around, he gives me a look... *the look.* "Tempest," he warns.

"Fine, yes," I tell him—appeasing him. "I'll lock my door."

Keeping his eyes on me for a few more moments, he grunts and opens the door. "If I come over here to check up on you and this door is unlocked, I might have Sheriff James put you in jail just to put my mind at ease."

"Daddy." Now it's my turn to warn him. Sometimes, he forgets that I'm twenty-eight and not eight. I guess, to him, I'll always be his little girl... and one of these days, if I ever get a chance, I hope to know what that feels like.

One of these days.

After he's gone, I do walk over and lock the door. Sure, this is Green Valley, but I feel a bit more exposed and alone being in an apartment as opposed to my safe little neighborhood surrounded by familiar faces. But I've also never felt freer—freer to be myself and do what I want... when I want, how I want... *who* I want.

Stop it, Tempest.

Knock that shit off.

I've barely got one box unloaded before my phone rings.

"Hey, Mama," I say, cradling the phone between my cheek and shoulder so I can continue to work.

"Tempest," she says and I get comfortable, because I can tell by her tone that I'm in for a lengthy monologue. My mama can give Shakespeare a run for his money. "Your daddy just got home and was telling me that this new... *apartment*," she says the word like it's displeasing her by existing, "isn't very safe... are you sure you don't just want to move home. It could save you money and save your father and I the grief of worrying about you."

I hear my daddy arguing with her in the background. I'm pretty sure there is a "leave that girl alone" followed by a "mind your own business", to which she shushes him and continues.

"I just think this is a rash decision and you haven't thought it through. What, with Asher's indiscretions and the untimely… *separation*." She's yet to say the word divorce. I want to spell it out for her and force her to repeat it over and over until she gets it through her head that we're divorced… finished, done, over. In the words of Taylor Swift, we're never ever getting back together. "You might not be thinking clearly," she continues. "I know you've been attending these sessions, but I think you need something more, like counseling. Pastor Johnson would be more than happy to see you until you can get past this and find it in your heart to forgive Asher."

She takes a breath, but barely, before pressing on.

"We are all just human, Tempest, Asher included, and it is not our place to judge. But it is our place to uphold the sanctity of marriage."

Oh, here we go.

Please, Lord, give me strength.

I clench my jaw and breathe out of my nose, slow and steady.

"You made a promise to God to love and cherish him. And part of loving someone is forgiving them. I know things don't seem fixable right now, but with some time… and *prayer*… I think the two of you can come to a place of understanding and move on with your lives."

When I've had my fill, I finally stop her. "Mama, I know you mean well." I've found over the years, it's always better to start with that, giving her the benefit of the doubt, because deep down, I know she does. She loves me. And she cares about my happiness. She just has a screwed up way of showing it sometimes. "But Asher and I aren't getting back together. Ever."

There's no sense beating around the bush. I might as well lay it all out there for her. Rip that bandaid right off.

"He and Mindy are married. They're having a baby. And even if he were to crawl back to me on his hands and knees, I still wouldn't take him back."

Her audible gasp has me rolling my eyes, but it doesn't deter me. "I'm staying in the apartment. I'm staying divorced. And I don't need counseling from Pastor Johnson. Actually, the last thing I need is one more person in this town knowing my business."

I almost add that I might need to get laid, but decide that I don't want to give my mother a coronary, so I skip that one.

"Thank you for being concerned about my well-being… but I'm fine on my own." Repeating my daddy's words, I tell her, "I'm going to be just fine."

"*Fine*," she replies, a bit of sarcasm in her tone. "Just fine… but don't call me when you're dead in a ditch."

"Mama!"

From the other end of the phone, I hear my daddy have a similar response.

"Oh, you know I'm not serious," she scolds. "Lord knows I'd lose my mind if anything ever happened to you… I just love you and want what's best."

"I know, Mama, and I love you too."

"Lock your door."

"Yes, ma'am."

A few hours later, I have every box unpacked and almost everything put away, except for a small box of random papers. With my hands on my hips, I blow a stray strand of hair from my face and admire my work. Since the walls are brick, and I don't have a drill, I just propped my big mirror against one wall and one of my favorite larger prints against another.

From my cozy new bedding to my dishes on the exposed shelves, everything about this space is just… me.

It's mine.

Spinning around like Julie Andrews in Sound of Music, I can't help the smile on my face.

After my little victory dance, I decide to break down the empty boxes and walk them downstairs to the back alley where the dumpster is. Having everything done before I go to bed will feel good, and hopefully, it'll help me sleep better and feel rested, because I haven't since the call from the realtor that the house sold.

I've laid awake every night thinking about the move and everything being final.

Actually, if I'm being honest with myself, that kiss has cost me more hours of sleep than anything else. That damn kiss and the man who gave it to me have consumed every waking moment.

I wish he was home.

No, no I don't.

Because if he was and I went over there… or he came over here…

My thoughts immediately turn to the heated scenes I've been conjuring up every time I think about him, and now that I know what it's like to feel his touch, I can't stop myself.

I know I need to, but I can't. I've tried, but it's futile.

Part of me wonders if my attraction to him is a way for my heart to rebound from the rejection and hurt, but something tells me it's not that at all. The way my skin tingles every time I'm around him and my heart skips a beat when he looks at me with heat in his eyes, I know it's something more. And it's not just the physical attraction, I like him. I like hanging out with him and talking to him. He's funny and smart and interesting. And he's unlike anyone I've ever met.

He doesn't judge me or try to change me.

He just accepts me for who I am and he makes me better.

The truth is: I might be falling for Cage Erickson.

And I want him, more than I ever wanted Asher.

And that scares me. And excites me. And worries me. And makes me hopeful. He makes me feel everything.

With Asher, it was a relationship that developed slowly. I didn't immediately love him. He eventually won me over. *Like* eventually turned into *love*. He was the only boy I'd ever dated. Hindsight being twenty-twenty, maybe I should've dated more and figured out if marrying him was really what I wanted, but I thought I knew. I thought I knew him and thought I could trust him.

Apparently, I was wrong.

With Cage, the attraction was immediate and it's gotten stronger as time goes on. I don't know what I'm going to do about it. But I do know I don't want to ruin the friendship we've developed. Besides, I don't know if I'm ready for another relationship or if he'd even be interested in having one, but the feelings are definitely there.

CHAPTER 20

CAGE

"I can't believe you got Julio to agree to fight," Val says incredulously, like I might be lying to him. "I just talked to his agent a few weeks ago and it was a hard no. The purse wasn't big enough."

Pacing the length of the room that's looking more and more like a legit studio every day, I huff. "Well, believe it. I called him… called in a favor and he's in." I want to add "don't say I've never done anything for you", but I'm trying to smooth the waters not stir the shit, so I keep my mouth shut.

"Thanks," he finally says and I can tell it's a struggle. He still wants to be pissed that I won't give in and fight a losing fight. Because regardless what he and Viggo think, I *would* lose that fight. Wilson is in the best shape of his life and he has a vendetta against me for taking his belt a few years ago. "But it would still be nice for you to be there. We could use the extra publicity. Maybe you could do an exhibition bout—"

"No," I say, cutting him off. "I'm not stepping foot in that ring."

He sighs and I can picture him running a hand over his short buzz cut. "Viggo said you were done… I guess I just didn't believe him."

"Well, I am," I confirm. Admitting it doesn't leave me with the gutted feeling it did eight months ago. Back then, I couldn't imagine a life outside of the sport, but now that I'm living it, I can. Sure, I'm disappointed and there's still a hole that hasn't been filled, but I'm getting there.

"Gunnar wants to fight," Val says and I stop pacing and turn toward the mirrors. "He wants you to train him."

Crossing the mats, I throw a punch at one of the bags, making the chains rattle. "What do Mom and Dad think about that?"

Out of all my brothers, Gunnar is the most like me. He's smart. Not that my other brothers aren't, but where Gunnar and I excelled in academics, the others just coasted by until they could graduate. Viggo and Val both have their business degrees from a community college. Ozzi went straight from high school to the gym. By the time he graduated, business was booming. I was fighting, Viggo was managing everyone, and Val was promoting fights.

We were a well-oiled machine.

And I do miss those days.

"He's graduating in December. He promised Mom he would graduate. He's doing it," Val says, but what I feel like he's implying is that *unlike me*, Gunnar is graduating.

Yeah, I already know.

I'm officially the failure of the family.

"Besides, he's twenty-one," Val adds. "It's not like he needs their permission."

True. It's hard to believe he's that old, but he is—plenty old enough to make his own decisions and blaze his own path. I'm proud of him for sticking with college and getting his education. I always knew he would, because the other way Gunnar is unlike me is that he actually wanted to go to college.

He even applied to Harvard, but didn't get accepted.

However, he's graduating from Rice with a degree in Exercise Science. If I had stuck with college, that's something I probably would've enjoyed, but being at Harvard, I felt stifled. I just didn't fit in with all of the pre-law and pre-med students. It wasn't the life for me. And as much as my family, my mom most of all, would like me to feel bad about my decision to quit and start fighting full-time, I don't.

I made my choices.

I lived my life.

And I don't have any regrets.

Gunnar is going to be a great addition to the Erickson MMA business. He'll probably be the one to fulfill all of the dreams placed on my shoulders.

"He's good, huh?" I ask. I know he is, but I haven't had a chance to see him fight recently, but according to Viggo, he's really come into his own in the last few months—more driven, more focused... stronger, faster.

"It's like he knows he has to pick up the torch, man," Val says and I can hear the smile in his voice... the pride he feels. "He's ready to step up."

And fill my shoes, that's what he leaves out.

Maybe I should feel bad about it, resentful even, but I don't.

"And he wants me to train him?"

"We all do," Val says. "You're the best."

"I'll think about it. And I'll be home soon, so we can all sit down and talk about it." I need to make a trip to Dallas to tie up loose ends. If I'm going to stay in Green Valley for the foreseeable future, there's no sense in keeping my house. Plus, I could use the money from selling it to invest in a studio.

There's a pause and it's then I hear the shuffle of feet behind me and turn to see a sight for sore eyes, my sore eyes.

Tempest is standing on the other side of the mats holding a box from the bakery. I haven't seen her since the day we went to Knoxville and ended up kissing in the truck... best fucking kiss of my life. But that was over a week ago and I was afraid she wasn't going to show today.

"Hey," I say to Val. "I've gotta go."

"Think about it," he says. "And think about coming home for the fight."

"Fine," I agree, ending the call and walking toward Tempest.

She gives me a small smile, biting down on her bottom lip.

"Hey," she says, pushing the box out in front of her, like they're a peace offering. "I made you these."

My payment.

So, I'm guessing we're still on for her reunion. After the kiss and the way she bolted after the call from her realtor, I thought she might've changed her mind.

"I wasn't sure if you were coming today," I admit and her eyes skitter around the room, looking anywhere but at me, and fuck me, this is what I don't want. If Tempest gets weird and feels uncomfortable around me, that would be the worst, because as much as I want her body, I want her presence even more.

"It's been kind of a shit day," she says, exhaling. "And I really need a friend… and something to take my mind off of everything."

I feel a tightening in my chest with her words and as much as I want to tell her to fuck being friends, I can't. She obviously needs that from me and I'm willing to be what she needs.

For now.

"You came to the right place," I tell her with a smirk, hoping to set her mind at ease—giving her a safe place to land.

The hesitant smile on her face tells me she really needs a good session. And by that, I don't mean with my dick. So I walk over and set the muffins down, grabbing her new gloves I bought in Knoxville.

"Try these on," I instruct, handing them over.

She takes them and her green eyes go wide. "What are these?"

"Your new gloves," I tell her, walking over to grab a roll of tape. "We're sparring today."

"You bought these for me?" she asks, disbelief in her tone as she slides one of them on and flexes her fist. When she looks back up at me, there's pure adoration in her gaze. You'd think I gave her a new car.

She looks down at the gloves and I see a soft smile on her lips… those fucking lips. When she laughs, I ask, "What's so funny?"

Shaking her head, she replies, "I can't remember the last time someone bought me something. How sad is that?"

My heart clenches and I have a sudden desire to buy her the world.

"What do you mean?" I ask, sure I've misunderstood what she's saying, but she simply shrugs.

"Just what I said." Looking back up at me, her eyes are a little shiny. "Usually for my birthday, my parents take me out for dinner, but they stopped buying me gifts when I was in college. For Christmas, we agreed to not exchange gifts a few years after Asher and I got married. I think…" she drifts off, but then continues, her voice an octave lower. "I think they thought we'd have kids… and that they'd start buying for them, but…"

That never happened.

Instead, her fuckwad of an ex went and knocked up someone else.

I feel that gut punch for her. My stomach literally hurts when I think about what she's been through.

"Wanna know something?" she asks, almost absentmindedly, her gaze fixated on the black leather of the gloves as a finger on her ungloved hand traces the flames. "Asher came into the bakery today to buy a dozen muffins… *Back in Baby's Arms*." She laughs, but this time, it's empty of humor. "I took the order and had no idea who they were for."

"So, I'm assuming," I start, but she finishes my thought.

"It's a boy." Her smile doesn't reach her eyes and even though I know she's over Asher, this hurts. "Mindy went into labor two days ago."

The fact that he intentionally brought her even more pain makes me want to go find him and make him wish *he'd* never been born.

"Wanna put those gloves to good use?" I ask, thinking of another gift I can give her.

When she nods her head in agreement, I take her hand in mine and wrap her knuckles in tape, taking care to not make it too tight, but tight enough to protect her hands. They are, after all, extremely valuable. The Duchess of Muffins couldn't make her magic with damaged hands.

"Just like shadowboxing," I instruct as we start to bounce around the mats. "Except now, you're going to make contact."

Her eyes grow wide. "I'm going to hit you?"

"Yep," I tell her, knocking together my gloves, which are just for show, because there is no way in hell I'm going to actually spar with her. All I'm going to do is let her blow off some steam and take her new gloves on a test drive.

"Hard?" she asks, still unsure of what we're getting ready to do.

"As hard as you want."

I hit my stomach for show, raising my shirt and flexing my muscles. When her eyes darken, I raise an eyebrow in challenge. She wants me… I know she does… as more than a friend. If only I could get her to see that we can explore this heat between us and still be friends.

The best relationships are built off friendships, after all.

"It's all about getting comfortable in the ring," I instruct. "This is your ring." I spread my arms wide to the mats around us. "Stay on your toes… stay moving."

She nods and begins to bounce around like when we're shadowboxing.

"Most importantly, breathe," I tell her, making eye contact and holding her gaze. "Breathe."

I watch as she inhales deeply and lets it out.

"Relax," I say, dropping my voice and raising my gloves up. "Eyes on me."

After a few more seconds, I see her begin to focus and forget about everything else—Asher, the baby… everything. "Now punch."

She starts off tentatively with a half-assed right hook and then a weak left jab.

"You can do better than that," I tell her, giving her shoulder a push as we dance around each other. "Give it to me… lay it all on me."

The next punch hits me in the arm and I can't say it stings, but I feel it and I give her a quirk of an eyebrow in approval. "Again."

Left, right… uppercut, jab.

"That's it," I coax. "Hands up, keep your face protected."

It's too pretty to take a punch.

When she starts to get the hang of it and realizes she's not going to hurt me, she loses herself in the sparring, throwing punch after punch. Some I dodge, some I deflect, and some I take like a man, letting her take out her frustrations and disappointment on me.

I must get too lax in my protective stance, or maybe I'm losing my touch, because she lands a wild right hook to my jaw and it kind of knocks me for a loop.

"Oh, my God," she exhales, bracing her hands on her knees as she catches her breath and tries not to laugh. "I'm sorry… I didn't mean to punch you in the face."

Her genuine laugh is a soothing balm to any injury I might've sustained, which is minimal, maybe a sore jaw, but probably not even that. But that doesn't keep me from playing it up. I cup my jaw and turn my back to her, bending over as if I'm in pain.

She immediately comes to my side, concern in her voice. "Cage… are you okay? I… I didn't mean to… I'm sorry."

Just as she squats down to look me in the eye, I grab her and toss her over my shoulder.

"I should body slam you for that," I growl, earning a squeal.

"I'm sorry!" she exclaims. "Put me down. Please!" Her padded fists hammer at my back and I twist.

"A little to the left," I tell her. "My lat has been tight for a few days." My own laugh rumbles through my chest as she starts pounding harder. Without thinking, I smack her ass and she practically jolts right off my shoulder.

Letting her slide to the floor, I can't help the way my body responds to hers.

"Did you slap my ass?" she asks, eyes wide.

I nod. "Yeah, I did… you had it coming."

Her mouth drops open and she huffs out another laugh in disbelief, but I see the way her eyes change—darkening, lids lowering—just like the other night in the truck. She's thinking about kissing me… maybe more.

I'd bet money on it.

To preoccupy myself, I take the Velcro closure of my gloves and rip it open, freeing one hand and then the other, before working on hers.

She barks out another laugh as she uses her freed hand to brush wayward strands of hair out of her face. “I think I had some pent-up aggression to get out,” she admits on a huff. “That felt good. Not the hitting you part.” Biting down on her bottom lip, she fights back another laugh. “But the sparring part… that was just what I needed.”

Her words of *pent-up aggression* and *need* are going straight to my dick, which is entirely too close to her to be getting hard. At this proximity, she’d feel it… she’d know exactly how much I want her.

That intense connection from the other night is back and I feel something in my chest pull, like it’s tangling with something inside her, pulling me to her.

“I, uh,” she hesitates for a moment, her eyes boring into mine. “I wanted to say that I’m sorry for kissing you… I crossed a line and it was really—”

“Fucking great,” I tell her, cutting off her bullshit apology. I was hoping she’d bring it up, but only because I wanted to do it again and tell her how much I love kissing her… touching her, being near her. When she leaned across the cab of the truck and kissed my cheek, I lost my mind. I’m also confident if we’d have kept it up and her phone hadn’t rang, I would’ve had her in my lap, grinding on my dick in no time.

I wanted her.

I still want her.

Her cheeks tinge pink as she looks away.

“Tempest,” I demand, gently taking her chin and turning her gaze back to me. “It was more than great… best kiss of my life.”

The blush on her cheeks deepens and she swallows hard.

“Don’t overthink this,” I say, barely above a whisper, leaning toward her and praying to God she lets me do what I want—what I need. “And before you say anything, we can still be friends and kiss… lots of friends kiss.”

Smirking, I get a small smile from her and lean my forehead into hers, breathing her in.

A second later, her hands come up to my chest and she grips my T-shirt in her fists, taking some deep breaths.

"What are you thinking?" I ask, not wanting to mess this up because I love being this close to her, feeling her body against mine, but I'm going to go fucking crazy if I can't touch her. But I won't if she doesn't want me to, so she's going to have to say something, either putting me out of my misery or pouring cold water over my heated body.

"I'm thinking I want you," she murmurs, her voice barely audible, but I heard her… and I heard the need in her tone. It mirrors my own and I want nothing more than to give her what she needs.

Running my nose along her cheek and over to her ear, I lower my voice and tell her, "In three seconds, I'm going to kiss you. If you don't want me to, you should walk away now. No harm, no foul. However," I pause, nipping at her ear and loving how her entire body shivers in response, "if you stay, I plan on devouring you. I have four hours until I have to be at work and I'll spend every second worshipping your body… if you'll let me."

She stills and I'm afraid I've crossed the line and she's about to bolt, but then she practically melts into my arms. Her body feels amazing against mine, sending thousands of feelings and sensations all at once as she presses against me.

"I want you too," she whispers, her tone sounding relieved at the admittance, like it's something she's been holding inside for too long and needed to get out.

Breathing against her soft skin, drinking her in, I move my lips to hers and kiss her.

Hard.

Tempest meets me beat for beat as our mouths collide. Her hands go from gripping my T-shirt to gripping my shoulders as she uses me for leverage to get closer. Sliding my palms down her body, I cup her ass and hoist her up. She never breaks the kiss. I'm not sure she even realizes her feet are no longer on the ground as I carry her toward the stairs.

That intense, crazy feeling from our first kiss quadruples as her arms move around my neck and her hands glide into my hair… her breasts—those luscious mounds I've dreamt about—pressed against my chest.

I need her.

Naked.

Now.

CHAPTER 21

TEMPEST

I'm dreaming.

This has to be a dream, right? Because, only in my dreams would I be lying in Cage's bed, watching him undress. Only in my dreams would a man's body be so incredibly perfect. Only in my dreams would I be naked and ready for him without any inhibitions.

And, yet, here I am.

And I've never wanted a man or to be with a man more.

Even when I was with Asher, we either kept the lights off or had sex under the covers. I was comfortable with him, but I didn't feel sexy or beautiful or powerful. I assume I turned him on but he never made me feel desired.

Cage makes me feel all those things and more and we haven't even gotten to the good stuff yet.

After Cage carried me to his room, he carefully undressed me before laying me down, allowing me a front-row seat to his undressing. Where he was quick to remove my clothes, he's taking his damn time taking off his own and it's driving me crazy.

I'm pretty sure he knows it, too.

His eyes haven't left mine and I feel like I could come from his gaze alone. I've seen him with his shirt off, but only briefly and not like this.

"Like what you see?" he asks, and I can't hold back the disbelieving laugh that leaves my mouth. It's teetering on unstable. I want to pinch myself… or slap myself… or yell, "*What the hell are you doing, Tempest?*"

If I was in the business of answering myself, I'd yell back, "*CAGE ERICKSON. And don't you mess it up for me!*"

When Cage pushes his loose-fitting shorts to the floor—his boxers with them—and stands up, the laugh dries up on my tongue like a raisin in the sun. My mouth suddenly feels parched—all the fluid in my body rushing straight between my legs.

Squeezing my thighs together, I try not to gape at him and his… cock.

Have I ever thought that word before?

It's now my second favorite C word. The first being its owner.

"Get out of that pretty little head of yours," Cage says, his voice low as he swipes his thumb across his bottom lip, looking like an erotic advertisement for everything manly and good in the world.

"I… uh," I stutter, opening and closing my mouth as I try to get my wits about me.

Between the way my body is responding to him without a single touch and how vulnerable and exposed, yet wanted, I feel, I might combust.

Cage wraps his hands around my ankles, gently at first, stroking my legs up to my knees as he takes me in… and I let him. There's nowhere to hide, and somehow, I'm okay with that.

Better than okay.

I love it.

When his hands slide back down to my ankles, he grips and pulls, bringing me to the edge of the bed and mere inches away from his cock being exactly where I want it. I'm about to ask him to just put it in when he drops to his knees at the foot of the bed.

"Wha? What are you doing?" I ask, swallowing hard as I brace myself for the unknown.

Cage is so tall that even kneeling he still towers over me. "I told you, beautiful… I'm going to devour you." His words are deeper than usual, almost a growl, and I'm still trying to comprehend them and the fact he just referred to me as *beautiful*, when his mouth descends on me.

"Oh...oh, my God… Cage." I don't know whether to breathe or scream or lose my ever-loving mind, because his mouth is… "Oh… my… God." My hands instinctively go to him, reaching and grabbing for anything to hold onto, to draw him closer as his tongue flicks and licks at my clit making my hips rise off the bed.

Asher never did this, and he was the only man I've ever been with. I thought it was fictional, something women made up or only happened in pornos.

Cage's hands circle my waist and he pulls me even further down the bed. His nose nudges at my opening… and then his tongue strokes up and down.

Oh, my God.

My legs begin to shake and Cage's large hands move to my thighs, holding me open, giving him even more access to my most intimate parts. When he releases one of my thighs and slips not one, but two fingers inside, curling them up and pumping them inside as his tongue circles my clit, the tiny ledge I've been clinging to slips out of my grasp and I fall. When I scream his name as my orgasm surges, I honestly can't believe this is happening to me.

It's sublime—otherworldly—and I had no idea it could be like this.

My head feels like it's floating in a cloud.

"Are you alright?" Cage asks, his face coming into view as I lazily open my eyes. I'm Jell-O. My bones have turned to mush and I'll have to spend the rest of my days just oozing through life.

I swallow, mentally taking inventory, and a small smile creeps up on my face. "I'm… fantastic. That was… I don't know. I thought stuff like that only happened in pornos," I blurt out, still reeling from the best orgasm of my life.

"Wait," Cage says, bracing his arms on either side of my head as he hovers above me. "No one has ever gone down on you?"

I shake my head once. "Nope. That was, uh… that was my first and it was fucking amazing."

His expression shifts from something that resembles anger to an unmistakable cocky smirk.

"I don't know whether I want to beat the shit out of your past partners—"

"Partner," I correct. "I've only had… one." I won't say his name because I don't want to taint this moment with the mention of him.

"Then I'm glad I'm the only one who's ever given you pleasure like that, even though you should've been given it time and time again… over," he says, leaning down and kissing my jaw. "And over." He drops an open-mouthed kiss to my neck. "And over." This time, his lips find my breast and he sucks a nipple into his mouth and lights my body on fire.

It doesn't take much. The inferno is still blazing from my orgasm. Something about Cage's mouth on me makes me lose all control. I can't think or overthink or second-guess. All I can do is give into to the tidal wave of emotions and just feel.

"I want you," I tell him, wrapping my arms around his neck and holding his head to my chest.

I want him in every sense of the word.

I've wanted him since the first time I laid eyes on him, even in my drunken, damaged state, it was like something deep inside me called to him… or maybe it was something inside of him that called to me.

"Please, Cage," I groan, loving the way his body feels as he lowers himself on top of me, pressing his body against mine. The weight of him… the feel of our skin touching… I want to stay in this moment forever, right here in limbo between the best orgasm I've ever had and whatever is coming next.

CHAPTER 22

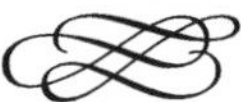

CAGE

I'm not even inside Tempest yet and I already feel as though I'm about to lose control.

God, this woman.

Tasting her was something I've been dreaming about for so long and now that I've done it—felt her writhe beneath me and scream my name as an orgasm wrecked her body—I don't know how I'm going to stop. I've moved from her pussy to her tits and everywhere in between and I'm still starving for her.

"Please, Cage. I need you," Tempest groans, her body mirroring her words, begging for more.

Fuck, she sounds as desperate as I feel and I love it.

I'm still covering her body with nips, licks, and kisses because I can't get enough of her but, also, as a distraction. It's been a while since I've been with a woman and I'm so fucking turned on, it's possible I'll blow my load as soon as the tip of my dick is inside her and that's simply unacceptable.

I made a promise I was going to devour her and take my time doing it and I plan on never breaking a promise to Tempest.

There's not a chance in the world I won't enjoy every moment we're together, but I want it to be even better for her. I want to erase every bad experience she's had and show her how good this can be. I can't fucking believe her asshole of an ex denied her the pleasure she deserves, but that shit stops now.

I'll gladly take care of her needs.

Once I feel a bit more in control of my body, I sit back on my knees and just look at her. Her body is flushed and primed for me, glistening in all the right places.

"You're the most beautiful woman I've ever seen," I tell her and it's the absolute truth. It's like she was fucking made for me, designed with my desires in mind, even though she's nothing like anyone I've ever been with before. She's different in every way, the best ways.

Her stunning red hair, plump lips, penetrating green eyes—I've been attracted to those since day one. Now that I've seen the rest—her perfectly placed curves and luscious tits… a pussy I could feast at for days—I'm fucking gone. Done.

I can feel her eyes on me as I lean over and grab a condom out of my bedside drawer, hoping she doesn't ask me why I have them, because I'd have to be honest and tell her I'd hoped that things would progress with our *friendship*, and I wanted to be prepared.

I bought them with her, and only her, in mind.

Locking my eyes on hers, I rip the package open and take the condom out, discarding the foil and positioning the latex at the tip of my cock. Her green eyes widen and then go hooded as I roll the latex down my length, gripping my shaft and then stroking back up, pinching the tip.

When she visibly swallows and then trails a hand across her stomach, inching toward her sweet pussy, I close my eyes and bite down on my lip, willing myself to get the fuck under control.

Deep breaths.

"Cage," she whispers, making me open my eyes back up and I see the hesitation on her beautiful face and I want to shut that shit down, so I lean forward, positioning my face inches from hers.

"You're so fucking perfect, Tempest… I want to make this good for you," I tell her, pressing my cock against her so she can feel just how hard and ready I am for her. "You do this to me, every fucking day…

every time I think of you. Do you know how bad I want you? It's all I can do right now not to come on contact." I lean closer and take her mouth with mine as I stroke my cock against her wet center, sliding between the lips of her pussy.

She moans into my mouth and I can't take it any longer.

I have to be inside her.

Holding my weight on one arm, I slip my other one between us and replace my cock with my middle finger, running it up and down her slit and then stroking my cock. When I position it at her opening, I pull back enough to lock eyes with her. I want to see her and I want her to see me.

This is us, Tempest, and we're great together.

When I feel her tense a little as I start to push inside, I brush her cheek with my lips, whispering in her ear. "Breathe… relax… eyes on me." Just like earlier, when we were sparring, after a few seconds, she does as I instruct. Her thighs fall open, giving me freedom to move.

Slowly, I start to thrust… once, twice…

Holy fuck.

For the first time in my life, I'm thankful for the thin latex barrier, because without it, I would be coming like a freight train.

Tempest is perfect.

Her body fits mine like a fucking glove and I feel like I've died and gone to heaven. When she cries out and grabs my shoulders, it brings me back to the moment and out of my head.

"You okay?" I ask, my body already glistening with sweat as my muscles contract. Fighting off an orgasm takes work, but I'm determined to make this last.

She releases my shoulders and wraps her arms around my neck, taking a deep breath before responding. "Never better," she says, her voice a bit shaky.

"You're so fucking perfect," I tell her, my own words becoming breathless and choppy as I continue to move inside her. "You know that?" Nuzzling my nose into the crook of her neck, I lick and kiss, feeling completely overwhelmed by her—tasting her, feeling her, hearing her, being inside her. It's too much and not enough all at the same time. "So fucking good."

"You," she starts, but stops, sucking in a breath as I shift my hips and change positions, rubbing against her clit. "Oh… God… you feel… amazing… so good… best… ever." Her words are choppy and strung together with moans and cries but they take my ego to all new heights.

I can't help the smirk against her cheek and I know she must feel it because she laughs breathlessly. "I would make a joke about your head getting big, but… ahhhh," she cries, panting as she grips my shoulders and I thrust harder, faster. "It's big enough… so big."

Oh, fuck, yes.

"Tell me more," I say, pushing myself above her, letting my hips and thighs do all the work.

Her arms stretch out, grabbing fistfuls of the blanket beneath her.

The look on her face is pure bliss and I'm feeling like the smuggest bastard on earth, knowing I did that… I'm doing that. I'm making her feel good. It's the headiest feeling. I could get addicted to it, to her… she's like the best drug.

Sitting back on my heels, I pull her body up, gripping her waist and pounding into her. We've had gentle and slow, but I'm ready to feel her walls spasm around my dick. I need her to come again, just in case I don't last much longer.

"Oh, God… Cage," she screams and I fucking love it. I love that she's screaming my name and not afraid to express herself. It's sexy as hell. "I'm gonna come." She swallows back a cry and her eyes squeeze shut as another orgasm hits her, making her entire body tremble.

Slowing my pace, I allow her to ride it out, milking my dick in the process.

Dead puppies.

817-222-4561

$x = -b \pm \sqrt{b^2\text{-}4ac/2a}$

3.14159265

"Cage?" she asks, her voice tentative and breathy. When I feel her hand touch my chest, her fingers trailing down my six-pack to the base of my cock, I stop breathing.

"Fuck."

She huffs out a laugh and I feel the vibration in my dick. "You did that already," she says coyly.

"Oh, beautiful… I'm not done with you yet," I tell her, slipping my cock out of her and flipping her onto her stomach. "On your knees."

The wide-eyed look she gives me over her shoulder makes me think this might be something else she's never experienced. What the fuck was that douchebag doing? He should have his dick surgically removed and given to someone who wants to use it properly.

"On your knees," I repeat, giving her amazing ass a light slap.

She huffs out a laugh but follows my command, pushing herself up on her hands and knees. "Like this?"

"Just like that."

I could come in any position. Shit, I've been holding off since she practically climbed me like a tree downstairs, but I want to be deep inside her when I do. And I'm pretty confident I can give her one more orgasm from this position. "Brace yourself," I warn, lining my cock up with her opening and sliding in, nice and slow.

Tempest moans, throwing her head back, her red hair in disarray against her creamy, white skin.

Looking down to where we're joined, I can't take my eyes off my dick moving in and out of her. "You like that?" I ask, loving the sounds she's making and wanting more of them… more of her.

With one hand gripping her hip firmly, I glide my other up her soft back and twist it into her silky hair. "Tell me, Tempest… I want to hear you."

"Ahh," she cries out as I gently pull on her hair, bringing my mouth down to her ear. "So…" I thrust harder. "Fucking…" My balls begin to tighten and the intense tingle starts at the base of my back, radiating up my spine. "Good." She exhales loudly—part moan, part cry. "I'm going to come… I'm…"

"Touch yourself, Tempest," I instruct, closing my eyes and letting the sensation wash over me. "Touch yourself… come with me."

A few seconds later, my climax shoots through me—earth-shattering and mind-blowing—leaving me gasping for breath with a death grip on Tempest's ass as I hold her to me. Her body, in return, is trembling again beneath my touch and I lean forward, peppering her back with light kisses, tasting the saltiness of her sweat.

I feel her arms and legs begin to give out, so I roll over onto my back and take her with me.

"That was…" she starts, but can't finish.

Brushing her sweaty hair off her face, I kiss her cheek and then her neck. "I'll be right back," I tell her, slipping out of the bed and walking over to the bathroom to toss the condom and grab a warm washcloth for her, but when I get back to the bed, she's out.

Not like gone, but passed out… asleep.

I would think she's faking it, maybe to avoid an awkward conversation, but her heavy breathing tells me she's really and truly asleep.

The cocky smirk on my face is inevitable. "Well, Miss Cassidy," I whisper, crawling back onto the bed and curling up beside her. "I must confess… this is a first for me."

As I glance over at the clock on my nightstand, I see I have a couple hours before I need to get around for work, so I decide a midday nap after the best fuck of my life doesn't sound so shabby. Grabbing my phone, I set an alarm and wrap my arm around Tempest's waist, pulling her as close as possible and drifting off into the best sleep I've had in a long time.

When I hear the obnoxious beeping from my phone, I instinctively reach over to press snooze, but then I remember… Tempest, amazing sex… but my arms that were full of the most beautiful woman on the planet are now empty, as is the opposite side of the bed.

Sitting up, I look around the open space and start to panic when Tempest walks out of the bathroom, fully dressed.

I know before she even says anything that she's either regretting what happened or she's feeling embarrassed about it and I hate both options.

"Hey," I say, climbing out of the bed and walking toward her.

The intense blush on her cheeks travels all the way down her neck and now I know, it doesn't end there, and it's all I can do to keep my hands to myself and not get her naked again so I can see just how far it goes.

"Hey," she replies, pushing a strand of hair behind her ear. "It's, uh… almost five and I thought… well, I was just going to go." Her brows pull together and she licks her bottom lip nervously.

"No," I tell her and I mean it for more than just her suggestion to leave, especially without telling me or waking me. I mean it for everything. She doesn't need to feel nervous or embarrassed or weird. This is still us, and regardless of what happened, we're still friends. "Let me get dressed and I'll take you home on my way to work."

"I can just walk," she says, stepping around me to grab her shoes.

Shaking my head, I bite down on my lip and growl. "Tempest." As I pinch the bridge of my nose and turn to face her, she's leaning down slipping her shoes on and not looking at me. "Look at me… please."

Finally, she tilts her head back up and I walk toward her. Grabbing my shorts, I slip them on, letting them hang at my waist, but at least my cock is covered, and I can have this conversation without my balls hanging out.

"Don't do this, okay?" I ask, sitting on the edge of the bed and pulling her to stand between my legs. "I know you're overthinking this and probably going in a million different directions, but nothing has to change, okay?"

She nods and swallows, but averts her eyes over my shoulder.

"I'm going to need some verbal communication."

Huffing, she rolls her eyes and fights back a small smile. "Okay, no weirdness."

"Zero," I tell her, pulling her closer and wrapping my arms around her waist. "The only thing that's changed is I made you come with my tongue… and gave you two more orgasms."

Her eyes go wide and she laughs, the tension between us dissolving. "Oh, my God." She tries to hide her face in her hands, but I don't let her. Instead, I take her wrists in my hands and put her arms behind her back, bringing her close enough so I can kiss her.

"And I'm kissing you from now on," I tell her. After a few minutes, I release her hands and stand, placing one last kiss on the top of her head. "Let me take a quick shower and I'll drive you home."

She nods, stepping away. "I'll just go downstairs."

"Stay," I tell her, walking toward the bathroom and dropping my shorts by the door, giving her a nice show. "You can even join me, if you like."

When I glance back over my shoulder, she's standing with her arms crossed, one hand at her mouth as she watches every inch of me. Noticing me watching her watch me, she rolls her eyes and picks up one of my shoes, tossing it in my direction. "Go shower!"

"Such anger… you might need to get that checked."

She laughs, incredulously, chucking the other shoe in my direction just as I shut the door and deflect it.

As I turn the shower on, waiting for it to warm up, it's all I can do to not go back out there and toss her over my shoulder and bring her in here with me. But I can tell she needs time to adjust to this new us, so I'll give it to her.

CHAPTER 23

TEMPEST

Closing the door, I lean against it and take a few deep breaths and give myself a mental pat-down: all my limbs are still attached, I'm breathing, my heart is still in my chest, even though just a few hours ago it felt like it exploded into a million pieces.

What did I do?

I'll tell you what you did, Tempest… you had the best sex of your life. That's what you did.

With. My. Friend.

"Ugh," I groan, dropping my head forward and covering my face. "What was I thinking?"

That's the thing, I wasn't.

From the moment Cage told me he was going to kiss me, my brain shut down and my body took over. It was sublime. Every second of it was mind-blowing. At one point, I didn't know what was up and what was down. I was so wrapped up in Cage and the way he made me feel, I could've died right then and been happy with my life.

Here lies Tempest Cassidy. It took twenty-eight years, but she finally found out what it was like to have multiple orgasms and cunnalingus. And then she died.

Laughing maniacally, I bang my head against the door a couple of times, trying to get the images to stop playing on replay. My body still feels like it's on fire, smoldering from the inside out. How is that even possible?

A cold shower.

That's what I need.

When I inhale, I can still smell him… us. I smell like sex and I'm not hating it, but I need to clear my head and it's not helping. So I'll shower, and then, I'll get dressed and run to the grocery store. After that, maybe I'll stop by Anna and Cole's and check on the baby.

Maybe I should whip up a quick batch of muffins to take over there?

Yeah, that should do the trick.

It's only five thirty and I need to keep myself busy. If I don't, I'll spend the rest of the night overthinking the last few hours and I don't want to do that. I promised Cage no weirdness, but I feel my freak out boiling under the surface, just waiting to erupt, so I'm guessing I won't be able to keep that promise if I don't get out of the house and out of my damn head.

An hour later, when I walk into Cole and Anna's house, it's utter chaos.

Blankets, baby clothes, and diaper cloths are in piles on the floor with random pacifiers strewn about. There's also fast food bags littering the house and I'm tempted to close the door and check the house number to make sure I'm in the right place.

I've never seen Anna's house like this and to be honest, I'm scared. Is this what having a baby does to you? I mean, I know they need a lot of stuff, but I thought all they did was sleep at this age.

Even though the place is a mess, it's quiet, so I continue to walk carefully to the kitchen, placing a box of muffins on the only cleared off counter space I can find.

"Hey, you. We're over here." I jump at the sound of Anna's voice and follow it to the living room where I see the most beautiful sight. In the midst of what looks like a detonated bomb's aftermath is my friend. Her hair looks like a rat's nest and she has bags under her eyes, but she's completely in her element as she nurses her son. She looks so calm and happy.

She's breathtaking.

"Look at you, Mama. You're a pro at this!" I pick up a stack of folded laundry that's close to Anna and move it to the coffee table, sitting in its spot.

"Well, I'm obviously not a pro at multitasking but I really don't care." Her voice is carefree and I cannot believe this is the same Anna I've known all my life. Where's the uptight, judgmental woman who lovingly bosses me around? It sounds crazy, but I kinda miss her.

"You know I can come over here and help with the house stuff, if you want. I don't mind."

She shrugs. "The house will be cleaned one of these days. I can't believe it's not bothering me more than it is, but I'm just really enjoying my time with Matthew. Yeah," she coos, gently stroking his sweet face with the most content smile I've ever seen in my life.

"You can hold him after I burp him, if you'd like."

"Sure." I smile at her.

If I'm being honest with myself, I thought it would be hard being here, surrounded by baby things, when just a few months ago, it was all I wanted. All I could think about. But I'm okay, I really am. Of course, I still want a baby of my own, but I can wait.

In hindsight, I think I was so obsessed with having a baby because I felt like something was missing in my life, but now, I realize that something was love. True, unconditional love. It's like my subconscious knew things weren't good in my marriage long before my conscious mind caught up to speed.

Maybe there were signs.

Maybe I missed them.

Maybe it was intentional.

But now, I'm living life with eyes wide open, and I'm okay with waiting. It'll happen when it's supposed to happen. Deep down, I know I'll be a mom one day and it'll be the best gift I've ever been given. Until then, I'll just dote on this little bundle of joy.

Reaching out, I sweep my hand gently over his soft head.

"He's so small," I whisper. "Are you sure Cole is his daddy?"

Anna chuckles, shaking her head. "Stop."

While she burps the baby and changes him, I go into her kitchen and grab the box of muffins for us to snack on. I also use the opportunity to start a load of dishes in the dishwasher and wipe down the counters before I return to the living room.

"How about you sit," Anna instructs once I'm back. "I'll situate him the way he likes to be held."

I do as she says and soon I have a precious baby sleeping in my arms. *Good gravy, he smells so good.* I always thought it was weird when others would remark about baby smells because I assumed they all smelled like poop or spit up most of the time, but now I get it.

Inhaling deeply, I close my eyes and smile, brushing a kiss on his cheek.

"So, tell me how you've been doing," Anna says, dragging a laundry basket over to the couch and pulling out a tiny little onesie. "I feel like I've missed out on so much lately. Are you still doing your anger management classes?"

I nod, glancing up at her. "Yeah, I'm still going, but I'm almost done with my required sessions."

"Do you think it's helped?" she asks, adding another clean, folded onesie to the pile at her side. "You seem calmer… more at peace."

"I am," I say, taking a deep breath and loving the way Matthew feels in my arms, so snug against my chest. "Gosh, how do you not sleep the day away with him… he's like the best sedative."

"Tell me about it," Anna says with a laugh. "A sleeping baby is better than all the chamomile tea and melatonin in the world combined."

I sigh. "Maybe I'll just come steal him the next time I can't sleep."

"Give us a few more months and he can have a sleepover at Aunt Em's."

"Aunt Em," I coo, looking down at Matthew. "I like the sound of that."

There's a long minute of silence and I know there's something

Anna wants to ask or say, so when I can't stand it any longer, I look up at her. "Spill it."

"What?" she asks in mock confusion, her brows that are typically well-defined fading into her light complexion as they scrunch up. Even without a stitch of makeup on, Anna is still one of the prettiest people I know.

"Whatever you're wanting to say or ask," I tell her.

Her shoulders relax and she places the cotton fabric she's holding in her lap. "Cole said he's seen you around town with that… with Cage." Her eyes lock with mine, an eyebrow raising, and I prepare myself for the typical, holier-than-thou Anna, yet she surprises me once again. She smirks, "Are the two of you… you know?"

The blush on my cheeks is immediate and flashes of my time in Cage's bed come to mind in vivid bursts of imagery. Swallowing, I clear my throat. To tell the truth or not to tell the truth: that is the question. But I've never been one to lie, so I go with, "We're friends."

"And," she encourages.

"Oh, Anna." I huff, trying to keep my voice low so I don't wake the sleeping baby. "You don't want to hear this."

That damn eyebrow raises even higher. "I wouldn't have asked if I didn't."

In my mind, I'm thinking about Cage… on top of me, behind me… between my legs, and the fire in my belly is back. This is so inappropriate with a baby in my arms.

"Tempest," Anna prods.

"Fine," I say, giving in. I could use someone to talk to and she's always been there for me. Sure, some of her advice is a little too pious for my taste, but it always comes from a good place. "We're… a little more than friends. We, uh… well, I kissed him last week and today we… you know," I tell her, using my eyes to tell her what I don't want to say in front of the baby.

"Today?" she asks, and I don't miss the way she leans forward, engaged in the conversation.

"Yeah," I tell her, nodding my head, my eyes wide in affirmation. "It was…," I pause, swallowing. "Well, let's just say, I had more…

you know..." Giving her more nonverbal cues, I know she's picking up on what I'm throwing down from the way her expression changes. "More of *those* in one afternoon than I've had in the last year."

"*Oh*," she says.

"Yeah."

She exhales, folding the blanket she's been holding and letting what I just told her sink in. Then she places it beside her on the couch, starting a new pile, and picks up another pale blue one from the basket. "So, do you think this is…"

"I don't know what it is," I tell her, feeling the freak out from earlier trying to surface. And I'm thankful for the baby in my arms, because he's keeping me calm… and centered. "It's all so new and different," I whisper, keeping my eyes on Matthew as I pour out my soul. "I was with Asher for so many years. He was my first everything. No one had ever seen me... *like that* besides him, until today. And it was so… different. I felt different. Not weird different, but good different. Even before the cheating, there was always something off when Asher and I were together. But it wasn't until I was with Cage today that I even noticed it. You know, when you don't have anything to compare something to, you just accept it for what it is and assume it's normal. But never, in all of the years I was with Asher, did I feel the way I did today."

When I stop for a breath, I glance up to see her watching me so intently. "And how did you feel?" she asks.

I can't believe I'm saying this to Anna of all people, but I am. "Sexy, desired… wanted…" I drift off and bite down on my lip at the way he spoke to me. "He called me beautiful."

"Every woman should feel that way," Anna says and it shocks me. "Oh, don't look at me like that. I'm a woman too, you know. Just because I don't talk about it doesn't mean I don't like sex."

When I cover Matthew's ears, Anna laughs.

"Stop," she says with the most carefree expression that for a split-second I wonder where my friend went. Is this a case of the body snatchers? Have we had an alien invasion? "I know I was pretty unbearable before the baby, but hormones can really do a number on you."

You think?

Her expression turns more solemn and she furrows those expressive brows, clasping her hands in front of her. "But Tempest," she says gently, like she's getting ready to break some bad news and I brace myself as she tilts her head to the side. "Don't just jump into bed with the first guy that comes along and calls you beautiful. You *are* beautiful. And you don't need a man to tell you that." Sighing, she pauses. "Don't give your heart away too soon. It'll just set you up for more heartbreak and I don't want that for you."

I ignore the twinge in my chest.

"And I'm not as delusional as your mama," she continues. "I know that you would never be able to trust Asher again, so I'm not praying y'all back together. I stopped that a long time ago."

Did she just call my mama delusional?

I can't disagree with that.

Matthew squirms in my arms and I shift to hold him a little closer, rocking until he settles back into a deep sleep.

"I've been doing some reading on moving on after a divorce," she tells me and my head pops up. "What? I'm your best friend and I needed to be educated so I know how to help you navigate this time of your life."

Looking down at the baby, I roll my eyes and have to fight back the urge to whisper to him that his mama is crazy, but it's okay, because his Aunt Em will be here to be his voice of reason.

"Rebounds are typical," she continues. "They're normal… Even though I'm not an advocate of sex outside of marriage, I understand the need to… *get back in the saddle.* Your confidence was shattered and you need to get that back. I get that. So, let this just be that… a rebound."

A rebound.

It's not a foreign thought to me. Actually, it's something that's been niggling in my brain for a while, but I've shut it down, because I've been telling myself that Cage and I are friends. Which we are. But now that we've crossed the line, I don't know what to think and I'm afraid that we won't be able to go back and that sucks.

Tears prick my eyes and I blink them back, not even sure where they came from or why I'm feeling so emotional. I sniffle and lean forward to kiss Matthew's hair, breathing him in.

"Oh, honey," Anna coos, like I'm the baby. She walks over and wraps an arm around my shoulder and hugs me to her… again, so un-Anna.

I make a mental note to call Cole when I leave and make sure she doesn't need some medication. Some women suffer from postpartum depression. Is there such a thing as postpartum cheerfulness? Because she's kind of freaking me out.

But I don't shrug off her hug, instead, I lean into it.

That's what else I loved about today… just the contact, having someone hold me. I've missed that and I didn't even realize how much until I was in Cage's arms. It just felt… right.

"You're going to get through this," she whispers, squeezing into the seat beside me. The three of us—me, her, and Matthew—in a group hug. "I'm sure your heart and head are both confused, but it's all going to be okay. You'll figure it out and move on, and one of these days, the right man will walk into your life. You'll see."

I want to tell her that Cage is that perfect person, but I don't even know if he's looking for something that permanent. For all I know, I could just be a casual fuck. He doesn't seem like the type of person who sleeps around, but do I even know him that well?

Earlier today, when I got to the studio, I walked in on the tail end of a conversation he was having with one of his brothers. I heard him say he'd be home soon.

Stupid me for letting myself fall for someone who has no plans of sticking around.

Stupid me for making something more out of this than it is.

Stupid me for opening my heart up to someone who was just going to walk out… again.

Later, that night, when I'm back in my apartment and lying in bed, trying to sleep, my mind is a black hole I can't escape. Thoughts of my time with Cage mix and mingle with Anna's words and my own fears and uncertainty. It's a horrible combination and keeps me awake most of the night.

When I can't take it any longer, I grab my phone and think about calling Cage, but that's when I realize, I don't even have his phone number.

I had sex with him… three orgasms… and he had his head between my legs, but I don't even have his telephone number.

Then my thoughts turn to where he is and what he's doing and the gross, unwelcome feeling creeps over me.

Can I trust him?

Is he screwing other people?

Have I ever even asked him about his past relationships?

What are his plans?

My heart begins to beat rapidly and I have to sit up in bed and take deep breaths. When that doesn't work to calm my nerves or my mind, I climb out of bed and start going through some Tai Chi movements Cage has taught me. Starting simple, I roll my head to the side and then around in one slow motion before stretching my back as I bend down and touch my toes.

Moving my arms and legs in the fluid motions eventually brings me some peace.

What I've loved about this martial art since Cage first started teaching me is that it has purpose and flow. Moving into the single whip, I bring my arms up and out at shoulder height, one hand curved into a beak hand. From there, I move into a white crane, balancing my weight on one leg and then kicking with the other.

Better.

Deep breaths.

Even if Cage is a rebound.

Even if he goes back to Dallas and forgets all about me.

I'll be okay.

Maybe what Anna was saying is true. Maybe I'm feeling so invested in him and our relationship because I'm craving the closeness.

Maybe my feelings for Cage have nothing to do with him and everything to do with me.

There's a small voice in my head—and a feeling in my heart—telling me I'm wrong and it's bigger than that. I feel like he came into my life at the right time and that we were meant to meet, and I think we're good together.

But there was a time when I thought Asher and I were good together.

And I see how that turned out.

When I realize there's no chance I'm going to get any sleep, I shower again, make a cup of coffee and drink it while I go ahead and dress. I might as well get a head start on the muffins for the day.

**SM*

It's almost four when I walk out of my apartment and start walking down the street. Not for the first time since I moved into the apartment and started walking to work, I find myself checking my back, but there's not a soul out at this time of the morning.

All the lights are out down the block. Cage's entire building is dark.

Is he losing sleep?

Is he laying there thinking about me?

Do his sheets smell like me… us?

I almost skip the bakery and walk to Cage's instead, but stop myself. I really do need to get some muffins going and I also need time to think and sort through my feelings. And hopefully, not be weird the next time I see Cage.

Unlocking the bakery door, I walk to the back and flip on some lights. Breathing deeply, I love the sweet smell that always lingers here. This is definitely my happy place and I throw myself into baking and creating, coming up with a perfect Muffin of the Day.

Crazy—loaded with nuts (all puns intended) and chunks of dark chocolate.

After a couple hours of baking like crazy, the open sign of the bakery gets turned on and my mind is feeling better, less frazzled and more focused.

It's a busy morning from the get-go, a couple customers were actually waiting for the door to be unlocked and it hasn't slowed down since. So, when the door chimes and I'm unloading another tray of muffins into the display, I call out, "Good morning! Welcome to Donner Bakery!"

"Good morning." Cage's deep, smooth voice makes me snap my head up in his direction, my heart practically jumping out of my throat.

"Hey," I manage to say without sounding too off. Hopefully.

He smiles, scratching at the back of his head. "Hey…"

"Can I get you something?"

Checking the case, he peruses the options. "What's the Muffin of the Day?"

Clearing my throat, I lick my suddenly dry lips. "*Crazy*… loaded with nuts and chunks of dark chocolate."

The look he gives me over the top of the display case is downright sinful. He should be arrested for giving a look like that. Earlier, during my baking session, I'd convinced myself that I needed to try to get back to just being Cage's friend. That's a safer zone for me to be in and there's a lot less risk of getting my heart broken if and when he leaves. But now, I'm not so sure.

Maybe there is no going back.

"Crazy, huh?" he asks, a lazy smirk on his face. "Are you feeling crazy, Tempest?" His voice is a low whisper, meant only for me, but I can't help looking around to see if anyone else overheard. It's not the question he asked so much as the tone he used—seductive, like liquid sex.

"Uh, yeah," I say, probably a little too loud, now that I think about it. Laughing nervously, I brush some hair behind my ear. "It's got that perfect… crunch and hint of salt from the, uh, nuts… mixed with the bite from the dark chocolate… ninety percent cacao… full of antioxidants. I mean, it's basically a health food… Crazy, huh?"

"So crazy," he says, but I feel like his words hold a double entendre. "Can we talk?"

I nod, but my feet stay frozen in place behind the counter… my safety zone.

"Maybe outside… or over at that table," he suggests, pointing to an empty table in the corner by the window.

"Okay," I agree, making eye contact with Mikey and motioning over my shoulder. "I'll be back in five minutes."

Cage and I sit and he reaches across the table and takes my hand. I have to force myself to not close my eyes from the sensation of his skin on mine, which *is crazy*. You'd think after yesterday, I'd be used to it… maybe would've built up some sort of immunity, but no. I crave it more. Now that I've had the full dose, a measly little hand hold won't do.

"Hey," Cage says, getting my attention. "You okay?"

Yes.

No.

"Sure," I say, giving him a small smile. "Why?"

He cocks his head to the side and looks at me speculatively. "You didn't say much yesterday when I dropped you off. I thought about you all night… even drove by your apartment when I got off work, but I couldn't tell if you had any lights on or not, so I circled the block and went home." Breathing in deeply, he puffs his chest up and then exhales. "I just don't want you to think anything has to change between us, because it hasn't. Don't freak out or stress, okay?"

I swallow down the small lump in my throat.

Why does he have to be so damn intuitive and in my fucking head?

"The ball is in your court," he adds, squeezing my hand to bring my eyes back to his. "Your pace… okay?"

"Okay," I finally say, feeling a little of the tension I've been carrying around since yesterday dissipate.

"The reunion is this Friday, right?" he asks. "We're still on for that?"

I smile, grateful for the shift in conversation and for him just being… Cage. He's wonderful and I'm reminded of how grateful I am that above all else, he's my friend.

"We're still on," I confirm.

"Anything I need to know?" he asks.

I shrug, trying to think of anything I should tell him. "I was going to have to walk onto the field with Asher," I tell him. I'd kind of forgot about it, but a few days ago, I got an email from the planning committee that plans had changed. "It's tradition that the king and queen from the ten-year reunion class presents the crowns to the current king and queen."

"So what happened?"

"I guess Mindy decided she didn't want me that close to her husband."

Cage's look of disgust makes me laugh. "This whole situation is so fucking twisted," he mutters. "On one hand, I want to beat the shit out of him for what he's done to you, and on the other, I want to buy him a fucking beer."

"Well, he's not worth either… the ass-whipping or the beer, so don't waste your time."

"Would you have done it, if they hadn't changed their minds?" he asks, curiosity thick in his tone.

Thinking for a second, I reply honestly. "I was married to him for eight years. What's five minutes?"

"So you're going to be okay seeing him and Mindy together at the reunion?"

Smiling, I quirk an eyebrow. "Are you worried I'm going to embarrass you?"

"No," he says adamantly. "I just need to know if I should bring bail money."

CHAPTER 24

CAGE

I haven't been to a Friday night football game in several years.

Ozzi and Gunnar both played when they were in high school, but none of the rest of us ever played. Even though football is life in Texas, I was so dedicated to kickboxing and martial arts I never had the time. I spent nearly every single evening in the dojo or gym. Viggo and Vali were also gym rats, following in our father's footsteps and putting on the gloves at an early age.

But I've been to my fair share of football games, so this should feel familiar.

However, tonight, I'm feeling anxious. Not so much for me, but for Tempest. I get why she wants to go—needs to go—but it doesn't mean I like it. There's a protectiveness inside me when it comes to her that knows no bounds. After the amazing sex we had the other day, those feelings have only grown stronger. I wish I could shield her from all the bad shit in the world—past, present, and future—but I know I can't.

I can only be there for her, be her friend, which is what I'm going to do.

Pulling up in front of her building, I turn the truck off and hop out.

I haven't been inside Tempest's apartment yet. When I drove her home the other day, she insisted I just drop her off, and since I needed to get to work, I did as she asked.

But tonight, I feel the need to walk up to her door like a proper gentleman.

When I knock on her door, Tempest opens almost immediately.

Her hair is pulled up in a ponytail, making her look so much younger than her twenty-eight years. The freckles on her nose and those fucking green eyes on full display, my cock stands at attention. "Ready?" she asks, a plaid blanket draped over her arm.

Fuck yeah, I'm ready.

Ready to take her back to my bed.

Ready to fuck her senseless right here on these stairs.

Ready to push her up against the wall and claim those sweet lips.

But I remind myself, and my dick, that I'm here tonight as her friend. "Yeah," I say, stepping aside to let her by. She pauses long enough to shut her door, sticking a key into the deadbolt and locking it. "My dad insists I use the deadbolt," she says with an annoyed expression and a shake of her head. "I think he forgets I'm an adult sometimes."

"Well, I'm fully aware you're an adult and I'm with your dad," I tell her, following her down the stairs and appreciating the view from behind. "Lock the deadbolt."

Once we pull up to the field, I drive around until I find a place to park.

Putting the truck in park, I turn it off, but Tempest doesn't reach for the door, so I sit and wait, letting her take the lead. "You good?" I ask, reaching over to take her hand.

She allows me to thread our fingers together and I'm grateful for the small contact. All I've been able to think about is her—her body, her sounds, her taste. I want to tell her how much I want her and need her… how much I crave her, but I don't want to scare her off, so I'm going to let her come to me.

"Yeah," she eventually says, her eyes glued to our hands.

"Do I have any rules… anything I should or shouldn't do?" I ask, wanting to know my boundaries. Because if she doesn't want me to touch her or show her affection, I'm going to need to know that now.

"No," she says quietly. "I don't think so."

"So, it's okay if I want to hold your hand?"

She gives me a small smile, nodding her head. "Yeah… I guess that'd be okay."

"What about kissing you?"

Her blush tells me she's probably not much into PDA, so I don't push it.

"Okay, hand holding," I tell her. "And maybe I can slip an arm around your shoulder and cop a feel?"

Covering her face with her free hand, she tilts her head back and laughs.

"Hand holding… like we're back in third grade," I mutter. "Got it."

"You held hands with girls in third grade?" she asks, turning to face me.

It's my turn to smirk—a cocky, self-assured, you-don't-even-want-to-know smirk.

"I didn't even kiss a boy until I was in the tenth grade," she admits.

Inwardly, I cringe. "Let me guess, Asher?"

She nods, biting down on her lip and averting her gaze to the floor.

"Hey," I say, reaching over and tilting her chin up so she's looking at me. "You don't have anything to be embarrassed or ashamed of, okay? Everybody is different and I like who you are, regardless of your past. If anyone has anything to be ashamed of, it's Mindy and Asher, got it?"

"Got it."

"Alright," I say, opening my door. "Let's go watch some football and give these people something to talk about." She laughs, and instead of exiting out the passenger door, she slides over and follows me out of the truck, our hands immediately joining back together.

I feel her squeeze my hand a little tighter as we approach the gate, and I get the feeling she's holding my hand for moral support more than anything else, and I'm reminded once again of my role.

Friend.

Part of me wants to ask her if she feels like having sex with me was a mistake, but I'm not sure I want to know the answer. The way she freaked out wasn't unexpected. I should've seen it coming. She's guarded her heart so closely since the day we met. It shouldn't surprise me that us giving into our desires would cause her some distress.

The mind can be a scary place.

All I want is for her to not try to put what we have in a box. We don't have to just be friends. We can be friends and more. But if she's not ready, I understand… and I'll wait.

Following her lead, she guides us to the bleachers and I see her take a deep breath before she releases my hand and makes her way to a sectioned off portion of the stadium.

Welcome Class of 2009

"Tempest," a woman with platinum blonde hair says, as we take a few steps into the reserved section. "I was wondering if you'd show." Her blue eyes bounce between us scrupulously. "Who's your... *friend*?"

I feel Tempest tense, her spine going rigid. Placing my hand gently at the small of her back, I non-verbally tell her everything she needs to know.

I'm here.

I've got your back.

"This is Cage… Erickson," Tempest says, glancing briefly over her shoulder and giving me a tentative, but grateful smile.

"I don't believe we've had the pleasure," Blondie says, reaching around Tempest to shake my hand. "I'm Stella Wilson, Class of 2009 class secretary and captain of the cheer squad. Go Pirates!"

Choking back my laugh, I cover it with a cough and then finally shake her hand so I don't make this any weirder than it already is. "Nice to meet you."

"So, Tempest tells me you're from out of town," she continues, her eyes all over me. "What brings you to Green Valley?"

"I work at the Pink Pony," I tell her, hoping that will effectively shut her up so we can move to our seats and away from her. She's poison. My bullshit detector is usually spot on, and without Tempest even telling me anything about Stella, I could probably describe her perfectly.

If I had to guess, she's probably always walked around with her nose in the air, thinking her shit doesn't stink. When in reality, she's insecure, so she has to make other people feel weak in order for her to feel strong. She preys on those she views as less than her. And unlike ninety percent of society, who move on from high school and realize none of that shit mattered, she's stuck there.

Those were her glory days and she's taking up permanent residency.

Stella's expression changes and a look of complete and utter disgust paints her fake-ass features. Pulling her hand back, she not so discreetly wipes it down the leg of her over-priced jeans. Batting her obviously glued on lashes, she says, "There are a few seats up there." Pointing to the top of the bleachers. "Enjoy the game."

Giving her a smirk I hope conveys what I can't say, like *suck a dick*, I nudge Tempest. "Let's go… I need a better view."

When we finally settle into a seat, sitting on the blanket Tempest brought, I ask, "So where is he?"

"Who?" Her eyes are on the field, watching the game, or at least pretending to.

"You know who," I mutter, not wanting to draw the attention of anyone sitting around us since we're packed in like sardines.

Sitting up a little straighter, she cranes her neck, sweeping her gaze one way and then the other, before groaning quietly. Leaning over, she points her finger to the right. "There," she says. "Three rows down… dark hair… popped collar."

Looking like the douchebag he is. I can't see his face, but when he turns to follow a play, I catch a side profile. He kind of looks familiar. Maybe I've passed him at the Piggly Wiggly or when I've been out on a run. This is a small town, there's a good chance we've crossed paths and I didn't even know who he was.

That's probably a good thing.

"Is *she* here?"

Tempest shakes her head. "Doesn't look like it. If she was," she whispers, "she'd be sitting with Stella. They're kind of a packaged deal. I wouldn't be surprised if they've had a threesome." She snorts and I hold back a chuckle.

I love when she's candid and just speaks her mind.

Keeping one eye on Asher, I try to enjoy the game, rooting for the home team—cheering and booing when it's called for—but the whole time, my mind is on Tempest. She's so close I can feel the warmth of her body and I want nothing more than to get closer. Shit, I'd pull her onto my lap if I thought I could get away with it, but I settle for slipping my arm around her back.

At first, she tenses, but then eventually relaxes into it, leaning over and letting me hold her to me.

It's enough.

For now.

"I have to be to work by eight," I tell her, looking up at the scoreboard and watching the seconds until halftime.

"We can leave whenever you want," she says, glancing up at me. "I've made my appearance. That's all I needed to do. Besides, tomorrow night will be a late one."

"I've asked for tomorrow night off," I tell her. "So, we can stay as long as you want."

She laughs. "Probably not long…again, I just need to make an appearance, see a few old faces, and do what I need to do."

Show them they haven't beat her. I already know, without her telling me, why she has to do this. It's like when you eventually stand up to a bully and they leave you alone after that. This is Tempest standing up to her bullies, putting them in their place.

We stay through halftime. The old guy in the press box announces the class of 2009 and Tempest smiles and shakes her head as the stands around us erupt. "Go Pirates," I tease, mimicking Stella from earlier.

"Woo," she says, laughing.

The band takes the field and we watch their performance. When the third quarter starts, Tempest stands and looks down at me. "Let's go."

As we make our way down the stairs and across the bleachers to the ramp, I chance a glance up at Asher, wanting a good look at his face. Leaning down and placing my lips near Tempest's ear, I lock eyes with him, whispering, "I know him."

Her steps falter, but she quickly recovers.

"Where from?" she asks as we squeeze past people coming back to their seats for the second half. It's like swimming against the tide. I put my arm out in front of Tempest, clearing a path for her and keeping people from knocking into her.

"Pink Pony," I tell her once we're clear of the crowd. "He's a regular."

She stops in the middle of the gravel parking lot, a few feet from the truck. "What?"

"Yeah, he comes in once or twice a week with a couple of the guys he was sitting by."

"Asher?" she asks, confusion clear on her face.

"Pretty sure."

Frowning, she shakes her head. "I don't think so." She laughs, giving me a look like I'm crazy. "He never goes anywhere. If it doesn't have anything to do with a book he's working on, he's pretty much not interested. I was always begging him to go out and do something, but he never wanted to. He doesn't even like to drink."

I hate to break it to her, but she's wrong, or maybe he's changed since they split up, but he's definitely a frequent flyer… or rider… at the Pink Pony. I'm sure of it. It's my job to see every person who comes and goes, and I'm damn good at my job.

"Am I taking you home?" I ask, as we approach the truck and I open her door for her.

She pauses for a second, half way in her seat. "You know… I think I'll go hang out at the bar while you work… if that's okay with you?" She's hesitant, like I might not be okay with that, which is crazy. I'd have her with me every second of the day if I could.

"On one condition," I tell her, sounding serious.

Her eyes move to mine and she furrows her brows. "What?"

"Two shots… three tops," I say, holding up my fingers. "And when I ask you to get off the fucking bar, you do it."

Swatting me in my shoulder, she tries to look mad, but fails, adorable nonetheless.

When we get to the bar, Tempest takes her same seat from the first night I saw her—the one I usually occupy while keeping watch—and smiles at Floyd.

"Hey, Em," he says with a wide grin. "What brings you in here tonight?"

"I'm with him," she says, tossing a thumb over her shoulder in my direction and earning me a look from Floyd. He knows we're friends, but that's about it. What happens between Tempest and I is none of his business, or anyone else's for that matter.

She orders a shot of tequila and a Coke with lime while I turn my attention to the patrons.

With the football game going on, the place is pretty quiet. Although, there are some regulars occupying the front tables, and the girls are putting on a good show.

"Do they do the same routines every night?" Tempest asks, turning on her barstool to face the stage, leaning her elbows back on the bar. And looking so fucking hot doing it.

"Uh, no," I answer, watching Fuchsia do her thing. "They probably have a dozen routines each and an equal amount of costume changes… wig changes. Some of these men who come in here probably think there are a dozen different dancers."

"Wow," Tempest says, watching intently. "That's a lot of work… and coordination," she adds, her head tilting to the side as Fuchsia shimmies across the stage. "Not to mention incredible balance."

"Don't get any ideas," I tell her.

She laughs, sipping on her Coke. "Don't think I could do it?"

"I'd have to beat up every guy in here for looking at you."

She's quiet for a second and I'm worried that I might've overstepped. "What?" I ask when she fights back a smile.

"Nothing."

About that time, a large crowd filters through the door, a few of them nodding a greeting as they look for a suitable table.

"You've gotta be fucking kidding me," Tempest mutters, causing me to follow her line of sight. And that's when I see him—Asher—walking in with the other two guys I recognized.

I don't want to say I told her so, but I told her so. At least now she can see it for herself.

When he notices her sitting at the bar beside me, his eyes widen. And for a second, I wonder if he sees how hot she is leaning against the bar, and thinking about what a horrible fucking mistake it was to let her go.

If I was him, that's what I would be thinking. But then again, I'd never be him. I might not be known for having long relationships, but I've never had a problem with monogamy. I think it's why I haven't been in more serious relationships. If I don't see it going somewhere, I don't invest the time. There's no point in it.

But Tempest is worth it.

She's the girl you take home to meet your parents.

She's the girl you snatch up, because if you don't, someone else will, and you don't want to look back and think, I should've married her.

"You want me to take you home?" I ask, glancing over at her. She's glaring daggers at Asher's back and I wonder if he can feel it. He better be glad looks can't kill, because if they could, he'd be dead.

"No," she says, her lips pursing as she turns around and faces the bar. "Another shot of tequila, Floyd." He obliges, pouring one and setting it down in front of her. She takes it and tosses it back.

"You okay?" I ask, keeping my eyes on the growing crowd.

"Fine."

But I can tell she's not. I'm not sure if it's just seeing Asher or the fact she has to be in the same vicinity as him, but she's definitely pissed about something.

After a few minutes, one of the guys from Asher's table walks up to the bar and asks for a beer. He really doesn't need to, that's what we have waitresses for, so I watch him closely.

"Hey, Tempest," he says, sliding onto a barstool beside her.

"Jimmy," Tempest says through clenched teeth, not looking at him.

He smirks and leans over onto the bar. "Didn't know you frequented the Pony," he says mockingly. "Isn't it too late for you to be out… time to make the muffins?"

I'm about to step in and tell this guy to fuck off when Tempest slides off her barstool and stands up to him. She's not tall and tonight, she's wearing tennis shoes, so there's no added height from heels, but the way she stands with authority, it makes Jimmy back up.

"Whoa," he says with a smile, hands in the air. "I thought those anger management classes were paying off, but maybe not." The cocky grin on his face is getting ready to be wiped off if he doesn't shut his mouth.

"Jimmy," Tempest says, venom in her tone, but she covers it up with a syrupy-sweet smile. "I know you're not making fun of my job, seeing as how you haven't had one in over a year." Her hand comes down on his shoulder. "My mama told me they've been praying for you. You know how those prayer circle women are." When she feigns innocence, I know something else is coming. "Speaking of, how is Heidi? My mama said she's been hosting their Tuesday night bible study. I'll have to let her know I ran into you."

Jimmy's face pales and he grabs his beer and walks back to the table without another word.

"That's when it pays to listen to gossip," Tempest says, sliding back into her seat. "What a fucking douchebag."

I huff a laugh, shaking my head. "Tell me how you really feel."

"Duped," she says after a few seconds, something like sadness and hurt in her tone. Looking over at her, she swallows and shakes her head.

"Wanna talk about it?" I ask.

She shakes her head. "Not right now." Taking a deep breath, she blows it out. "I just want another shot of tequila and to see something naked."

"I could help you with that," I murmur, leaning closer.

"Your job requires you to remain fully clothed," she says. Turning back to the bar, she lifts a finger to Floyd, who reads her sign and gives her what she wants. "Their job is to take it off." Tipping her shot glass toward the stage, she brings it back to her perfect pink lips and throws it back. "I typically don't swing that way, but they'll do in a pinch."

I can't help the laugh that erupts. She's something else and I love it. I love that I never know what she's going to say. I love that she fights back and doesn't shy away from tough situations. I love that she's strong and fierce and sexy as hell.

CHAPTER 25

TEMPEST

Thanks to the tequila I drank last night and staying at the bar so late, when Cage finally drove me home, I came straight upstairs and crashed.

He asked me if I wanted to come to his apartment, but I knew what that would entail and honestly, my head is still reeling from our first romp in the sack. I don't think I'm ready for another. Besides, I hardly ever get a Saturday off work and I had plans of sleeping until eight.

Glancing over at the clock, I see it's only six thirty, which is still sleeping in for me, even though I didn't go to bed until after two in the morning. I'm used to baker's hours.

I lay in bed, staring at the ceiling for what feels like forever, but when I turn back to the clock, it's only been ten minutes. Frustrated with myself, I toss the blankets off and throw my legs over the edge of the bed, toeing into my slippers.

It's already starting to feel cooler in the mornings and evenings. You can tell fall is upon us and that makes me happy. It's my favorite time of year.

Shuffling over to the coffee pot, I think about how much I love living here. I'm sure for some people, it might feel claustrophobic and they would probably be dreaming about more space, but this is perfect for me right now.

As the coffee permeates the air, I inhale and let it coat my lungs.

That's what I'm talking about. There's nothing like your first hit of caffeine in the morning. Something about the smell of coffee soothes my soul and sets me up for a productive day. Without it, I'm lost and grumpy.

Sipping my first cup, I lean against the brick wall and peer out the window to the street below. From here, I can see that there are customers arriving at the bakery. I start to feel bad about not being there, and then quickly shut that shit down.

Besides, I made extra muffins yesterday for today, so it's not like they're going without.

With so much time to spare, I glance around my apartment and make a mental list of things I could check off my to-do list.

There's a box of clothes I need to either donate or find space for under my bed. I also have a basket of clothes I washed at the laundromat earlier this week that needs put away. Plus, there's still one small box of random papers I need to go through.

Most of the junk can probably be thrown away, but I need to make sure there isn't anything in there that's important. My luck, if I just trashed the whole box, I'd accidentally throw away a winning lotto ticket or my birth certificate.

Although, I'd have to buy a lotto ticket first.

And my birth certificate is safely tucked away in a fireproof box.

But I can't throw it away without easing my mind first, so I set my half-drank cup of coffee on the island and lean down to grab all the papers out of the box.

One pile for trash.

One pile for keep.

The first few items are old bills, mostly utility bills, from the old house.

Trash.

A credit card statement from one of Asher's cards.

Trash.

A letter from Asher's Aunt Patricia for his birthday last year.

Trash.

I start to move through the stack faster, only adding one receipt that I'll need for taxes to the keep pile, until a folded piece of paper catches my eye.

Fertility Institute of Knoxville

Patient Information: Asher J. Williams

Scanning the paper, I'm confused at what I'm looking at. Asher was never a patient at the fertility clinic. But I've never seen this paper before. As I skim the information, it's like I'm reading gibberish, until I come to one line.

Semen Test

Flipping the page, I still can't make out what any of the numbers mean, but at the bottom of the third page, there's a section titled: *Conclusion.*

Again, most of it is Greek to me, but when I come across one line in particular, I pause. My heart starts beating a little harder and a little faster.

A result of 0 percent NF usually means in vitro fertilization (IVF) may be necessary for conception.

Flipping back to the first page, I scan it looking to see what it says for NF… NF… NF…

2.

Asher's result was 2 percent NF.

What does that mean?

He's what? Infertile? Has bad swimmers?

Going back to the conclusion portion, I read over it quickly one more time. *IVF may be necessary for conception.* Meaning, we might have never conceived again on our own? Which must mean that the one time we did, it was a miracle.

My heart squeezes, just like it does every time when I think about the baby I lost. I wasn't pregnant long, but it was long enough for me to get attached to the idea. I loved that baby for eight weeks and wanted it more than anything in the entire world.

But that also means that if he got Mindy pregnant, that's some freak of nature shit.

Lightning striking twice?

My wheels start turning and I spend the rest of the day doing my least favorite thing—thinking about Asher Williams.

Between the sperm analysis and him showing up at the Pink Pony last night… and Cage recognizing him as a regular… I feel more confused today than I did the day I walked in and found him and Mindy in bed together.

Something about all of it makes me feel like a fraud, like I was living a lie. It leaves me second-guessing Asher and who he is as a person, which in turn makes me second-guess myself.

Why didn't he tell me about going to the fertility clinic?

Did he go before or after he started sleeping with Mindy?

And since when does he hang out at the Pink Pony?

How did I not see him for who he truly is?

How could I let myself trust him so completely and get blindsided so severely?

By the time six o'clock rolls around, I'm dressed and ready to go, but my head isn't in the game. Taking another look at myself in the big mirror, I stare at my reflection.

If I'm not Asher Williams's wife, who am I?

I thought I was starting to figure that out, but now, I'm not so sure.

But this pant suit I decided to wear is fucking awesome. The second Stella mentioned that everyone was wearing their prom dress, I made up my mind I wouldn't be. I wouldn't put it past them to tell me one thing and everyone else do the opposite, like that scene in *Legally Blonde* when Reese Witherspoon's character shows up to the party in a bunny costume.

Yeah, that's not happening.

Also, I've seen *Carrie*, and there won't be any blood spilled tonight, pig or otherwise. I refuse to let them get to me. I'm going, showing them that I'm not ashamed. Why should I be? I'm not the one who cheated. I'm also no longer intimidated by them. They can have their washed-up reputations and high school accomplishments.

Let's not discuss that my mental pep talk and decision making is based on movies.

There's a knock at my door at precisely six-fifteen, exactly when Cage said he'd be by to pick me up, and my heart does a little flip.

I just saw him last night, but that doesn't mean I'm not looking forward to seeing him again. He's the bright spot in all this mess. If it wasn't for him, there's no way in hell I'd be doing this.

As I walk to the door, the realization hits me that I've only ever seen Cage in workout gear and jeans and T-shirts. For a second, I let myself daydream about what he's possibly wearing now, pressing my hand against the door, I take a deep breath before I twist the deadbolt.

Yeah, not prepared.

Breathe, Tempest.

Just breathe.

But that doesn't help either, because now, when I recite those words to myself, they sound like Cage when he was pushing inside me.

Standing in front of me—in black slacks and a white dress shirt, with his sleeves rolled up and his thick forearms on display—is the most beautiful man I've ever seen.

I open my mouth to say something, but the words die in the back of my throat when he smiles at me. Those pale-blue eyes twinkling. His blond hair a bit shorter than it was last night, which means he must have got a trim today. And his beard he's been growing since he arrived in Green Valley is still there, but also trimmed.

Deadly, deadly combination.

"Wow," Cage says, stealing the words right out of my mouth. "You look… damn."

Swallowing, I feel the blush creep up on my cheeks. "Thanks, but you stole my line."

"Tempest," he murmurs, taking a step closer and reaching his hand out to grip my waist. "This is the sexiest fucking outfit I've ever seen."

With his hand touching me, my eyes close on their own accord and my body wants to lean into him, craving him. Even though my mind is out of the game, everything else is all in. His lips brushing my cheek startles me. Jumping a little, I laugh nervously.

"I wish I could keep you here all to myself, but it would be an absolute shame to waste this delicious ensemble," he whispers and then kisses my cheek once more before stepping back. "Ready?"

"As I'll ever be," I tell him, giving him a grateful smile. "And you look fucking hot."

When I turn to lock my door, I hear him chuckle behind me and take a deep, fortifying breath.

"I hope there's an open bar," he mutters.

"You and me both."

Walking into the Lodge, I'm instantly on high alert. The first person I see is Mindy. She's standing at the welcome table with Stella and Catalina, who I haven't seen in years. Back in elementary school, we were friends, good friends, but then we got to junior high and she became a cheerleader and I started eating lunch in the library.

"Tempest," Mindy greets as Cage and I walk up. "Welcome."

I'm so glad I didn't eat, because I'm pretty sure I could puke right now. All over her ridiculous hot pink dress.

Stella was serious. They're all squeezed into their prom dresses, even Mindy, who just had a baby. I watch as she places her hands on her waist, almost as if to say, "*look at me*."

"Hi," I deadpan, forcing a smile, and then move to Stella and Catalina, giving them a forced one as well. And that's when I see the look on Catalina's face. She wants to say something, but Mindy probably has her on a tight leash, and a gag order.

If I had to guess, their pre-reunion pep talk probably went something like this: "The last ten years didn't happen. Asher and Tempest were never married. If anyone brings up our affair or their divorce, you're kicked off the island."

"Catalina," I say, focusing my attention on her as Mindy looks through a stack of badges. "I haven't seen you in what… ten years? Oh, wait. You came to my wedding! That's right. How have you been?"

I'm being petty. I know. But I can't help myself. If Mindy can stand here acting like she's the love child of Mother Teresa and a Victoria's Secret runway model, then I can get in a passive dig.

Catalina's face drops, but she quickly recovers, eyes darting toward Mindy and then back to me. "Yeah, it's been…" she pauses, swallowing, "years. How have you been?"

"Great," I say, glancing over at Mindy. "Never better."

"Oh, pardon my rudeness," I say, placing a hand on Cage's firm, muscular chest. "This is Cage Erickson. My date."

Cage's hand slides around my waist and he pulls me to him in a possessive gesture. And I don't just let him, I relish in it. If I could meld my body with his, I would.

Looking up at Cage, I make quick eye contact and give him a genuine smile. "You know Stella," I tell him, turning my gaze to the bleached blonde at Mindy's side. "And this is Mindy, who you've heard a lot about, and this is Catalina, we all go way back."

He doesn't miss a beat, stretching out his arm, shaking each of their hands. "Nice to meet you, ladies," he says, effectively charming the pants off of them. Literally. Even though Stella acted completely put off last night when he mentioned working at the Pink Pony, she seems to be fully recovered from that now. I want to tell her to close her mouth. Drooling is very unladylike.

When Mindy screeches, my head whips in her direction, expecting for someone to be bleeding out or the building to be on fire. Instead, her cheeks are so red she looks like her head is getting ready to explode. I don't miss the piece of paper she tries to discreetly crumple up in her hand as she lets it fall to her feet.

"Looks like they forgot to print you a badge," she says, speaking through gritted teeth and a strained smile. "Stella, fix it."

I glance up at Cage who's fighting back a laugh and it dawns on me what must've happened.

If I had to guess, someone—not sure who—made my badge with my married name. That's the only thing that would elicit that kind of reaction from her. And that's just not going to fly tonight. No way. It would put a huge crack in the facade Mindy is so painfully trying to maintain. That's okay, because I wouldn't have worn it anyway.

But I would love to know who did that.

And give them a high five.

Tell them to stop by the bakery.

Muffins on me.

After Stella scribbles our names down on two blank badges, she hands them to us. "Have a nice night," she sneers. "Bar's at the back. Dinner will be served at seven."

Deciding to be the bigger person, I smile back and make it as genuine as I can manage. "Thanks… and good to see you, Catalina."

She gives me an awkward half wave and then turns to the people who walk in behind us.

Breathing a sigh of relief, Cage keeps his hand around my waist and squeezes. "Well, that was fun," he chuckles, his lips brushing the ridge of my ear. "You handled that like a fucking boss."

"I'm not so sure about that," I say, feeling the adrenaline from the interaction begin to subside, leaving me feeling a little numb and tingly… or maybe that's Cage being so close and whispering in my ear. I smile at a few familiar faces as we walk into the ballroom and scan the place for a place to sit, preferably away from all the assholes.

"I think Catalina forgets that I always came to her defense when people used to tease her about being a salad dressing back in fifth grade," I mutter. "We actually did used to be friends, before all the bullshit of popularity kicked in and people started picking sides."

When Cage's lips brush my hair, I falter a little and he steadies me. "Every eye in here is on you," he whispers.

"Nothing I'm not used to," I tell him, feeling the familiar fortress I've built inside me close up the gate.

"And it has nothing to do with Mindy… or Asher," he mutters, his warm breath hitting my neck and sending chills up my back. "But everything to do with how fucking hot you are."

"Stop," I say, swatting at him as I swallow down my desire and give myself a mental fist bump for my choice of attire. I've never been more thankful to be my own person and unattached from all the bullshit that came with having Asher in my life.

Mindy's minions are so obvious as they flounce around in their prom dresses. It's laughable.

"I'm serious," he continues, his voice low and gravelly as we make our way into the main room.

"Okay, now I'm being serious," I tell him as we approach an empty table. "Because every time you whisper in my ear or touch me all I can think about is having sex with you and it's distracting and I've really gotta keep my wits about me and make it through this night." My words spill out in a rambling mess, per usual when I get flustered, and Cage's cocky grin tells me he knows exactly what he does to me… what he's *doing* to me.

He laughs, biting down on his lower lip and I have to force my mind to stay out of the gutter.

"Think you can keep the vultures at bay while I go hunt us down some drinks?" he asks, those stunning blue eyes twinkling as he pulls a chair out for me. "Or do you want to go with me?"

"No," I tell him, grateful for a moment of solitude. "I'll be fine here… and you know what I want."

If I didn't have to interact with another person tonight, I'd be happy. I'd rather ride out the night, here at the table, with Cage by my side, and hopefully escape unscathed. If Mindy and her flock of fakes is all I have to deal with this evening, I'll consider it a win for Team Tempest.

But of course I'm not that lucky.

Cage has barely been gone a few seconds when I feel someone walk up behind me and place a hand on the back of my chair, brushing my hair.

"Interesting choice of attire," Asher's familiar voice says from behind me, making me tense.

Taking a deep breath, I focus on centering myself before replying. "Last I checked, you don't have a horse in this race, so what I wear shouldn't concern you."

He huffs a laugh, walking around and occupying the chair to my left, forcing me to look at him. "Come on, Tempest. We're not strangers. You and I spent over a decade together. I'm always going to notice."

"I think your wife would have something to say about that."

Sighing, he pinches the bridge of his nose. "About her," he starts and it's crazy, but I know what he's going to say before he even starts. "Could we keep it between us that I was at the bar last night? Old friends catching up. So, if we could let bygones be bygones, that'd be great… what do you say?"

"Bygones be bygones?" The laugh that escapes me is a little crazy, I'll admit, but his audacity knows no bounds. "Are you kidding me? Oh, and let's not pretend like that was a one-time occurrence," I scoff, scooting my chair back to put some distance between us.

I need some fucking air. All of a sudden this huge room feels small and Asher is sucking up all the oxygen.

When he gives me a look, daring me to cross him, I hold his gaze and stare right back.

I'll fucking cross you, alright, Asher Williams.

Try me.

Because after all the shit I've discovered in the last twenty-four hours, I could ruin him. The little piece of paper I found earlier, after some well-spent time with my friend Google, is enough to put a stop to half of this bullshit.

"I was just having a drink with old friends… for old time's sake," he says, feigning innocence. "You know I don't normally go to places like that."

Biting my lip, I close my eyes and pray for patience. Good Lord knows I don't want to end this night in jail, but Asher Williams is currently testing all my strength.

"You know, Asher, I thought I knew everything about you. I mean, you *were* my husband," I tell him, looking him straight in the eyes as I say it, wanting him to feel the words like a weight on his soul. "For eight years."

He lets out an exaggerated breath, running a hand through his dark hair. "We're not doing this tonight," he warns. "It's not the place."

"I'm not the one who waltzed over and struck up a conversation," I retort. It's a little petulant, but I can't help it. He did this… all of it. I'm tired of taking the blame and being the villain. "So, since I have the pleasure of your presence, let's go ahead and get a few things out in the open, shall we?"

"Who's the beefcake you've been hanging out with?" he asks, trying to change the subject and turn it around on me, just like he's always done.

"None of your business," I say, glancing over my shoulder, part of me willing Cage to materialize and the other part of me praying he stays away until Asher leaves. I have a feeling things could go from bad to worse if he walked in and found Asher harassing me.

"Are you fucking him?"

Whipping my head around to face him, I look at him like he grew three heads. "Are you kidding me?" I laugh, but it's lacking humor and its only purpose it to keep me from screaming. "I guess I should've been asking you that about Mindy a long damn time ago. How long were you fucking her, anyway? You've never really given me a straight answer about that."

"Tempest."

"No, Asher," I say, sliding my chair back even further, just in case I need an escape. "You don't get to do that anymore… you can't talk to me like I'm a child, no one can, but especially not you."

"Okay," he says, standing from his chair. "I'm leaving. I can tell it was a bad idea to think I could have an adult conversation with you. You're fucking crazy," he mutters, turning away from me. Those words. He has to know what they do to me. And the tone he used when he said them, if I didn't know better, I'd guess he's looking for a rise out of me. He wants me to cause a scene.

The rational part of me is telling me to *let him go*.

But that irrational part of me, the one I'm always battling, is saying *fuck no*.

"How long?" I ask, my voice getting louder to get his attention. "Or did you forget? Kind of like how you forgot to tell me about your little trip to the fertility clinic?" I say, dropping that bomb.

The look on his face as he turns around is one of horror and realization… *understanding*.

I'm not going to lie, it thrills me. His discomfort feeds the beast inside me.

Maybe I am crazy?

Maybe I'm a sadistic bitch?

Because I can't stop. "Yeah, I found those results as I was going through some papers today. It's like the universe is finally on my side for once… just dropped them right in my lap." Laughing again, I don't even recognize my own voice. It's a little detached, a bit unhinged. "And, you know me, I can't help but Google shit. Apparently, that time we got pregnant, it was a fucking medical miracle. I mean, like one in a million kind of thing."

My pulse is racing as the words rapid-fire out of my mouth. I feel eyes all over me. Everyone in our proximity now has a front-row seat to the show. My skin crawls, itching, begging me to lash out and release the pent-up anger.

"Tempest," Asher warns. His eyes begging, pleading me to stop.

I swallow and close my eyes, trying to center myself and regain a little self-control.

"Why her?" It's one of the many questions that has plagued me for months now. Why her? Why Mindy? What does she have that I don't have?

When he doesn't answer, I continue. "If you were tired of being married to me… if you knew you didn't love me anymore… you should've ended it. That's what someone with integrity would do, but you have none. You threw eight years of marriage away and jumped in bed with someone else." The pounding in my chest is now reverberating all over my body. "You're fucking weak… pathetic," I seethe.

Asher's anger flares, and it's so fucking satisfying. Through everything—me walking in on them, the trips to jail, the divorce, selling the house—he's never once shown any emotion. So, I'll take his anger. I'll devour it like a starved animal.

"You think this has been easy for me?" he asks, taking a step toward me as his finger comes between us, inches from my chest, but I don't back down. Regardless of the nerves coursing through my body, he won't win this battle. Or the war.

"Everything has always been easy for you, Asher. That's the problem." I pause for a second, reining in my emotions. *Deep breaths, Tempest. Deep breaths*. "You don't know how to fight. You've never had to. And personally, I feel sorry for you."

"He was never happy with you." Mindy's voice carries across the ballroom, gaining even more attention. "You've always been a wannabe," she sneers. "If it hadn't been for Asher, no one would've even remembered your name."

I swallow, her words pouring salt on old wounds.

"And how dare you speak to my husband like that," she finally says, coming into view as she takes her place next to Asher, her arm snaking around his possessively.

That's right, Mindy… *stand by your man.*

"Hey," Cage's strong hand is immediately at my back as he walks up, moving to put himself between me and Mindy and Asher, but I push him back. I don't need his help. This is my battle, and I want to be the one to fight it.

Taking a step toward them, I close the distance. "I'll speak to him however I want… and how dare you steal what doesn't belong to you. Don't think people can't see through your facade. You're bullshit is stinking up the whole damn town."

Mindy's eyes flare with anger. "Look who's talking… *felon.*"

"I'd rather be a felon than a whore."

The gasps echo around the room and it's only then I realize the music in the background is no longer playing. Everyone's eyes are on us.

"He was never yours to begin with," Mindy screeches, tears brimming in her eyes. "You're just so stupid, you never saw it. Do you know what he did the night before your wedding?" she asks.

"Mindy." Asher's voice is low and lethal. "Stop."

"No," she says, pulling away from him. "She needs to know." Crossing her arms over her chest, she glares at me. "Me."

It takes me a second to realize what she just said.

She slept with Asher… the night before our wedding.

My eyes go to him, but he can't look at me. Nausea and anger paints his face, telling me Mindy is speaking the truth. That feeling from earlier, about my life being a lie, is back and it brought friends—hurt, regret, and humiliation.

"That's right," Mindy says, glancing down at her perfectly polished nails. "It's always been me. We're meant to be together… it just took him a while to realize it. And now, we're a family." She pauses. You can hear a fucking pin drop and then, Mindy drops her final bomb.

"I gave him something you couldn't."

Tears sting my eyes as they threaten to spill, but I refuse to give her, or anyone else in here, the satisfaction of seeing me break, so I turn and start making my way through the now-crowded ballroom.

Not running, but walking… holding my head as high as I can. As I pass by people, Cage's arm comes up to clear a path, his strong hand never leaving the small of my back, something in me snaps. Kind of like the day I walked in on Mindy and Asher, but unlike that morning, I have clarity.

Pausing, I turn back to them. The crowd is parted like the Red Sea, Mindy and Asher standing there in the wake.

"I wouldn't be so sure that baby is his," I say, raising my voice to make sure I'm heard clearly. "You might want a paternity test. Apparently, Asher's swimmers are damaged goods. Isn't that right, Asher?"

There are a few gasps and a few laughs, but I don't stick around for his response or anything else. I'm done here.

I'm done with Asher.

I'm done with Mindy.

I'm done with the whole fucking thing and I need some air.

When I get to the parking lot, I stop, bracing my hands on my knees and breathe. The tears that have been threatening to come finally do and a sob breaks free from my chest. Before I can crumble into a heap on the ground, Cage's strong arms are there—catching me, keeping me from falling.

"I'm here," Cage whispers. "I got you."

He's right. He's got me and he holds me until I can finally stand on my own two feet again, walking me to the truck and helping me into the passenger seat, even going as far as reaching across and buckling my seat belt for me.

I let him, because right now, I feel so numb.

What was I thinking?

How could I have ever loved someone as vile as Asher Williams?

How did I not see the real him?

The hurt and betrayal from Mindy's revelation are tangible, feeling like weights on my arms and legs.

"Where do you want to go?" Cage asks, concern and tenderness in his voice.

"Anywhere but here."

After he gets into the driver's seat and starts it up, we sit for a minute in the parking lot, Cage's hand on mine as we let the last half hour sink in.

"I'm sorry," he says. "I should've been there—"

"No," I tell him, my throat feeling raw. "That needed to happen. Don't be sorry."

Eventually, he puts the truck in drive and we make our way out of the parking lot and back to the main road. As we drive back to town, my mind whirls and I just want to shut it up… somehow, some way.

"Want me to take you home?" Cage asks when we get closer.

"No."

"Tell me what you need, Tempest. Anything, I'll do it."

"Help me forget… just for a little while."

CHAPTER 26

CAGE

We're barely inside my bedroom when Tempest attacks me, her mouth on mine and her hands on my belt.

I know what she wants… what she needs and I'll gladly give it to her. I'm hers to use for as long as she desires, but I hope she knows I'm here for her in all aspects, not just the physical.

That doesn't mean she has to do all the work, though.

While she undresses me, I start removing her clothes, as well. "As gorgeous as you are in this suit, I've been dying to take if off you all night." When her top is gone, my mouth goes straight for her nipple, sucking it until she cries out. Tempest stops working on my clothes and grips onto my head when I switch to her other breast, throwing her head back and gasping in pleasure.

"I need you, Cage." Her words are breathless and full of passion. She's so beautiful when she's vulnerable like this, but I want to see her strength right now. I want her to take charge.

I brush my lips across hers and slide my fingers through her hair, holding her gaze on me. "I'm yours, Tempest. I'm yours to use however you need to tonight. All of your anger and pain, your frustration and resentment… use my body to purge all that negativity."

She looks uncertain, like she doesn't think she can do what I'm saying or that she'll hurt me in some way. The truth is, the only way she can hurt me is by shutting me out and not allowing me to help her.

"I don't know how," she whispers.

"Take me. Take my body and get your pleasure however the fuck you want. Clear your mind and just feel. Break yourself into a million pieces, if you need to. All I ask, is that you let me help put you back together."

I watch as her eyes tear up, brightening the green of her irises. "Do it." My voice is soft but firm, showing her the truth behind my words. After a brief moment, Tempest releases a deep breath and where there were tears is now fire.

Yes.

My shirt already on the floor and my pants undone, she slides them and my boxers down to my feet before pushing on my shoulders until I'm sitting on the bed behind me. I quickly kick off my shoes so the rest of my clothes can follow, leaving me naked and hard for her. So fucking hard.

Tempest takes the rest of her clothes off as I watch but, thank fuck, she leaves her heels on. How I haven't come all over myself yet is damn miracle.

She stands directly in front of me, between my spread legs, and I think she's going to straddle me but she doesn't. Instead, she sinks to the floor and grasps my cock, her eyes never leaving mine.

"Tempest," I warn, my voice strained. "Don't do anything for me, do it for you."

"I am," she assures me. "I want this. I've wanted to do this for a long time. You'll tell me if I do something wrong, though, right?"

Shit. I'd rip Asher apart right now, if I could, but I refuse to let him ruin this moment for her.

"You won't do anything wrong; you're perfect, trust me."

"I do trust you."

She kisses my tip then slides my entire length into her mouth and holy shit, she's a natural. Her grip is strong at my base and the amount of suction she's providing as she moves up and down my cock is absolutely perfect. Too perfect, in fact, and when I groan out her name, she looks up at me. My dick is still in her mouth and the vision before me causes my eyes to squeeze shut because it's just too much.

The cold air on my shaft as she takes her mouth off is jarring but it gives me a brief reprieve and allows me to collect myself.

"Was I doing okay?" she asks. "I couldn't tell because your eyes were closed."

"Oh, my God, Tempest, it was so much more than okay. It was amazing. I had to stop watching because I didn't want to come yet."

She smiles and my dick twitches in response, causing us both to laugh.

"I didn't expect to enjoy that so much, but I did. It really turned me on." When she admits this, there's no shyness or embarrassment and that thrills me to no end. It's exactly what I want for her.

"Can I feel for myself?"

Her eyes darken as she nods her head yes and I waste no time slipping my fingers through her folds, finding her pussy soaked.

"Fuck, Tempest. Tell me what you want. How do you want me?"

"I want to be on top," she replies confidently.

After I put on a condom, I pull her on my lap with her legs straddling mine. She immediately lowers herself on my cock and begins rocking her body in a perfect rhythm. I love her being on top while I'm sitting up because it allows me to stay close to her, but I want her to be able to use this position to her full advantage, so I lay back on the bed and give her more room to move the way she wants.

Tempest leans forward, instinctively moving to where her clit rubs against my pelvis. I keep one hand on her ass, guiding her just a little, and use the other to hold her tits close to my mouth. I love flicking her nipples with my tongue as she moves over me and the way her walls are tightening around my dick tells me she likes it, too.

"Yes! Cage! Oh, shit, I'm coming," she gasps out. I grab her ass with both hands and slam her down on me harder, faster until our orgasms take us over, leaving us both sweaty and spent.

Later, after we've cleaned up and calmed down, Tempest is snuggled in my arms, running her fingers over the planes of my chest.

"I didn't realize how much I needed that," she admits. "It's kinda crazy that you knew what I needed more than I did, but I'm really thankful."

I laugh as I kiss the top of her head. "Anytime." Her body feels so perfect against mine and I can't help the feelings building inside me. "I mean it," I whisper, my lips brushing her hair. "Any time… all the time… whatever you need. I'm here."

CHAPTER 27

TEMPEST

When I wake up, I'm covered in sweat. My heart is beating wildly like I've been on a long run. But it's the lingering vision from my dream that I can't shake.

I was standing in the middle of the hallway at my old house—mine and Asher's—the door to the bedroom was partially open and I could hear voices. There were loud moans accompanied by a man's grunts. It was so vivid. I remember the way the Berber carpet felt under my feet and the smell of the candle I always burned in the bathroom down the hall—apple cinnamon.

In my dream, I looked down at myself and I wasn't wearing any clothes, kind of like those horrible dreams people have where they're standing in front of a crowd naked, but there was no crowd… just me and…

Pushing the door open, I could feel the rush of adrenaline and spike of fear. When I stepped into the room, my heart dropped, along with the shoe in my hand, getting the attention of the man who was driving into the woman only seconds before.

The woman smiles at me as the man speaks, "Like what you see?"

Cage.

Bile rises into my throat and I have to force it down. I know my subconscious is playing tricks on me, playing on my fears and insecurities, but the dream was so real. Looking over at Cage, I watch him for a second as he sleeps soundly, his arm draped over my stomach, and I have the worst thought.

How do I know I can trust him?

Unlike Asher, I've only known Cage a short amount of time.

Who's to say he doesn't have a wife and kids back in Dallas?

I thought I knew Asher. I trusted him with my life and bound myself to him, assuming we'd uphold our vows with only death parting us. And look how that ended up… how terribly wrong I was.

Tears sting my eyes and I press my palms against them to keep them from falling. Feeling dirty and used and so unsure of myself, I can't stand to lie here any longer.

Slipping out from under Cage's arm, I ease myself off the bed. I think about showering in his bathroom, but I need some air and I need to think, and I can't do either when I'm this close to him. He makes me feel things that cloud my judgment.

Maybe that was what was wrong with me and Asher?

Maybe I just latched onto him because he was the first boy to show interest?

What if I'm doing the same thing with Cage?

Anna's words from a few days ago come back to haunt me. *Don't jump into bed with the first guy that comes along and calls you beautiful.*

Am I really that weak and starved for attention?

What the fuck is wrong with me?

Filling my lungs with air, I try to put into practice all of my coping mechanism I've learned over the past few months, but nothing works. As panic starts to set in, I look frantically around the room. Grabbing my clothes from the floor where they fell as I lost myself in Cage, I quickly put them on, forgoing my shoes.

"Where are you going?" Cage asks, his voice groggy from sleep. My back is to him as my hand grips the frame of the door. Pausing, I try to think of something to say to get him to go back to sleep and just let me leave, but I know that's a lost cause. He's too much of a gentleman for that… too nice… too caring. And why is that? What would he want with a girl like me?

"Tempest?"

"I… I just need to go," I tell him, still not turning around, biting my lip to keep from crying, not from sadness, but pure fear. I'm afraid of myself—of what I've done, of how I've let myself fall for him, of my ability to make good decisions. Nothing is making sense right now and it's freaking me out. "I would call you later, but I don't even have your phone number," I say, something between a sob and a laugh catching in my throat and that's when I feel it, that snap in rational thinking. The one I'm always fighting so hard against, but it overtakes me.

"How crazy is that?" I ask, finally turning to face him. "We've had sex twice and I don't even have your telephone number… or know what your favorite food is? Maybe you're married? Or are a member of the Communist Party?"

Cage rubs his eyes and sits up, the sheet falling away, exposing his amazing torso.

"Cover up," I tell him, my voice taking on that tone of insanity it's become accustomed to lately, especially in moments when it feels like my life is falling apart. "I can't think straight when you're naked… or when you look at me like that. Actually, I can't think when you're around period. It's like my brain takes a hiatus and hands over the controls to my hormones."

"And that's a bad thing?" he asks, still trying to wake up and get his wits about him as he runs a hand through his hair.

"Yes!" He doesn't get it. "It's a very bad thing. Don't you get it? You're so… you, and when I'm around you, I'm not myself. I think what Anna said is right… you're the first man to show me any interest and I think I've been using you… like a diversion… or a rebound…" I pause, knowing those words don't settle well in my chest, but I can't take them back now. "You shouldn't want—"

"817-222-4561."

"What?"

"That's my phone number," he says, standing up and grabbing his slacks from the floor, making quick work of pulling them up before he turns back around. "I should've given it to you earlier… meant to a few times, but kept forgetting. I'm sorry."

His tone is no-nonsense and the look on his face is fierce as he walks around the bed and into my space, but doesn't touch me. Just stands close enough that I can feel his warmth. And it's all I can do to keep from reaching out to him, knowing a touch from him would make all the crazy thoughts and second-guessing fly out the window.

But I can't.

"I've never been married." His tone is the exact opposite of everything I'm feeling—rational, right-minded, calm, cool, collected. "I've only had two serious girlfriends. My last long-term relationship was in college. I've had sex with quite a few people, but always wore a condom and I've been checked for STDs on a regular basis. My favorite food is steak. I'm a Scorpio. My birthday is a month from tomorrow. My mom's name is Janice and my dad is Kristoph. I was born in Dallas. Moved to Boston for college, but moved right back when I dropped out, so Green Valley is only the third place I've lived, but I've been practically everywhere, in and out of the country. I'm an Independent, but hate talking politics."

He finally stops, taking a deep breath and scratching the back of his head. "Anything else you want to know?

I shake my head, but not in response to his question, because deep down, I want to know everything about Cage Erickson, but I can't… I don't trust myself.

And that's the bottom line. That's the real problem here. It has nothing to do with the man standing in front of me and everything to do with me.

"You shouldn't want to be with me," I tell him, finishing my thought from a second ago before he began pouring out his heart on the floor. "I'm damaged goods and I'll probably never be able to trust anyone ever again… let alone myself. So, if you want a relationship with someone, I'm not your girl."

"I want whatever you want," he says, crossing his arms over his chest. "I told you already… the ball's in your court."

"For how long?" I ask, my voice rising. "I know you don't have plans to stay… I overheard you talking to your brother about going home. Back to Dallas. And I can't stick around and get my heart broken again. So, let's just end this now and save ourselves the trouble."

And by us, I mean me.

Because as much as I'd like to deny it, I have feelings for Cage… big feelings. He could easily break me, far worse than anything Asher has done.

When he stands there, stoic and rigid, not budging, I try another tactic.

"I… I don't want to be with you..." I stammer, struggling to get the lie out of my mouth. "You were a fun time… and you, uh… helped me clear my mind, but that's it. Thanks for that," I say, my eyes going to the floor because I can't look him in the eye. "And thanks for playing the part and going to the reunion with me."

We stand in silence for a moment, but I can't stand this any longer. As I turn to go, he reaches for my hand, but I hide my face from him, tears already trickling down my cheeks.

"Tempest," he pleads. "Don't do this."

The slight break in his tone is what sets my feet in motion. I'm a horrible person. I must be, because it would take a monster to break a heart as good as Cage's.

"I need… I have to go," I say, turning for the stairs. "Please don't follow me."

CHAPTER 28

CAGE

I did follow her, from a distance, watching her until I knew she was safely inside her apartment.

But then, I walked away, letting her go.

CHAPTER 29

TEMPEST

"Well, you're early," Jenn says, walking in the back door and scaring me just a little.

I've been here for over two hours, but I don't tell her that. "Couldn't sleep."

With a heavy sigh, Jenn walks around the workspace and faces me, hands flat on the stainless steel worktop. "Alright," she says, drawing my attention up to her and away from the batter I'm working on… my fifth one of the morning because nothing is sticking. It's like every good idea for a muffin has left the building. "Enough of this."

"What?" I ask, looking around to see what she might be talking about. "I know I made two chocolate muffins yesterday, but this one will be different… "

How? I'm not sure. I haven't figured that out yet.

The only thing I've decided on is I'm calling it *I'm So Lonesome Tonight*, not because it has anything to do with the muffin, but because I'm *so fucking lonely…* and I literally could cry… or die. I've felt dead the past few days.

"No," Jenn says, slapping the counter. "This." She waves a hand in my direction. "You… moping around. It's depressing and your muffins are uninspired. The names you've been giving them have brought the mood in the bakery down to Prozac level. Even the customers have started commenting on it." She sighs, her beautiful eyes looking concerned. "Mrs. Dillon said she wasn't coming back until your muffins stopped making her weepy. That's a direct quote."

"Please, don't fire me," I beg. My eyes go wide as I realize this may be her way of telling me she doesn't want me working here anymore. I have been pretty hard to deal with lately. "I need this job…" I'm two seconds from getting on my knees. I'm not above begging. "I promise, I'll do better. I was, uh, actually thinking of making a muffin with... pistachios," I say, pulling it out of my ass, because I remember seeing some in the pantry and at least it's not the same, sad chocolate muffins I've been making lately.

"I'm not firing you," Jenn says, rolling her violet-blue eyes and smiling sadly. "I just… I'm worried about you. You've been worse this past week than after… you know," she says, waving her hand in the air, and I do know. It's true. I've felt sadder since the morning I walked out on Cage than I ever was after Asher.

"Do you want to talk about it?" Jenn asks. "I know you said you didn't, but maybe it would help."

Stepping back from the counter, I brace my hands on it and let my head hang between my arms, sighing in defeat. Maybe I do need to talk it out.

"The muffins are sad," I say, after a few moments, "because I'm sad… and I can't get past it. I thought a clean break was what I needed, but the edge left behind is so sharp… I feel like I'm bleeding every time I breathe."

"Asher?" Jenn asks, confusion in her tone. "I thought you were—"

"Not him," I say, my eyes still trained on the floor at my feet. "I wouldn't piss on his leg if it was on fire."

"Then who?"

Lifting my head, I look across at her and realize she doesn't know about Cage and I. The last thing I told her was that he was going to the reunion with me.

"Cage." Just saying his name makes my chest ache.

She tilts her head in confusion. "I thought the two of you were just friends?"

I laugh, humorlessly. "That's the lie I was telling myself, too."

"So… you like him?"

Swallowing, I look away, rummaging through the feelings I've been digging through over the last few days—longing, desire, understanding. Each time I've tried to make sense of everything, I get lost in a deluge of memories. In a short amount of time, Cage became my best friend. He was understanding and supportive when everyone else in my life was judging me. He got me, made me stronger, and helped me be a better version of myself. He's funny, smart, strong… so strong, yet sensitive when he needs to be. It's all such a heady combination.

Everything I wasn't looking for, but needed.

"I think…" I start, but stop, afraid of the words that are on the tip of my tongue. But if I can't be honest with Jenn, who can I be honest with? Even though she's my boss, she's also always been there for me and never judged me, not even at my craziest. Taking a deep breath and closing my eyes, I let the truth tumble out. "I think I love him."

"Oh," Jenn says, a little surprise in her tone and I hope I don't regret confiding this piece of information. I've held it close to my heart, afraid it wasn't real… or validated… but the longer I mulled it over—flipping it this way and that—the more I knew it was true. There's also the lingering fear that maybe I can't trust myself. That may never go away. But love is the only explanation for the way I've felt.

I spent hours overthinking the dream I had and why it bothered me so badly and the only explanation is that I love him. Seeing Asher with Mindy brought out rage, but seeing Cage with someone else, even in a dream, it crushed me.

I care what he thinks.

I want to be around him more than any other person.

I miss him the second he walks out of the room. Walking away from him was the most painful thing I've ever done.

I want him… so bad… so much.

"So, if you love him… what's the problem?" Jenn asks, nothing but honest curiosity in her question.

"How do I know I can trust him?" Looking back up at her, she frowns. "Anna said he's probably just a rebound. She told me not to fall into bed with the first guy who tells me I'm beautiful… I mean, I lived with Asher for eight years and I didn't even know the man I was married to. I had no clue who he really was. How do I know I can trust myself?"

"Honey, listen," Jenn says, sighing as she leans onto the table and reaches for one of my hands, forcing my eyes to hers. "You can't be held responsible for Asher's indiscretions. That's all on him, but it doesn't cheapen your love and it doesn't make you wrong. You… you're everything right in the world." She squeezes my hand and I roll my eyes, brushing away a rogue tear. "You are," she insists. "You're kind, caring, thoughtful… you're a hard worker and you're passionate about your craft. You accept those around you for who they are. Don't let Asher mess that up for everyone else. He's a bad apple, but it doesn't mean everyone else is… it doesn't mean Cage is."

Deep down, I know what she's saying is true, but the doubts still linger.

"I don't know how to get past this," I confess, feeling exhausted. "He doesn't deserve my distrust. He's good… the best person I know. I don't want to hurt him, and I don't want to give him a chance to hurt me. I'm tired of heartbreak."

Jenn is quiet for a moment, but she finally lifts her chin up, confidence filling her tone. "Everyone in life has the possibility of hurting you. If you allow yourself to love and be loved, you risk being hurt. That's just how it is. It's the risk you take when you give your heart away. But if we never give it away, we never have the chance to find true happiness."

We stand there in silence for a few minutes and I think about what she said. Loving people is risky, but what is life without love? I know these last few days without Cage have been horrible. I can't imagine going my entire life without him… I need him, want him. And I know we were meant to find each other. Him moving to Green Valley wasn't a mistake.

He's not a mistake.

"What are you thinking?" Jenn asks.

I sigh, letting my heart do the talking. "I know Cage isn't a rebound," I tell her, feeling my heart stutter at the memory of telling him that. I was wrong… so, so wrong. "He's the best thing that's ever happened to me. On paper, we probably don't make sense… this big, badass cage fighter and me, a cardigan-wearing muffin maker." I laugh, wiping away a tear that slips out, but it's not entirely due to sadness. For the first time in a long time, I can see my life clearly. "But we're good together."

Now she's the one wiping away a tear. "That's good," she says, patting my hand she's still holding. "Because you deserve to be loved… with a deep, fiery passion."

I know Jenn speaks from experience, because that's the way Cletus loves her. It's so complete and authentic. You can see it every time he looks at her. I think I've seen the same look on Cage's face when he looks at me… how stupid of me to discard that—him, his feelings.

"Asher stole years from your past," she continues. "Don't let him steal your future too."

The following day, after my next-to-last anger management class, I linger, waiting for Lana to finish talking to a couple other people. She's helped me work through my anger, so I'm hoping she can help me with my newest issue.

"Tempest," she says, walking up to me. "How are things going?"

"Good," I sigh, nodding my head. "I mean, when it comes to the anger and self-control stuff… I've been doing much better."

She smiles. "Good, that's what I like to hear… and I just want to say, I've noticed a significant change in you. Next week is your last required session and I'll be signing off on your completion letter back to the judge."

"Thank you."

"Was there something else you wanted to talk about?"

Feeling a little unsure, I consider just leaving, but Jenn's words keep playing on repeat… *don't let him steal your future.* What if Cage is my future? I don't want to live with the regret of letting him go and never finding out. "This is probably going to sound crazy," I start, hesitating for a moment. "But, how do I learn to trust myself again?"

"That's a good question," she assures me, setting me at ease with a thoughtful expression on her face. She's been a great sounding board over the weeks I've been coming here. Getting a sentence to anger management classes was probably the best thing that's happened to me… well, second best.

"I think the biggest thing is coming to the understanding that we're all human and there is no one hundred percent guarantee that we won't fail ourselves," she finally says. "Or that other people won't fail us. It's going to happen, multiple times over the course of our lives."

Sighing, she sits down in one of the chairs and pats the one beside her.

"And then," she continues, "you've got to realize you're stronger than you think and you can survive your mistakes."

Now I'm sighing, but deep down, I know she's right. Even after everything Asher put me through, I'm still here. And if I'm being honest with myself, I feel stronger now than I did eight months ago. I also feel so much more… me, like through the struggles and trials I've experienced, I've found myself.

"I know when you're going through the pain… hurt, betrayal… it's easy to be consumed by it. You think you'll never recover, but then one day, you wake up and realize it doesn't cut as deep… and you move on."

I nod, giving her a small smile. "I think I'm ready for that," I tell her… and myself.

She smiles, looking like a proud parent. "I think so, too."

On my drive back to Green Valley, I decide to go straight to Cage's once I get to town and apologize. It might not fix everything, but it's definitely a step in the right direction. Besides apologizing, I just really, really need to see him.

It's been almost a week since the reunion and even though I've been laying low—going to the bakery at ridiculous hours and straight back home after work—I thought I'd at least catch a glimpse of him… or he'd show up at the bakery after one of his early morning runs.

But he hasn't.

I should be happy, right? I mean, he's only doing what I asked him to do: not follow me.

But I'm not.

Driving down the main road, I slow when I approach Cage's building, parking in the spot right in front of the window. From here, I can tell the downstairs is empty and all the lights are off, but that doesn't necessarily mean he's not home.

Checking my phone, I see it's not quite time for Cage to go to work, so I hop out and walk up to the door. I knock once and wait. When he doesn't show, I walk over to the window and peak inside. The place looks locked up tight, but I decide to knock once more.

And then on the window.

Nothing.

As I walk back to the truck, I turn to look at the upstairs window, but there's no movement… no lights on, at least not that I can tell. Maybe he's at the store? Come to think of it, I need a few things, so I turn the truck around and head to the Piggly Wiggly.

Once I'm in the parking lot, I know right away Cage isn't here. I would recognize his truck in the parking lot, and I've made two sweeps up and down each row. I'm thorough if nothing else.

And a fucking stalker.

Forgoing a shopping trip for now, I turn the truck around and head back out to the main road, sitting at the turn-in as I try to decide my next move. I can't just go back home now. I'm a woman on a mission and I won't be able to rest until I've talked to Cage.

When my truck's tires hit the gravel of the parking lot at the Pink Pony, I do another sweep, not seeing hide nor hair of Cage or the truck. But since I'm here, I go ahead and park.

"Hey, Tempest," Floyd greets as I slide up to the bar. "What can I get for you?"

I look around and realize I've never been here this early. It's kind of weird to see the dancers on stage with only a few people at the tables. "Running the skeleton crew, huh?" I ask, gesturing over my shoulder.

Floyd smiles and nods, using a bar towel to dry a glass. "Regulars."

"Have you seen Cage today… by any chance?"

His expression shifts. "No," he says, shaking his head. "He hasn't worked all week. Boss said he's off the schedule."

My heart drops into my stomach.

"Did he say why?"

Floyd looks thoughtful for a second before answering. "Nope… not that I recall. He's had Roger filling in for him."

"You wouldn't happen to have his phone number, would you?"

If I could only remember, Cage actually gave it to me, but it was in the middle of my meltdown and I could barely remember my name at the time, let alone ten digits.

Floyd glances around the bar, and then back at me. "I'm not supposed to give out personal information, but I know the two of you are friends...so—"

"I won't say anything," I tell him, making a show of zipping my lips and throwing away the key.

After a few seconds, he tosses the towel over his shoulder and walks to the back. When he comes back out, he has a folded piece of paper and he hands it to me.

"Thanks, Floyd. I owe you one."

Once I'm back out at my truck, I climb in and grab my phone, unfolding the paper and dialing Cage's number before I can chicken out.

CHAPTER 30

CAGE

"Now, that's what I like to see," my brother, Viggo, calls out as he walks into the gym. I thought I'd be able to get some quiet time here, just me and the bags, but unfortunately, I was wrong.

I should've known better. Alone time in a big family is like a mythical creature.

"Don't get so excited. I'm just getting in a short workout before I meet with my realtor."

"I can't believe you're really leaving the city for a small town... in Tennessee, no less. I never pegged you for the type." He stands on the other side of the bag and holds it for me while I continue my punches, working out the pent-up aggression that's lingered for the last week.

"What type are you referring to, exactly?" I cut him a look, daring him to say something offensive.

"You know what I mean. Small town-type—seeing the same people and the same things every day, a slower pace, nothing exciting to do…"

My mind immediately flashes to Tempest, because I'd love nothing more than to see her every day and she's far from *nothing exciting*, but I shut that shit down. No sense in pining over someone who doesn't want me. But that's the crazy thing… I know she does. She's just fighting it.

"You've never been there, so you really shouldn't be judging Green Valley. I like the pace and the people and I don't have to be constantly entertained like you do. Where you are never satisfied, I'm actually quite content with my life."

"Aww, my little bro is growing up." He pretends to wipe a tear from his eye.

"Yeah, you should try it, dickweed." I move as though I'm going to punch the bag, but instead, I hit Viggo in the shoulder, catching him off guard.

Laughing, he rubs at where my glove made contact. "Asshole."

Ready to take a break and change the subject, I hold my gloves up to my brother and nod my head, silently asking him to untie them for me. "Did you know Gunnar is thinking about coming to stay with me and train in a few months?"

My youngest brother and I have been talking a lot this week about his future in the ring. He's excited to take his training to the next level, but I know he's been avoiding telling Viggo. Being the oldest of us Erickson boys, Viggo feels like he's in charge and he doesn't always welcome change, unless it's approved by him. Hence, his unhappiness with my early retirement.

It's not that he doesn't understand my injury or the fact that I refuse to fight under anything less than the best conditions, but he wanted a say so in the path my life took after the ring.

He's always had a vision of the five of us living close to each other and working together forever, but life doesn't always turn out the way we plan. It's a great vision, don't get me wrong. And I love my brother and don't want to crush his dreams, but Dallas isn't for me.

At least, not right now.

"I had a feeling this was coming," Viggo says, tossing my gloves to the side. "And I knew he wouldn't have the balls to tell me himself."

"He looks up to you, man," I tell him as I stretch out my bad shoulder. "He doesn't want to disappoint you."

"The only way he'll ever disappoint me is if he doesn't work his ass off to achieve his goals. He's got the talent and it'd be a shame if he pissed it away."

I look at my brother, trying to gauge whether or not that was meant to be a sly jab at me and my situation, but I see nothing but honesty on his face. Maybe we're all growing up a little.

Miracles never cease to exist.

We walk over to a bench where I left my towel and water bottle, and I make great use of both while Viggo updates me on the latest gym gossip. There really isn't a difference between big cities and small towns when it comes to this kind of shit, but I keep quiet and let my brother continue his story.

"So, what's the pussy like in Green Valley?"

Nearly choking on my water, I take a quick glance around us to make sure no one heard him.

"What the fuck is wrong with you? Why would you ask me that, especially in our place of business?"

Viggo huffs, rolling his eyes. "Get your fucking panties out of a twist, would ya? We teach fighting here, not etiquette. No one's offended by my mention of pussy but you, which makes me think you've found yourself a girl… or at least a steady lay."

I don't answer. I don't even look at him because I don't know if I can have a conversation about Tempest with him. He's never been in a serious relationship. He's definitely never been in love. If I tell him what's been going on between Tempest and me, he'll just tell me to get over it and move on, and that's not what I want to hear right now.

"Come on, man. You can talk to me. I know you say you really like being in Tennessee, but my gut tells me it's not working at the strip club that's making you want to move there permanently. I mean, I'd totally understand if that was it, but I know you. There's gotta be something or *someone*, so spill it."

Fuck it.

I toss my towel onto the bench and sit down. When he sits by me, giving me his full attention, I tell him everything. I tell him about how I met Tempest and a little bit about her history and how that lead to her taking lessons from me. Then, I tell him about how my feelings started changing for her and how the last couple of weeks were between us. Lastly, I tell him about Tempest freaking out, leaving me completely dumbfounded. After I've said everything I want to say, I take a breath and brace myself for his response.

"So, you're gonna go back and prove her wrong, right?"

That's not what I was expecting him to say.

"I haven't decided yet, to be honest."

"Bullshit. If that were the case, you wouldn't be selling your house here."

Okay, so he has a point.

"I'm going back because I have plans I want to see completed, but I don't know if those plans include Tempest. I'm not sure she's ready and I don't want to push her. She's been through a lot."

Her words ring in my ear like a fucking gong—*just a rebound.* I don't believe that. I don't want to believe it. I think she's scared so, maybe, I need to go back and demand she give us a shot, which makes me laugh. Me demanding anything from Tempest, outside of the bedroom, that is, would only result in her kicking my ass. I'd gladly let her.

An ass kicking from her would mean she's near me, and as masochistic as it sounds, I'd rather be close to her, taking whatever she wants to give me—even an ass kicking—than to be without her.

"I've never seen you this worked up over a girl before. Not even with what's-her-name. She must be really special."

I smile at my brother. "She is. She's fucking amazing and I'm crazy about her."

"Well, sounds like you need to grow a pair and go get your girl."

Ah, there's that brotherly advice I was waiting for.

Walking into the arena the night of the big fight has me feeling on edge. This is the first time I've even been near a ring in a year and I'm nervous. I mean, I'm not fighting, so I don't have to worry about that, but this is my first bout to attend since my injury and I don't know what to expect.

I wouldn't miss it, though.

Vali has worked hard and has a lot riding on tonight. I still feel a little bad about not being able to fight, knowing that had been his plan all along—to get me back in the ring. But I'm proud of him for all he's accomplished and I want to be here to support him.

"Hey, there you are!" Speak of the devil. Vali walks up, looking sick as fuck in a black suit and tie, something a mob boss would wear.

"You going to a funeral?" I tease.

"You stepping in the ring?" he shoots back, a gleam in his eye. "All you'd have to do is smile and wave. And, maybe, take your shirt off."

When I go to punch him, he laughs, pulling me into a hug. I respond with a very enthusiastic smack to the back of his head. "Watch the hair, jackass!" This makes me laugh, so I give him a genuine hug in return.

He's a persistent little shit, but I still love the guy.

"You've really outdone yourself tonight, Val. I'm proud of you."

He tries to play off my praise, but the way the tips of his ears turn red, I know my comment means a lot to him, even if he's a little embarrassed. But hey, isn't that what big brothers are for?

"I mean it," I assure him. "When I open my studio in Green Valley, you'll have to come out and plan something."

"I'm not a party planner, Cage. I'm a promoter."

"I know that. You can come out and promote the studio. It'll be great, you'll see."

The more I talk about running my own studio full-time, the more excited I get. I wasn't even sure it was what I wanted to do until I came here and saw how well the family studio is doing. Mine will be different though. Not as big or as flashy, but I'm hoping it'll be something the people of Green Valley and the surrounding areas need.

Now, that my house here in Dallas is officially on the market, I can think about moving to Green Valley permanently. My realtor assured me the house would sell quickly, but I know he can't really make that kind of promise. Still, the quicker it sells, the quicker I can finish fixing up the space and have a grand opening.

And I'll need more clientele. As much as I've loved training Tempest, being paid in muffins won't get me to where I want to be.

As I walk around, I smile and nod at the people I pass, remembering I'm here to make the family look good. A few of the guys I see stop and chat for a bit while even more people ask to take a photo with me. I haven't been in this kind of situation in so long, I'd almost forgotten what it was like.

I'll admit, it's not my favorite part of the business, but being seen is necessary when you're building any kind of brand. The Erickson brand just so happens to have been built around my face. So, it's vital for me to make this appearance, smile and play the part.

And even though I'll be back in Green Valley soon, I don't plan on abandoning my role. My family has always been a top priority and that won't change, even if my zip code does.

"Hey, Cage," a familiar looking blonde says, smiling as she walks up with a friend. "Good to see you around… we've been wondering where you took off to."

"Ladies," I say, dipping my chin in greeting. A year ago, I might've taken advantage of a situation like this, invited them to sit in the box with me and my brothers, showed them a good time. But that was before Tempest… before she showed up at the Pink Pony and reeled me in without ever even saying a word.

"Will you be here all night?" the brunette asks, handing me a card. "We've got a great party planned for after the fights, and we'd love to have you make an appearance."

I said I'd be at the fight, and I'm here, but that's where it ends.

Smiling politely, I shake my head. "Sorry, I've got an early day tomorrow."

"You sure?" the blonde one asks, stepping closer and running a finger down my shirt.

Taking her hand, I pull it away from me and place it back in her space. "Thanks, but no thanks." Turning, I walk away as quickly as possible, looking for any of my brothers to use as a decoy.

I'm off the market, ladies, but have you met Viggo… or Val… Ozzi?

Not Gunnar, because I plan on keeping his ass very busy for the foreseeable future.

A funny thought hits me as I walk up the steps toward the box I'll be sitting at during the fight.

What would Tempest say to all of this?

I've thought about her a dozen times since I arrived… hundreds since I've been back in Dallas. Would she think this is all ridiculous? She seemed pretty intrigued the night we were at the restaurant and the guy approached me. Would she be jealous about the women? Does it make me a sick fuck to hope that she would be?

There's just no telling with her. She's constantly surprising me. And I love that about her… along with a million other things.

I'm halfway up the steps when my phone buzzes in my pocket, but when I look at my screen, I don't recognize the number. It's a Green Valley area code, but it's not Hank. It could be someone at the club, Floyd or one of the workers. Swiping my thumb across the screen, I place the phone to my ear, "Hello?"

"Hi."

One word… that's all it takes.

My heart jumps up into my throat and for a second, I can't speak. Does she have ESP? Did she know I was just thinking about her? Then, my instincts kick in. "Are you alright? Is something wrong?"

If Asher or Mindy have done anything to harass her or make her life miserable… *so help me God.* They do not want to mess with what is mine.

"No," she says in a rush. "I'm… I'm fine."

Lie.

Tempest rarely lies to me, but I know it when I hear it. And just like the night she told me I'm a rebound… basically writing me off for good… I heard it then and I'm hearing it now. "Can you hold on for a second?" I ask, turning toward one of the exits and quickly making my way to it. "I'm going to go outside so I can hear you better. Don't hang up."

"Okay."

Her response is direct and not the usual way she speaks to me, but maybe she's just nervous.

I know I sure as hell am—sweaty palms, heart pounding.

What the fuck is wrong with me?

Once I'm outside the building and away from everyone, I take a deep breath. "I'm here."

"Where are you?"

"Dallas," I tell her, looking around at the parking lot that's quickly filling up and feeling a million miles away from Green Valley… and her. At this point, they could be on a different planet. "My family is hosting a bout… and it's kind of big deal, so I'm here to lend a hand."

"You left." It's not a question; it's a statement. And it sounds like she accusing me of something, but I'm not sure what. She sounds pissed. What does she have to be angry about?

"I did, yes."

She lets out a frustrated grunt before continuing. "You left without saying anything and I didn't know how to find you."

If I'm not mistaken, there's a hint of panic to her voice and even though I shouldn't, I'd love nothing more than to reach through this phone and pull her to me.

"You told me you didn't want to see me anymore," I tell her, feeling the weight of her words as I pinch the bridge of my nose to gain a little composure. "Why would I tell you I was going to Dallas?" Now, I'm getting pissed. "You're kind of giving me whiplash, Tempest. One second, we're just friends… the next second, you want me… and then you tell me I'm off the hook and I shouldn't follow you. What am I supposed to do?"

This is not how I wanted this conversation to go.

"I don't know!" She sounds just as confused as I'm feeling, which does little to calm me. "I… I looked for you," she stutters. "But the studio was empty and so was your apartment. I even went to the Pink Pony, but Floyd said you had the week off. And I couldn't fucking remember your goddamn phone number!" She's yelling at this point and I don't know what to do or say, so we sit in silence, both of us breathing heavy from frustration.

"I know I shouldn't be angry," she finally says, her voice dropping to a near whisper. "But I can't help it." Her words break on that last note and I feel it all the way down to my toes—*hurt*.

I rub my free hand up and down my face, willing myself to calm down before I speak again. "What do you want, Tempest?"

She doesn't say anything for what feels like ages and I know this is a struggle for her. She wants to speak her mind, but she's afraid to do so. I loved helping her before, back when our relationship wasn't so damn complicated, but I'm not bailing her out this time. She can say exactly what she wants to say to me or she can hang up. If she wants to be on her own, then that's what she'll get from me.

I'm done playing games.

Finally, she finds her voice. "I want to apologize," she begins, sounding more certain than a few seconds ago. "I need you to know I'm sorry for all the awful things I said to you. I was just angry and hurt… and *so confused*." She pauses, taking a deep breath. "I want us to be friends again. Actually, I want us to be more than that but, if you don't want that anymore, can we at least go back to being friends? I miss you and I need you in my life, Cage."

Fuck, fuck, fuck.

Why did she have to call and tell me these things? Why couldn't she wait until we were face to face again? I don't want to have this conversation here, like this. Going against every instinct in my body—fighting the part of me that wants to hop in my car and not stop until my feet are on Tennessee soil—I reply, "I can't talk about this right now, Tempest." Pausing while I swallow down the bile that's in my throat, practically choking on my own words, I manage to say, "I'll call you when I get back to Green Valley."

And I hang up.

CHAPTER 31

TEMPEST

"*I Fall to Pieces*?" Jenn asks, walking into the kitchen with the Muffin of the Day message board in her hand. "I thought we were past this."

Sighing, I let my head drop. "I'm sorry," I groan. "I can't help the way I feel, though. And you know my muffins are always inspired by what's happening in my life. It's not my fault that I'm in a constant state of turmoil these days."

Jenn just looks at me—one hand holding the board, one hand on her hip. "This is the last day," she huffs. "Do you hear me? Tomorrow, there better be some happiness on this board, so help me…"

"Tomorrow," I tell her, wiping my hands on my apron and walking around the counter. "I promise. I'll think of something and it will be sunshine and fucking rainbows."

Her pointed stare burns through me. "It better. This is Donner Bakery—Home of the Banana Cake Queen. People come here expecting to leave feeling good. Carbs… sugar… happiness. If you keep this up, we're going to have to get our liquor license and I just don't have time for one more thing on my plate."

Releasing a breath as she walks out, I press a hand to my forehead.

"Get it together, Tempest… you're better than this… stronger."

After a brief self-help talk, I decide to make myself useful while the muffins are baking and take out the trash. We might be royalty around here, but that doesn't excuse us from menial tasks.

Dumping my bowl, I keep on the counter for all the baking refuse —egg shells, empty wrappers from chocolate, banana peelings, etc.—I tie the bag up and make my way to the back door. It's still dark outside, not even six o'clock in the morning, but I feel like it's midday. Ever since my fight with Cage, I've started coming in super early, earlier than usual—two o'clock… three—which makes for a long day. But I'd rather make myself useful instead of lying in bed, trying to solve problems I don't have the answer to.

Why did Cage hang up on me?

When is he coming home?

What will he say once he gets here?

Do I have a chance to make things right between us?

I rub at my chest as I make my way over to the dumpster. "God, I hope so," I mutter, heaving the heavy bag over the edge. Before heading back inside, I take a minute to breathe deeply, assuring myself that whether or not I make things right with Cage, I'm going to be alright. He helped me see that and it's something I'll always be grateful for. It doesn't mean I don't miss him or that I don't want him back… but I'll survive.

When I get back inside, I continue with the muffin making until every tray is full of my go-to recipes lately—*I Fall to Pieces*, *Crazy*, and *Going Through the Big D*. But I also made a last-minute addition of I Will Survive—an espresso and chocolate masterpiece—and my new favorite, *I Will Always Love You*—a lemon blueberry with buttercream drizzle… it reminds me of Cage. Lemon for his blond hair and blueberry for his eyes… even though his eyes are blue, blue… like a glacier-fed lake.

"Daydreaming?" Mikey asks, nudging my shoulder and pulling me out of my thoughts.

Quickly going back to my task at hand, I huff out a laugh. "No, just… tired, I guess."

I turn to help a customer who just walked in when I see a very disheveled-looking Asher standing at the counter. For a second, I think about turning the other way and forcing someone else to help him, but I'm not going to. I have nothing to hide and I've said my peace.

"What can I get for you?" I ask, treating him like any other customer, even giving him a smile, because I'm the bigger person in this situation and I refuse to let him bring me down to his level.

"A minute of your time," he says, his eyes on mine. "Please."

"We're pretty busy, so whatever you have to say, you can say it here."

Asher's eyes dart around the bakery, taking inventory of who's here, obviously having something to say that he doesn't want spread around the town.

Just as I'm losing my patience, he clears his throat and drops his voice low. "You were right," he mutters, leaning closer to the counter. "About... everything—the analysis, the baby—everything."

Something like sweet satisfaction sings through my soul.

Not that I care, because I don't, but it's just the joy in knowing that I at least had something about Asher pegged right. When I don't say anything in response, he continues. "I... I think I made a mistake."

"Which one would that be?" I ask, not taking any care to keep my part of the conversation hidden, but also not looking to make a scene... again. "The one where you slept with someone else while you were married to me. Oh, wait," I say, sarcasm thick in my tone. "That's right... you slept with her before we ever got married. You know, I'm wondering why you didn't just marry her in the first place. You could've saved us all a lot of grief and heartache."

"It was a mistake," Asher repeats, weariness evident all over his face. "Ever since the night at the reunion, I haven't been able to sleep. Mindy finally admitted that she knew all along the baby wasn't mine, but she wanted it to be." He rolls his eyes, stuffing his hands into his pockets. "So typical of her."

The smile that creeps up on my face is probably scary and cynical, but I couldn't give a rat's ass.

"Sounds to me like y'all might need some marriage counseling," I tell him, taking a fresh stack of boxes to the end of the counter and begin folding. If I'm going to stand around and jack my jaws, I should at least be productive.

"That's the thing," Asher says, following me down the counter. "I don't think I can do it… I'm sorry… for everything."

Pausing mid box folding, I look at him like he's lost his damn mind.

"Well, I appreciate the apology… even though it's too little, too late, but there is no way in hell I'd ever… *ever*," I repeat, holding his gaze so there is no misunderstanding here. "I'll never take you back and I will never trust you."

"We were great together," he insists, his voice losing any level of control he might've had. "You know we were, so don't stand there and pretend that you don't love me anymore."

Laughing, I can't hold it in any longer. "Oh, Asher… I don't. You know, I've been thinking about it a lot, and I think I might've stopped a long time ago. Trying to have a baby was my way of trying to miraculously fix everything. But now, I see I was badly mistaken. And one of these days, when I finally have a baby, it'll be with someone I am madly, deeply… crazy in love with. Not you."

He braces his hands on the counter. "What do you want me to do to fix this… I'll do it."

"Go home, Asher," I tell him. "Go home to Mindy and the baby… might I remind you that baby did not ask for this, so be a good dad, it might be your only chance. You should take it."

After a few painfully awkward moments of him staring at me, waiting for me to reconsider or change my mind, he finally turns around and walks out.

"What was that?" Mikey asks.

"Mikey, always remember: chickens come home to roost."

It's been four days since I talked to Cage, four painfully long, agonizing days, and still I've had no word from him. The last time I saw him was almost two weeks ago, and I miss him.

Lying in bed, trying to keep myself awake just a few more hours to try and reverse this ridiculously early rising, I pick up my phone and dial my mama. She's called me a few times over the past week, but I just wasn't in the mood for her reprimand or advice, which I'm sure she's been storing up.

I can only imagine the stories going around about me after the reunion.

After a couple rings, she picks up. "Tempest."

"Mama."

There's something frying in the background and I wonder if she wouldn't mind another mouth to feed, because I'm actually really hungry. Cooking for one is for the birds and after the last two weeks, I just haven't felt up to it, so I've been living off of a diet of cereal and beef jerky.

Don't ask.

I was trying to balance out my food groups.

"To what do I owe the pleasure?" she asks and I roll my eyes. It's time for her to play her part as the martyr. She should be up for an Academy Award the way she sells this role. "I was just telling your daddy the other day that we never hear from you anymore unless you need something."

"I'm sorry, Mama. I've been busy."

"Well," she huffs. "Don't start with me about busy. Mildred talked me into doing this beginner's quilting class on Friday mornings. Between that, women's bible study I started hosting here at the house, and bridge on Tuesdays, I'm swamped. And then, there's your daddy…"

"I know, Mama… you're busy too." I shake my head and bite my tongue. "I'm sorry I haven't called or been over."

After nothing but silence from the other end, I pull my phone back to check and make sure it didn't drop my call. "Mama?"

"I heard about the little incident at the Lodge…"

Oh, here we go.

"Donna Pemberton said her daughter, Cynthia… remember her, long black hair… so tall she could hunt geese with a rake? Anyway,

Cynthia was there and she saw the whole thing happen… told her mama it was a sight to behold."

Sitting up in bed, I brush my hair out of my face.

Am I hearing this right?

Does she sound… happy? Proud?

When she starts chuckling into the phone, I really start to get worried. Maybe this is all too much and she's snapping. I've often thought she was one freak out away from the loony bin. "She said the look on Mindy's face when you stomped out of the room was priceless… trying to pass that baby off as Asher's… well, I've never…"

This is where she's going to start telling me I should give him another chance—poor guy was duped, this isn't his fault… blah, blah, blah.

"If you want to know what I think," she pauses, but I already know she's not waiting for me to ask. "I think they're meant for each other."

"I couldn't agree more," I mutter into the phone, shocked those words came out of my mouth while talking to my mother.

She sighs, "Oh, honey… I know I said I was praying for a reconciliation between you and Asher, but that was only because you're my baby and I want what's best for you… I want you to be happy. That's all."

"Thank you, Mama."

We talk a little small talk for a few minutes, until there's a knock at my door.

"Mama, I've gotta go. There's someone here," I tell her, standing from the bed and walking over to the door. "I'll call you later."

Hanging up the phone, I put it in my pocket and place my ear to the door. "Who is it?" I ask, placing my ear up to the metal. I really need a peep hole.

"It's Cole."

When I swing the door open wide, my cousin is standing there with a mischievous grin on his face. "Well, hey… to what do I owe this honor?"

Cole tilts his head to the side, giving me a regretful smile. "I'm going to, uh… I'm here to take you in."

"Take me in?" I ask, confused as I start racking my brain, trying to think of something I've done recently that would require me being arrested.

Outside of the heated discussion with Mindy and Asher at the reunion a couple weeks ago, I can't really think of anything.

"I'd read you your rights," he says. "But I'm pretty sure you're familiar with those."

"Cole!" I demand, widening my stance as he takes me by the arm. "What is this about?"

"That, you'll have to take up with Sheriff James."

"Sheriff James?" I screech, twisting and turning as I try to release myself from his grasp. I think about using one of the self-defense moves Cage taught me during our sessions, but I don't want to hurt him. "What would Sheriff James want with me?"

"You'll have to ask him yourself," Cole says, huffing. "Now, you know this is my job… please don't make it any worse than it already is." He gives me the look that says "*Come on, Tempest, just cooperate for once in your stubborn ass life.*"

I stare back at him, pissed that he'd agree to arrest me. I don't care if it's his job or not, I'm his family, and damn it, that should account for something.

Plus, I'm hungry, which just makes all of this worse.

"Listen," I say, poking my finger into his chest. "I just got signed off on from my anger management counselor and I haven't done anything wrong. So, I'm going to need to see some kind of warrant… or something," I tell him, breathing heavily out of my nose as my emotions take over. "Give me something, Cole."

"You know that's not how these things work," he says, putting his hands on his hips all business-like. "Now, please, just come with me and don't make this any harder than it is."

We have a stare-off for a few seconds standing in the doorway of my apartment. When I see he's not relenting, my shoulders sag in defeat. "Fine," I grit out, forcefully grabbing my keys off the table beside the front door. "But I just want you to know, I'm not happy about this and Christmas is just around the corner."

In Cole's defense, he actually looks remorseful as he makes sure my door is secure before escorting me down the stairs and to his police cruiser waiting by the curb.

"Can you give me a hint?" I ask, as he puts me into the cruiser.

Cole scrunches his face as he runs a hand over his short, cropped hair. "Something about a misunderstanding, but Sheriff James wants you to come down to the station. It's something that needs to be worked out face-to-face."

I spend the next few minutes as we drive through town stewing and trying to rack my brain over what this might be about, but I come up empty-handed.

When we pull up, Cole gives me a reassuring smile, and I flip him off.

"Did you just flip off an officer of the law?" he asks in mock horror.

"I know my rights," I tell him with a huff, folding my arms over my chest. "Come open my door so we can get this over with."

Cole chuckles, muttering something under his breath I can't hear, but knowing what's good for him, he walks around and opens my door and then guides me inside. As we walk down the long, familiar hallway, I nod at Mary, the receptionist, giving her a forced smile.

"Well, Miss Cassidy," she greets. "We haven't seen you in here for a while."

I sigh, looking over at Cole and gritting my teeth. "Yeah, and I was hoping you wouldn't."

"Tempest," Sheriff James says, popping his head out when he hears us talking. "Step inside, please."

Giving Cole one last dirty look, I walk past him and into Sheriff James's office and the wind is knocked from my sails.

Cage is perched on the edge of the desk with the cockiest smirk I've seen in a while… at least two weeks.

And it's the best damn sight in the world.

CHAPTER 32

CAGE

"What…" She pauses, her big green eyes growing in confusion. "What are you doing here?"

I laugh, looking over at Sheriff James and Cole, who are standing by the door to the office. "Oh, you know… I was burning up the pavement, trying to get back to Green Valley in a hurry," I tell her, a smile pulling at my lips. "Might've forgotten to slow it down a little on my way into town."

"Oh," she says, her perfect lips pursing. "So… am I here to get you out of jail?"

Sheriff James laughs. "We'll leave you two to it… fifteen minutes, tops. I'm going to need my office back for official business." He turns to walk out, but then stops. "And no… funny business."

"Thank you, Sheriff."

"Am I not in trouble?" she asks as she watches them leave and then turns her attention back to me. "I'm confused."

Shrugging, I push off the desk and walk toward her. "Cole is the one who pulled me over. He was kind of giving me the pat down over leaving town… you know how those small town cops can be."

She smiles, shaking her head. "Total pricks sometimes."

"Yeah, well, I thought it was better to tell him that I was coming back for good… for you… so he didn't find a reason to arrest me. He's a little protective of you," I tell her, thinking back to how the big guy went from being an asshole cop to a squishy teddy bear when he realized my intentions, where Tempest is concerned, are honest and good. "I like him."

"He's good people." She smiles, her eyes sweeping over me, drinking me in. "Except when he arrests me," she adds. "Mind telling me how I ended up here?"

"We thought it'd be fun… apparently it's a slow night for the GVPD, so he made a call to Sheriff James and then the rest just happened," I admit. "We were going to cuff you and the whole nine yards, but Cole said he'd rather keep his balls intact. Apparently, Anna is already wanting another baby."

She laughs, biting down on her lip. "So you came back…"

"Yeah," I tell her, closing the distance between us. "See, there's this girl… and she drives me crazy…" Lowering my head until our foreheads are pressed together, I inhale deeply, getting my first good breath in weeks. Ever since I followed her home and turned around and left, I've felt like there's been an elephant on my chest. But being here, touching her, I already feel lighter.

"Sounds like too much trouble," she whispers, leaning into me. "You sure you want that kind of trouble in your life?"

"Wouldn't have it any other way," I tell her. "I'm also pretty crazy about her."

"That's good because she's crazy about you too." Wrapping her arms around me, she squeezes. "She's really glad you came back… and in case you need to hear it again, she's sorry."

"She's forgiven," I say, kissing the top of her head and hugging her to me.

Sighing, she laughs lightly. "Damn, I could kick your ass for this."

"Cole said you'd say that."

Leaning back, she tilts her face up to look me in the eye. "I can think of a way you can make it up to me."

"Oh," I laugh. "So, I'm now indebted to you? I thought you were the one with some groveling to do."

"You want me to grovel?" she asks. "Like on my knees?"

Grabbing her hand, I pull her to the door. "Where are we going?" she asks, a breathless laugh escaping. "I thought you wanted me to grovel?"

"We're going to need longer than fifteen minutes."

She stops, yanking my arm back until my chest is flush with hers. "How long?" she asks, her expression turning serious. "I need to know… how long are you here for? Because, as much as I want to be with you, I can't give you my heart if you're just going to leave me down the road."

"As long as you'll have me," I tell her. "I sold my house in Dallas… well, it's on the market. Drove my car back. I'm here to stay."

The next thing I know, Tempest has launched herself at me, legs wrapped around my waist… arms around my neck… and her sweet lips on mine.

EPILOGUE

TEMPEST

Islands in the Stream. It's not really the season for pineapple and coconut, but the song is speaking to my soul today, so that's what's on the menu. The base for it is a spice batter that I've added rum to. It's to die for.

Just like Cage.

The past couple months have been great—busy, but great. Tonight is the grand opening of Cage's studio. He's worked hard to get everything just like he wants it. The last thing he added to it, what he's been working on ever since he came back from Dallas, is a legit boxing ring. He has plans to buy the entire building from Hank, not just the portion he's utilizing right now, but the whole thing, expanding it to rival Erickson MMA in Dallas.

Everything is changing, but I couldn't be happier about these changes. Unlike the beginning of the year, when my life was completely turned upside down, the end of the year made it all worth it.

"What are you still doing here?" Jenn asks as she walks back into the kitchen. "I thought you were leaving early to go help Cage finish setting up for tonight."

"I am," I tell her, moving the cooled muffins onto the tray, saving a few out to take with me. "I just wanted to finish this last batch before I left." Picking up the full tray, I carry it to the front and slide it into the display. "Are you and Cletus stopping by tonight?"

"We wouldn't miss it."

Smiling, I wipe my hands on my apron before untying it and hanging it on the rack. "Great… there will be drinks and appetizers starting at seven."

"See you tonight," Jenn calls out as I make my way back to the front and out the door, a bag of muffins under my arm. Crossing the street, I walk over to the studio, pausing for a second to admire the new sign.

Viking MMA

Cage toyed with the idea of making this place part of the Erickson MMA brand, but decided he'd rather it be his own, something separate from the family business. I love it.

"Hello," I call out, walking through the front door. "Cage?"

"Up here," he calls back, his voice coming from the stairs leading to the apartment. An apartment we now share. Last month, he talked me into moving in with him. I was hesitant, but he said it could be on a trial basis and if it didn't work out, I could move back to my old apartment… or buy a house… or whatever I want.

It's one of the things I love the most about him—he lets me be me.

"I brought you muffins," I call back.

"*Hey Good Lookin*?" he asks.

"No," I yell back.

"Forever and Ever, A*men*?"

"No!"

"What the hell?" he asks, finally walking down the stairs so we can stop yelling at each other. "You know those are my favorites."

Holding the bag out to him, I wait for him to take a whiff. He mentioned a few weeks ago that his favorite fruit is pineapple, so I think he's going to be happy with this combination. When he takes the bag from me and opens it, the groan he makes goes straight to my core.

Cage's muffin approval is basically the same sound he makes when he's coming.

I can't be held responsible for my body's response to that.

"*Islands in the Stream*," I tell him, walking over and stealing a bite from the one he's holding up.

"Hey!" He pulls the muffin back with a look of disgust on his face… his beautiful, perfect face.

Giving him an unapologetic smile, I walk around him and over to the mats. "So, what's left to do for tonight? I'm ready for you to put me to work."

"I'll put you to work, alright," Cage mutters, his mouth half-full of muffin.

He actually is going to put me to work, and not just in the bedroom. When his regular classes start next week, I'll be helping with the self-defense classes. After this week, Cage will no longer work at the Pink Pony, going full-time at the studio.

Ignoring his sexual advances, I redirect the conversation. "You know, when this all started, I thought you were just going to teach me how to channel my anger," I say, thoughtfully. "But you taught me so much more than that."

"Like how to kick my ass," he says, a mischievous grin on his face.

"That," I agree. "And how to fight, not just physically, but for myself."

He sits the bag of muffins down and walks over to me, grabbing me by the waist. "You already had it in you… I just helped you find it."

"You helped me see I was worth fighting for."

Crystal-blue eyes bore into mine as Cage's expression turns serious. "You are worth it," he says, his voice full of earnest. "I've known it since the first time I laid eyes on you… I'm glad you finally caught up to speed."

Rising up on my tip toes, I press my lips to his. "I love you," I whisper, hoping he knows how much. "Thank you for everything… for being my friend and always being on my side… for helping me fight my battles."

"Always," he says, his lips brushing my cheek as he kisses his way to my neck, strong arms wrapping me up and pulling me closer. "I love you, Tempest Cassidy...and I'll always fight for you… for us. Never doubt that."

THE END

ACKNOWLEDGMENTS

First and foremost, we'd like to thank the Queen, aka Evil Overlord, Penny Reid for giving us this amazing opportunity to write in her world. We've been Reiders and fans of her work for a while now, often commenting back and forth between ourselves about how well our characters would fit in the Pennyverse. Then, low and behold, the heavens opened up and she offered us a chance to do just that.

Fiona "Finger Guns" Fisher, you're the woman! We don't know how you do all you do, but we bow down to your greatness. Thank you for everything!

Being a part of Smartypants Romance has been a dream come true. The other authors we're privileged to work with have been nothing short of amazing. Their camaraderie, championship, and creativity are invaluable. In no particular order, because we love you all equally, we'd like to thank Karla Sorensen, Daisy Prescott, April White, M. E. Carter, Cathy Yardley, Piper Sheldon, Ellie Kay, L. B. Dunbar, Katie Ashley, Stella Weaver, and Nora Everly.

To our fellow bakery girls—Karla and Ellie—DONNERBAKERY4LIFE.

For this book, we'd like to give a special shout out to Miranda Lambert for writing the album—Four the Record. Music is the key to our soul and the songs on this album unlocked the heart of our character, Tempest Cassidy.

We'd also like to tip our hats to the Country Western greats that made the muffins possible: Waylon, George, Hank, Willie, Johnny, and Merle.

We can never not thank our amazing families. Our mamas probably read these and they'd be offended if we didn't show them some love. Also, our kids, who thankfully are now old enough to fend for themselves when we hole up in our writing caves.

Pamela Stephenson is always the first to read our words and we appreciate her honesty and cheerleading skill. She's always there from the beginning, watching and reading as the story takes shape. Thanks for being you, Pamela!!

We'd also like to thank Nikki, our editor. Thank you for always approaching every new story we throw at you with an insightful eye. We kind of threw this one on you at the last minute and we appreciate you always working us in and making a place for us in your busy schedule.

Our proofreader, friend, and drinking buddy, Mrs. Karin Enders. Thank you for everything! We appreciate your time, effort, and most of all, your friendship!

A special thank you to Shannon for always catching the sneakiest mistakes. You're the best!

Thank you to our pimp team and everyone in Jiffy Kate's Southern Belles. All of you make our days better. It takes a village and we're so happy you're a part of ours.

ABOUT THE AUTHOR

Jiffy Kate is the joint pen name for Jiff Simpson and Jenny Kate Altman. They're co-writing besties who share a brain. They also share a love of cute boys, stiff drinks, and fun times.

Together, they've written over twenty stories. Their first published book, Finding Focus, was released in November 2015. Since then, they've continued to write what they know--southern settings full of swoony heroes and strong heroines.

Website: http://www.jiffykate.com
Facebook: https://www.facebook.com/jiffykate
Goodreads: https://www.goodreads.com/author/show/7352135.Jiffy_Kate
Twitter: @jiffykatewrites
Instagram: @jiffykatewrites

Find Smartypants Romance online:
Website: www.smartypantsromance.com
Facebook: www.facebook.com/smartypantsromance/
Goodreads: www.goodreads.com/smartypantsromance
Twitter: @smartypantsrom
Instagram: @smartypantsromance

ALSO BY JIFFY KATE

CHECK OUT THEIR OTHER WORKS:

Finding Focus Series (complete):

Finding Focus

Chasing Castles

Fighting Fire

Taming Trouble

Table 10 (complete):

Table 10 – Part 1

Table 10 – Part 2

Table 10 – Part 3

Turn of Fate (previously titled The Other One)

Watch and See

Blue Bayou

Come Again

Neutral Grounds

The Rookie and The Rockstar

(New Orleans Revelers Book 1 – standalone)

Made in the
USA
Middletown, DE

77338483R00179